D1521154

Fake It

LILY SEABROOKE

For the love that's kept me afloat
and able to love myself
from seeing the way
you love me:

thank you.

All my books are for you,
but this one especially,
my starlight.

CHAPTER 1

Avery

"Seriously, Avery," I said, leaning over the bathroom sink and looking at myself in the mirror, tired eyes that no amount of concealer could hide, and a smart outfit with a sleek black apron emblazoned with a logo that I'd dreamed about for years, "you need to get it together."

Avery in the mirror didn't do anything to get it together, which kind of left it to me. Which sucked.

I squeezed the beveled edges of the sink, a sleek thing in our modern bathroom with black-tile floor and smoky gray walls, and I pinched my lips in a thin line, even my lip gloss looking like it was too tired to sparkle.

"Okay. You got this. Look at yourself. You are a smart, capable young woman. You started a dream restaurant. You put in the work, you made it happen. This is going to be fine. You can do this. Fake it till you make it, girl. Come on. Chin up. Chest out."

Someone knocked on the bathroom door, and I yanked away from the sink like it was going to bite me.

"Sorry," I called. "I'll be out in a second."

God, that was embarrassing. I really hoped they hadn't heard me talking to myself. The bathroom wasn't exactly padded walls, so they probably heard me.

I washed my hands and straightened, checking my easy, confident smile—which I assure you was very fake—in the mirror before I left the bathroom, heading back out onto the restaurant floor.

And I swear, this place was *beautiful*. The architecture was complex, modern stylings on everything, sleek dark surfaces and full-wall windows overlooking the bay, art installations that had cost a fortune on the walls, all punctuated by plenty of plant life that wrapped around doorways and along trellises through the building. The floor was such a polished black you could practically see your reflection in it, and the place oozed sophistication, class, money, and, uh, a complete lack of customers.

But it was *fine,* I told myself. I had to act like it was fine, at least. I knew this was just how it worked after starting a business—that this was sink-or-swim, and by god I'd swim. So I adjusted my apron, straightened my back, and headed over to one of the few tables that was actually occupied, up to a beautifully-dressed couple, a man in a black suit who looked like a movie star and a woman in a red dress who looked like... well, a movie star. Bisexually, I panicked a little, but I kept it cool.

"Hello," I said, calling their attention up to me. "Thank you for dining with us today. Are you enjoying your meals tonight? Service has been well?"

"Oh, absolutely," the woman said, dabbing her face with our very expensive embroidered cloth napkins, smearing spaghetti sauce on it. I winced inwardly. "Our waitress has been wonderful, and the food is to die for."

"Fantastic," I said. "I'm the owner, Avery. Let me know if there's anything at all I can do to improve your experience today."

She shook her head, smiling. "Thank you so much. I don't think there's any way it could be better."

"Wonderful. I'll be counting on you to come back again sometime, then?"

She laughed, glancing around the building. "I don't know if you'll be open long enough for that."

I felt like that hit me so hard, my succulent at home withered from the blow.

I was still a little despondent when I got into the back, where I bumped into Liv traying up drinks for the couple who had just crushed my heart. She shot me a lopsided smile, the one artfully loose strand of blonde hair outside her preppy high ponytail falling over her face.

"Are you doing okay, Avery? You look worse for wear today."

I thumped my collar. "I'm making it work. Manifesting a better reality."

"Manifest some customers while you're at it," she said, picking up the tray. "I think that might be your best bet."

I sighed, hanging my head. "Table seventeen says you were wonderful. You're doing well, Liv."

She stopped at the door to glance back at me. "Hey, Aves, just to say, even if this place crashes and burns, I'm glad I got to work here. I think you're the only boss I've actually liked."

I laughed wryly. "Please don't sound like we're about to die. We only just opened recently. There's still time for things to change."

"You sure say that a lot," Dominic said as Liv pushed through the door and out onto the floor. He was one of only two cooks on duty right now—not a lot of volume right now, after all—and he glanced up at me. "For someone in a hopeless situation."

Ah, Dominic. The giant, standing at six four with a shaved head, never did mince words. I just smiled at him. "No such thing as a hopeless situation. There's only situations we haven't figured out how to resolve yet."

He looked back down at where he was cooking down a tomato reduction. "Any idea what you're doing after this?"

"If this flops? No idea. Burn your boats. I've got no course out of this but up. It's the only way to survive in this industry. You can never run a successful restaurant if you're comfortable."

"The Julius down the road a ways was opened by some guy who had a cooking show and a few million in property and has never had a slow day once, they seem to be doing okay."

I hung my head. "Dominic, look, you're great, I love you, but I'm going to need you to not tell me things like that or I might actually cry."

The doors swung back open behind me, and I glanced at where Liv was coming back in, eyebrows raised. "Hey, Aves, uh, someone wants to see you. At the front. Asked for the owner."

I paused. "He didn't even ask for the manager, he asked for the *owner*? And— furthermore, someone came inside? Did you try seeing if you could give him a menu?"

She squinted at me. "Are we that desperate?"

"I prefer *resourceful* over *desperate*."

She laughed, shaking her head. "He didn't look friendly. I wasn't about to try selling him food."

"Of course he didn't look friendly," I sighed, adjusting my collar. It never did feel quite right. "I'll go talk to him. Did he say his name?"

"Mike. Wearing a checkered necktie. He's sitting at table three."

I strode through the doors and across the restaurant floor, bringing a glass of water and a basket of bread rolls towards table three, where a handsome man in a button-down and tie with light brown hair and stubble, sort of dirty blonde, sat leaning way back in his chair.

He grinned at me, but it made my stomach sink, because I'd seen this guy before, and I hadn't liked a second of it.

Mike Wallace. Had his own YouTube series for a little cooking show or something, when in reality, all he did was stand there and talk about how great he was.

Ugh. God. He looked even more annoying in person than he did on TV.

"Hi," I said, setting down the water and bread on the table and sitting opposite him, under a trellis of roses. "I'm Avery Lindt, the owner of this place. Mike Wallace, right? It's... nice, to meet you," I lied, badly.

"Nice meeting you, Avery," he said, reaching across the table to give me an awkward handshake. "You got that right. Mike Wallace, owner of the Julius, just down the road from here, and star of hit YouTube cooking series *The Perfect Sear*. You might have seen me."

I forced a smile. "I have," I said, leaving all value judgments on his lousy show out. *He* was the douchebag running the Julius? It added up, but—talk about annoying.

"I thought I'd drop in and say hi, see how things are going over here. We restaurant owners, we need to look out for one another, you know?"

Right. The celebrity chef, owner of the massively successful Julius right here in Southport, just here to *look out* for me. Because that wasn't concerning. "Yeah..." I shifted in my seat, straightened my back, and told myself to *not* be so damn terrified and *smile*. I told myself *you got this* and didn't believe myself, and I said, "Definitely. I visited the Julius once, before I opened Paramour. It's a beautiful restaurant, and the food was incredible."

He smiled. "Oh yeah? What did you have?"

I'd seen the menu prices and walked back out. I smiled back. "The saffron souffle and lamb. I have to say, your chef makes the best souffle I've ever tasted."

"Nice call," he said, leaning back and crossing his legs. "Always been a big lamb guy."

"It isn't lamb, but help yourself to some bread and butter. We're partnered with a special butter house to get handmade, flavored butters."

"Patterson Butter House, right? I've heard about that."

Right. Of course he somehow just... knew which contracts I'd signed and which partnerships I was in. The way he kept talking with something just slightly held back in his voice, I felt like he was waiting for a chance to grind me into dust, and given the circumstances, well... I figured he was waiting for a chance to grind me into dust.

But nevertheless, he took a bread roll, split it in half, and spread the sea salt and fresh dill butter on one half, taking a bite. I felt myself draw a breath in anticipation, practically counting the number of layers that fell away from the outer crust of the bread as he bit in, making sure it was high but not *too* high. Dominic had a way with butter baking, and I owed him one.

"Mm," he said, talking through a mouthful of bread, one hand over his mouth. "Fantastic."

I breathed out. "Thank you. Henry Patterson is so passionate about his craft, I think it shows. Would you like a further sampling? I can bring you a small plate, a wine pairing—"

"Oh, don't tempt me," he said, putting a hand up.

"I'm in the business of tempting. Lamb skewers with a mint sauce and a half glass of chardonnay?"

He smiled. "Pulling out the lamb again? You're good at this tempting thing, Avery."

So I headed into the back, and it was quick work preparing the small plate for Mike before bringing it with a half glass of wine back out. I left the bottle behind because I knew he'd criticize the damn wine otherwise, and my heart couldn't take that.

But Mike didn't complain—he lavished praise upon the food, talked about how succulent the lamb was, the perfect consistency on the sauce and how brightly its flavors shone, the perfection of the pairing, and he didn't stop there. He went on to rave about the beautiful designs, the look that was right on trend, the stunning location and how the food was just a little bit novel to match the destination setting, until finally he settled back in his seat and said, "You know, Avery, I'm fond of Paramour. I think I'd like to buy it."

And that knocked down all my thoughts like a house of cards built on train tracks. I stared at him for a second just processing the words before I said, "You think what?"

He smiled wider. "As you know, the Julius is the best of the best in Southport—maybe all Port Andrea. But what you may not know is that we're not only in the restaurant business, but in the real estate business. We've been buying... you could think of it as sponsorships for restaurants one after the other here, and let me tell you, Avery, everyone's been so excited to get on board with this collective. You can think of it like a group of restaurants working in harmony, under one banner of leadership."

I blinked slowly. "You've been... buying up all the restaurants and conglomerating them."

"Not really a conglomerate," he laughed, swirling his wine in his glass. "Think of it more like a partnership. Avery—when you think of your restaurant, what do you really want from it? Freedom, your own decision-making, and the endless creativity of running a restaurant. Isn't that why you started one?"

"Yes, and—"

"And I think you'll find that under our leadership, you would even have *more* freedom. Now, what do I mean by that? What I mean by that is—right now, you're having a hard time finding customers. I know, I know," he said, putting his hands up. "It's a hard truth, but it's one lots of restaurants face. This is a tough market, Avery, and you're gutsy getting into it. A lot of other new owners around here run into the same problem, and a lot of them are eager to get on board with this, because with our leadership, you can experiment *without* having to worry about if it'll bring you customers. You'll have the room to just focus on making sure your food is delicious, your service is impeccable, and you can keep bringing back those repeat customers."

I stared for a minute before I said, "But the restaurant will belong to you."

"Technically, the filings will be under our LLC, and any leadership decisions will ultimately come down to our quality control—"

"You're going to be *quality controlling* me. To make sure I don't do anything too ugly and stain your big fancy conglomerate."

He smiled wider. "Now, Avery, I see what you mean. It's frustrating—"

"Don't get all salesy talk on me," I said, standing up and leaning over the table, planting my hands on it and shooting him the dirtiest look I could. "I worked my ass off trying to open this restaurant, and you're trying to drag me into some kind of pyramid scheme that ends with you owning my business once it's successful—and you have the audacity to come in here, eat *my* lamb skewers, and then try to buy my business? I ought to ask you to give the lamb skewers back. Hell, those things cost money. I'll bill it to your fancy-ass theme park of a restaurant. I didn't even eat your crappy saffron souffle. Who the hell puts saffron in a souffle? Just make a damn souffle and—you know what? Just go on. Get out of here."

He sighed. "Avery. I get why you're upset."

"You don't get a damn thing," I said. "I worked myself to the bone every damn day to scrounge up money, to get connections, to be the best damn restaurant manager anyone's ever seen, just to get my one shot at calling this place my own. A guy like you who—who just swings by with your millions in holdings I'll bet you got from Mommy and Daddy, and you start up a restaurant because it seems like fun and you like cooking on YouTube, and you start incorporating all your competition into one big soulless void of *quality controls* and—you wouldn't understand a damn thing. And Patterson is damn good, but for right now, so help me god, Mike Wallace, I hope that butter gives you diarrhea."

He stared for the longest time before I turned—spun on my heel, thrust my chin up, and stormed into the back.

I knew they weren't going to pay, but I'd send the Julius that damn bill anyway. Just to make me feel better.

CHAPTER 2

Holly

Dwayne shook his head. "I don't know how I'm supposed to thank you."

I just smiled, looking around the kitchen. "Just keep making food," I said. "Good food is more than just a meal. It brings a community together, it starts a conversation. And it has effects that ripple through the whole city. You keep on making food just like this, and it'll pay all of us back."

He just beamed at me, brushing his hands off on the apron he had on over his lean frame, and he offered a hand. "Holly Mason, you are really something else."

I took his hand and shook it firmly, aware of the cameras rolling, Mack from the crew chewing her cheek while she watched from behind the camera. "Been a pleasure working with you, Dwayne."

"And cut," Kyle's voice called through the kitchen, and I turned away from Dwayne, forgetting him the instant the filming stopped. Kyle, a tall and slender man with gelled blond hair and a scarf that was not appropriate for a kitchen but impossible to separate him from, and who just so happened to be our producer, gave me a sour look. "Holly, you looked like you were swallowing a bag of nails."

I sighed. "Fuck's sake, Kyle. Another take?"

"Forget it. We're already pushing the time on our filming for the day. We can only get so many takes *in*, you know."

"If you're going to yell at me, let's take it back to the studio first. We've gotten in Dwayne's way enough for one day."

He shook his head. "We're wrapping for the day. Union's going to be breathing down my neck if I push today too long too. We'll meet tomorrow in the studio to see what we can do with all of this."

The staff packed up behind him, folding up booms and camera tripods, wheeling equipment out through the back doors. I watched Mack and Jason go before I turned my attention back to Kyle, standing there with his hands in his pockets, hip out to one side. "That bad, huh? Can't wait for the official diatribe in your office come morning."

"Don't start giving me sass. You've got to start acting like you care about the damn job if you want people to watch. You used to be able to smile on the damn camera."

"I'm not an extra to just stand there and smile, I'm—"

"The star. I know. I know. And as the star, you've done enough to start rumors that you hate the job and just want it to end. Try looking like you're doing a little more than going through the motions."

I shook my head. It felt good to snap back at Kyle, but it wouldn't get me anywhere. "I'll talk to you in the morning, Kyle."

"Seven am, sharp!" he called as I turned and strode out through the back doors and into the murky dusk of a sunset over the water. Seagulls cried overhead, and the road to my right rumbled with light traffic, staff loading up cars in the lot to my left. I glanced for my escort, but I spotted Tay instead, making their way toward me, waving their hand.

"Hey, Holly," they said, giving me a sympathetic smile that said they knew how much Kyle had been laying into me. "Congratulations on the big wrap."

"I'm half expecting Kyle to bring me out here again tomorrow to just redo it. Like Sisyphus pushing the damn rock."

"Relax," they said, putting a hand on my shoulder and walking me towards the van. "Even Kyle wouldn't do that. Sorry he chewed you out like that. You did great."

"Tell it to someone else," I said. "I've heard it plenty. Apparently I just don't look happy enough for the damn show."

They shrugged. "You're just looking a little burned out lately, that's all."

"That's just the nice version of what Kyle was saying."

They laughed, holding open the rear side door for me. My agent Tay liked being hands-on— literally, too, with how touchy-feely they were— but I didn't know what I'd do without them. They were a skinny little thing, almost six feet tall and with platinum-blond hair in a ponytail down their back, along with the slick white suit they wore so well, and we were inseparable half the time.

Part agent, part emotional support. Or, judging by everyone else I'd worked with in my years filming, I think everyone's agent was at least fifty percent emotional support. Tay was good at their job.

"Kyle just likes to yell at people. I just want to see you actually enjoying the work. But it doesn't matter. Let's get you home and I'll give you the gossip while we go, to help you feel better. You wrapped a segment and that's something to celebrate."

I sighed, stepping into the car and sitting down, looking at the driver's eyes glancing at me in the rear-view mirror from the front. "Thanks, Tay," I said, just before they closed the door, and a second later, slid into the back next to me, signaling to the driver, who put us in drive and headed for the exit to the lot.

"I've got some juicy news," they said, shuffling around to shed their suit and fold it up neat and tidy in their lap before they buckled their seatbelt and sank back. "Someone got into a spat with Mike Wallace."

That already made me feel better. I smiled to myself. "Yeah? Someone I know?"

"Someone I don't know if anyone knows. She came in from out of town to open a restaurant here, an upscale place on the water called Paramour. Avery Lindt. Seems most likely he tried to buy her restaurant—"

"I'm so sick of that guy."

"Likewise." They shook their head. "He's been getting more and more bold. I hadn't thought he'd try to buy a place this soon after opening. But word is that Avery all but spat in his eye, and he went out with his tail between his legs, and he's been pissed off."

"Mike Wallace, upset about his fragile ego. What a surprise."

"Right?" They slipped their phone from their pocket, swiping in an unlock pattern and scanning their fingerprint both to open it. "Here's his handiwork since then. Been two days and his smear campaign's all across the area. He's gotten nearly a dozen blogs to publish nasty pieces about Paramour, all ghostwritten."

I took their phone and scrolled through a page of articles, mostly on personal websites and small food reviewers, but with one even from a major outlet, all panning this place as if rats had run clear across their tables while they were eating.

"He's as heavy-handed as ever," I said, handing the phone back.

"No kidding. Anyone looking over the big picture is going to see right through it, but ninety percent of people are just going to see one or two outlets saying it. They're pretty evenly distributed, anyway. He's aggressive and heavy-handed, but he's smart about it. Paramour is doomed at this rate."

I sighed, sinking back into the seat and staring out the window, watching the city roll by. Port Andrea was a beautiful place, clean roads and enough public transportation that those roads were relatively quiet, and views out over the sparkling waters of the bay. It was a popular place for celebrities, for foodies, and especially for people who were both.

"You were supposed to give me gossip with a happy ending," I said. "Although going out spitting in Mike Wallace's eye is as noble an end as any."

"Want to go?" they said, giving me a sly grin. "Together. We could see if it's really as bad as the reviews say."

I chewed my lip. Earlier in my career, I would have jumped at the opportunity. To explore the story behind it, what brought this Avery woman here to Port Andrea to open an upscale restaurant, to find where she'd come from and what style of food she brought. To find out what she *loved*, because you didn't open a restaurant just out of *liking* something. It was an endeavor of passion, of love, and especially if she was willing to send Mike Wallace out the door like that, she must have cared about it.

But hey. Maybe Kyle was right. I'd lost something over the past few years. Filming this same series about rehabbing lousy restaurants for three years, I'd seen the process enough times that I could act out a whole new season of it from imagination alone. It was the same damn thing over and over, and it was just so damn hard to care about anything anymore.

Tay was right—Paramour was done for. Even if Avery found a way to survive the smear attack, Mike had a million times the resources. He'd drive her into the ground.

Best not to get invested, I thought.

"Maybe another day," I said. "If the place is still around then."

"I'll be in the area for a while. If you decide to go any time, hit me up, and we'll go together. It's always nice when I'm home here and get to watch you criticize restaurant food in person."

I smiled wryly. "I'm glad I'm still good for something, at least."

But it haunted me still, when I got back to my penthouse and took off my makeup, changed into casual clothes, and sank back onto the sofa to stare out the full-wall window of my thirty-third story penthouse and sip my evening tea slowly, a ritual for stressful days.

I hated Mike. He was a big player in the industry around here, and he'd been to more than one event I'd attended, and every time, he would track me down and talk to me, as if he didn't get the hint when we...

Dating him had been the greatest shame of my life, back when I'd started my restaurant and he was planning on opening one of his own. And even though that lasted all of two months, he'd been acting ever since like it gave him some kind of right to me, like he could just invite himself to whatever I was doing, whenever he wanted. And sometimes, it felt like Tay and I were the only two people who didn't like him.

He strutted around events like a peacock flashing his feathers, and he schmoozed with everything that had a pulse. And people ate it up. His little restaurant conglomerate he'd started recently had been reaching its strangulating tendrils across Port Andrea lately, and I swear, there was too much damn salt in every single meal served by every single restaurant he—to quote him—*sponsored.*

Minus the flavor, plus the preserved crap. I wouldn't have been surprised if five years from now, all those poor places would be franchisees for Mike Wallace's garish taste.

Maybe it was because I was just relieved someone else wasn't taking Mike's crap, but I couldn't get Paramour out of my head. And one way or another, I found myself at the front door pulling on my sneakers, sweeping my hair up into a lazy ponytail, and pulling on sunglasses at night just to reduce the chances of anyone bothering me before I slipped out and down to my car, and one way or another, I found myself at the front doors of the Paramour.

And it didn't disappoint—the place was gorgeous, even from the front. It was *right* on the waterfront, and thank god it cleared out the Starbucks that had been in that zone, because even just looking at it, I could tell there was someone who *cared* running the place. I took off my sunglasses when I got into the antechamber at the front, admiring the live plants that were creeping along the walls and the use of glass and water to create subtle mirroring effects and expand the spaces, but even without the sunglasses I was safe as the hostess gave me a smile and directed me to a table without saying a word about who I was.

Either she didn't recognize me, or she was being nice about it. I'd spent a while hoping people wouldn't recognize me, but with the way my career had been declining lately, maybe I should have been concerned.

Either way, I wouldn't have needed celebrity status to get a table—the place was dead, and unsurprisingly so given the smear campaign Mike had waged. I didn't entirely mind, though. It was quiet, no sound but water running in the fountain, a few murmurs from the rare other people in here, low jazz music playing from the ceiling, and the sound of cooks from the kitchen. I looked around taking note of it all—it wasn't a surprise Mike had targeted the place, with a building as beautiful as this. No doubt he'd wanted to get his claws in on their profit potential early on.

"Hello, and thank you for your patience," a woman's voice said from behind me, and I turned to look at her—a woman maybe in her late twenties, looking stunning in a well-tailored navy suit. She didn't look like a waiter, not wearing the uniform everyone else was, but she held a pad of paper and a tray, and she swept across the room all grace and confidence until I made eye contact with her, and she stopped short. "Oh. Wow. You're... Holly Mason."

Maybe my career wasn't completely in shambles. I gave her a sly smile. "A fan? It's nice to meet you. Don't worry, I'm not here to criticize your kitchen."

She swallowed nervously, a pink flush creeping into her cheeks. She was, frankly, drop-dead gorgeous—maybe it was just the suit doing it for me, but with the brown hair ending in loose waves at her shoulders, bright green eyes, and a deep nude lipstick, it all made her look like elegance and class wrapped up in one very sexy, suit-wearing package with beautifully long legs.

"That's a relief," she said. "It's... wow. It's an honor. I'm—a fan. Yes." She shook her head, regaining her composure, putting on the professional's smile. "I'm so sorry. You're here for dinner, not for awkward fan interactions. Thank you so much for choosing Paramour. I'm Avery Lindt, the owner, and I'll be here to take your order tonight. Can I get you started with something to drink?"

Ah—and here she was herself. The one who'd spat in Mike's face and sent him packing, at the expense of her entire *very* luxurious restaurant. That made her two of my weaknesses—brunette *and* ready to tell Mike Wallace to go fuck himself.

But I wasn't here to check out anyone.

"I'd heard about you," I said, and her face fell. "My agent told me about a little firebrand here on the waterfront who told Mike Wallace to kick rocks, and has been on the pointy end of a rather ugly smear campaign. That would be you, then?"

She cleared her throat, forced a fake smile, and straightened her back. "It would absolutely be me. Avery Lindt, at your service. It's—an honor to know you've heard of me." She paused. "A dubious honor."

I laughed. "Relax. I came here after I heard the story because I was tired of being the only person who can't stand Mike. I was impressed how I heard you'd shut him down."

The mask she was wearing over her emotions slipped for a second, and I swear she had a complete crisis on the spot before she regained it. "Well, I never thought I'd impress Holly Mason, but if I'd known it would, then I would have told him the checkered necktie was a hideous look, too, just to sweeten the deal. As it is, I only told him I hoped he got diarrhea."

I liked this woman even more. I blinked once before I laughed. "I hope he did, too."

"I—shouldn't be talking about all of that," she said, going red and scrunching up her lower lip. "I apologize. Can I take your order?"

"I'd like whatever you have to recommend. And frankly, I'd like to have you for a conversation, if you're not busy tonight."

"I—" she sputtered. "I would be happy to oblige. Wine?"

"Just a little, please. I drove."

"Red or white?"

I licked my lip without meaning to. "Red."

CHAPTER 3

Avery

"L iv, I need you here in about two seconds," I said into the phone, my hand shaking. "Can you do that?"

"What?" Liv's voice, down the phone, was so distant and confused it was hard to hear it over the clattering in the kitchen around me. "Don't tell me we got customers? Did I nap into the Twilight Zone?"

"Very funny, Olivia. I need you to take over waiting tables for me because Holly Mason is here and she wants me to sit down and talk with her."

"Holy shit," Liv said, choking on food. "Okay. Yeah. Let me get changed and I'll be down there as soon as I can."

"Okay. It's—probably not that much of a rush, actually, because Diane can host and wait tables, since we have four tables filled right now. I'm just freaking out."

And I was still freaking out, even when I got the bread rolls and the specialty butters, and I

racked my brain to go over every episode of
Kitchen Rescue to remember anything Holly
Mason might have ever said she liked before I hit
upon mushrooms and practically threw
everything down to stand there in the kitchen in
my suit and make fried mushrooms.

I had to stop before the door out to the
dining floor, carrying the tray, and look at my
distorted reflection in the wine bottle, and I said,
"You've got this, Avery. You are charming, and
friendly, and you can talk your way through any
situation. To anyone. You are damn good at this."

"That's subjective," Dominic said. I shot
him a dirty look, and I pushed through the door.

When I got back to table twelve, I found out
I hadn't been hallucinating and Holly Mason was
still very much there and very much real. I felt
like anyone who hadn't seen every episode of her
show at least twice wouldn't have recognized her,
hair down and makeup gone, wearing a white V-
neck t-shirt that showed the outline of her bra
underneath and jeans with sneakers, but to me
she was still so ridiculously beautiful that my
entire body felt like it could melt. She was tall,

lean, with that television face that was just so perfectly designed it made my stomach fluttery, dark eyes and black hair she had pulled back into a simple ponytail right now. I admired the muscle definition on her arms maybe just a little too much as I approached the table and set down the things in the middle, and she looked up and gave me a stomach-melting, drop-dead-sexy smirk.

"You must have known I can't resist fried mushrooms," she said, and I could have cheered. Instead, I pretended I was even vaguely cool.

"I think I might have heard it on an episode of your show," I said, sliding into the seat opposite her. It felt so surreal, sitting at a booth across from Holly Mason herself, loose strands of her long hair falling across her face, looking as messy as if it were in my kitchen the morning after—

I wasn't supposed to be thinking things like that. I just—you gave me a celebrity chef who was a bisexual woman, it wasn't like there were a lot of others, I thought about how hot she was. It was a lot. Now here she was, sitting right across from me, even hotter than I'd thought.

"You're a dedicated fan," she said, brushing loose hairs out of her face before she took a bread roll.

"I've watched the show... more than once, maybe." And it was the reason I had my own restaurant today. The reason my dreams had stayed alive after Cecilia. And Holly did not need to have all of that gushing right now.

She smiled. "I've been told I'm less interesting in person."

She was listening to the wrong people. I cleared my throat. "If you didn't like Mike Wallace, I, uh... I'm already inclined to like you."

She laughed. *God,* her laugh. It made my insides tangle up like limp spaghetti. "Common ground, then," she said.

I had common ground with Holly Mason. I shoved the gay panic out of my mind. "We have a close partnership with Patterson Butter House—"

"I thought I recognized the butter whorls," she said, smiling wider, flashing her made-for-TV pearly white grin. My brain fritzed out. "I love Patterson's. This is the cracked black pepper, isn't it?" she said, swiping from one of the butters on the tray and spreading over the bread. "That one's my absolute favorite."

"It's—amazing. Yeah. Absolutely."

I had no idea what to do. Was I supposed to be selling something to her? Asking her for a partnership? Asking her to take my sorry restaurant on her show and tell me how to get customers? Or deal with angry and powerful men who hated me? I felt like there was a truck full of free money just slowly rolling by, and I was just standing there not sure what to do with it, but I had to do *something* before it just drove away and I couldn't do anything but stand there sadly and watch it go.

When she bit into the bread, my heart stopped, because it looked like it was just a *little* too much on the crust and it crumbled just the *tiniest* fraction, and I was about to break down on the spot, but she put a hand over her mouth as she chewed and spoke through a mouthful and said, "Oh, it's good. The flavor is so complex, and it's sweet without being overdone."

I nearly slumped out of the seat. "Thank you," I said. She shot me another smirk that had my stomach doing things.

"You're nervous, aren't you, Avery?"

I was so nervous, my succulent back home was biting its nails. "I'm not nervous at all," I said. My voice went a little too high-pitched. She raised an eyebrow.

"Of course," she said. She didn't believe me. She wasn't even being subtle about it.

"I—swear I'm normally cooler than this," I said, which was in of itself probably the least cool thing I could have said.

She laughed. "It's fine, Avery. I'm a human being. Pour the wine. It'll help you with the nerves, too. And we'll try your mushrooms."

I swear, she was seducing me. I nodded a little too hard. "Of—course. I brought a cabernet—"

"Emiliano Russo, vintage 1995. I've had a Russo vintage 2005 before, but nothing longer than that, so I'm excited to try it."

Right. She could read the bottle. And she probably knew more about it than I did. I chewed my lip. "I, uh, might be nervous."

"Honesty is the best policy," she said. "I figured you were."

I sighed. "What gave me away?"

"You forgot wine glasses."

Crap. I forgot wine glasses.

But somehow or other, after I ran to the back and grabbed the wine glasses, I poured two glasses of cabernet—one for me and one for Holly Mason, which I still could not get my head around—and we clinked our glasses together, and we ate.

Somehow, talking got a little easier with some time. Maybe it was the wine. Probably it was the fact that the more I sat there staring at her, the more it sank in that I was actually sitting with Holly Mason, and she was just a human being like she said, not some kind of otherworldly entity. A human being who was put on camera to show failing restaurant owners what they were doing wrong and paid an absurd amount of money while the whole world watched her, but a human being, and as I realized that, it helped take the edge off.

And, well, the wine didn't hurt.

"So, let's hear it," Holly said after a little while, talking and eating, giving me vivid descriptions of the food that—*somehow*—sounded positive. "I'm sure you have questions for me too."

I blinked. *Are you single* was the first question to mind, and the last question I should have been asking. "Questions—like what?"

She raised an eyebrow. *How* in the world was she so hot with that one little gesture? "About me. My career. You've heard all the rumors, I'm sure."

Well—I'd heard rumors she secretly hated the show. There'd also been talk of her sniping the starring role on the show from someone else, and there was some growing movement demanding she give the show to them, seeing how she hated it anyway. But I'd never put any stock in rumors to begin with. So I just chewed my cheek and said, "I don't really follow rumors, to be honest with you. I think there's always people looking to take whatever you do in bad faith, especially when you're in the public eye. I believe in growth, in improvement, and as far as I see it, your show has been about that for so many people."

She studied me for a long time, slowly sipping her wine, before she said, "What even is your story? My agent told me the owner of Paramour had come from out of town. What brought you to Port Andrea to open an upscale restaurant?"

I took a long breath. I'd practiced the sales pitch a lot. Given it to myself in the mirror a million times. Given it to my friends, who helped me refine it. And now that I was here, I completely blanked on what the hell I was supposed to say. "I... like food."

She stared at me for a second. It took me that full second to actually process the words I'd said and realize how badly I'd just dropped the ball.

I took a sharp breath. "I—*love* food. Not just as something to eat when we're hungry, but as a way of self-expression. Every dish, every recipe, has its own history that can go back through generations, that can cross the world, all refined time and again into a single moment for a diner. It draws people together to share an experience you've cultivated for months, sometimes years. And when I managed a restaurant before, I was so inspired by that message, by that vision, that I wanted to bring people like me together in a city I'd fallen in love with, years ago."

She narrowed her eyes at me slightly, studying me. I was running completely on adrenaline, hoping I wasn't sounding completely ridiculous, and just when I was accepting that I'd gone and utterly embarrassed myself, she said, "And that city was Port Andrea."

"It was five years since the last time I was in Port Andrea. It had been a city of love and heartbreak for me. I'd moved here for someone I thought was the love of my life. It was a year of the highest highs and the lowest lows. But one thing I never forgot was the food we shared while we were here. She and I were so different, in so many ways—and that's what made it so exciting, and what made it crash and burn in the end—but when we shared meals, at restaurants like this one or out of takeout containers on her sofa with a movie on, for a second, we shared the same experience, spoke the same language. And when it all ended, I packed up my bags and went home, but even though I got over her, I never got over the city. It called me back. When I got funding to open a luxury restaurant... I knew Port Andrea was calling me." I sucked in a long breath, wondering how much my hands were shaking. I wasn't sure whether to kick myself or pat myself on the back for talking that long to Holly Mason. Ditto for accidentally outing myself to the hottest queer woman in the food industry. "And I might have screwed it up right at the outset. You know—by getting Mike Wallace angry at me."

She nodded. "He's a dangerous man to piss off."

"Yeah. Well," I laughed nervously, looking around the restaurant, "truth be told, there weren't a lot of customers here before that, either. Maybe I just wasn't ready yet."

Holly stared a while longer, studying me, swirling her wine, before she took a small sip and said, "But you took a leap. Just like with that girlfriend. And it sounds like you didn't regret it then."

I paused. "I... yeah. I don't regret that at all."

She frowned, looking down into her wine. "Good on you, I think. For taking a leap. Whatever happens, I think you'll be happy you did this."

Suddenly, it all felt so much realer—that I was really sitting at a table with Holly Mason, in a restaurant I'd opened in Port Andrea, and also that it was all falling through as we spoke.

And even though she was saying all that— and even though she was *right*—I was realizing more and more I didn't want it to fail. I didn't *want* to lose Paramour. I didn't want to have another heartbreak with this damn city. Wasn't one enough?

But I was supposed to be cool about it. Law of attraction. I was going to picture nothing but success, and believe in success above all else, and bring it into being. And if I didn't have a clue what I was doing, I was going to fake it, and see where it got me.

So I said, "I think you're right. But... for what it's worth... I think it's going to survive. I think Paramour is going to thrive. And I think it's going to be a destination enough that Foodie Magazine is going to feature us right on the cover."

She gave me a wry smile. "And your plan for doing that?"

I sank a little. "I... am still working on figuring that part out."

"Unfortunately, you can't just will something into being," she said, taking another sip of her wine, and I swear the air got ten degrees colder around the table. "A realistic and well-thought-out plan is crucial to growth. And it doesn't sound like there's much of that at work here."

I straightened enough that my back hurt. "I think my plan is to roll with the punches, and to find a way to work with everything the universe gives me."

"Your call what you want to do with the restaurant," she said, which—the simple dismissiveness of it felt worse than anything she could have done to double down on criticizing me.

"The mushrooms are excellent, and the rolls are perfect. I've enjoyed visiting."

Panic shot through me. "Do you want to look over the menu for a main course—"

"I think I'll pass," she said, looking out the window, and that's when it hit me that I didn't know what it was, but I'd said *something* wrong and now she was just looking to get out of it. "I had filming today and we ate at the restaurant I've been filming at this segment, and I'm satisfied."

"What's it like, anyway? Cooking on camera, fixing up a restaurant that needs saving."

She shrugged. "Exhausting. And I have to talk to the producer early in the morning, so I really need to make sure I get to sleep at a reasonable hour."

I was so desperate, I'd have brought up any conversation topic under the sun to get her to stay a little longer. To say *something* that would help. To offer something, as if I was just here to wring things out of her. Was that what business was?

But I'd botched it. I'd lost faith in myself, and I'd screwed something up along the way, and she was leaving now—hurrying out, even—and I didn't think she was keen enough on coming back to make it before Mike drove me out of business.

So I just sank back and I said, "I hope that goes well. It's really been wonderful talking to you. You're more approachable than I expected from a celebrity, I think."

She looked back over at me, arching her eyebrows, and again it was *too* damn hot. I swallowed. "You think so?" she said, her voice an airy thing, aloof.

"Of course. I enjoyed the opportunity to eat with you. We're very different with our approaches to food, but... I think a shared meal unites two people who otherwise can't share a language."

She stared for a while longer before a smirk flickered over her features. "You are an interesting character, Avery Lindt."

I had no idea if that was a compliment. "I'd say the same to you," I said, not sure if I was insulting her.

"It's been a pleasure," she said, sinking back. "Check? I'll pay for the full thing, of course."

"I wouldn't ask you to—"

"Please. I'm not about to steal food from a failing restaurant. That goes somewhat against my whole career, doesn't it?"

Ugh. She'd described Paramour as a failing restaurant. It hurt because she was right. I forced on a smile and said, "It's not a failing restaurant. It's a restaurant that hasn't figured out how to succeed yet."

She just stared at me. After a second, I looked down.

"I'll bring the check out. It's been an honor to have you."

"Likewise," she said, with that tone that said it wasn't an honor, and I cringed a little inwardly.

Paramour was having a really hard time figuring out how to succeed.

CHAPTER 4

Holly

Paramour was a lovely restaurant, and it was a shame I wasn't going to eat there again, because there was too much chance of running into Avery again.

Too bad. She was sweet. Really passionate about her restaurant. And I should have been inured to that kind of thing, because I was used to working with owners of failing restaurants who had nothing to their name but passion, but...

Something about Avery was different. Maybe that obnoxious thing she had for trying to just *will* her success into existence, as if she had a direct line to God and it'd get through the connection sooner or later if she believed hard enough. If people could just *believe* their restaurants into success, I wouldn't have a show.

So I had no idea why I was sauntering into an ice cream parlor feeling like I was in the wrong, and that Avery had shown me up.

I ordered a lychee ice cream with a fried crepe and candied orange peel, and I sat down in the candy-red booth in the back of the obnoxiously colorful place with all its charming outdated décor, and I only got a few bites in before a voice I did *not* want to hear right now rang through the building.

"Holly," he said, dragging out the word, a voice that was just too damn self-satisfied, a little sleazy. *Very* sleazy. "Babe. What are you doing here, crying into a bowl of ice cream alone at night?"

I closed my eyes and let out a long, slow sigh, sinking back into my seat. I didn't want to open them again and see Mike Wallace's smug look, but the sound of the booth seat crinkling from the side opposite me told me I had no choice. "Getting stalked by a man I have no interest in, apparently," I said.

"Babe. Please. It's not stalking. I just saw you going inside and was wondering how you got to be so washed up. And don't pretend you haven't been interested before."

I sighed, opening my eyes and looking at the man sitting across from me, wearing a brown leather jacket and a light brown stubble on his square jawline. Mike Wallace always had that damn grin like he thought he was better than you and *loved* it, and those hazel eyes that were too pretty for such a thoroughly ugly man sparkled at me like gemstones—pretty and shiny and cold and lifeless.

"It was a time I have regretted every day since then," I said. "And don't get any ideas about trying to win me back, because my mind, once made up, is made forever."

"You shouldn't be so icy. It's not good for your career, now, is it?"

I took a spoonful of ice cream and savored it, sweet and refreshing lychee melting over my tongue and distracting me from his honeyed voice that, just like honey, left a sickly residue in its wake. "Tell me what you're here for."

"I can't just drop by to say hi to an old friend?" He leaned in closer, folding his arms on the table in front of him. "The Julius is doing well.

It's been a blast. I really owe you for all the practice I got when we were together."

"Very good of you to acknowledge you dated me to scalp me for culinary knowledge, and you're now making money off of it while I assume you're here again now to try kicking me off my own show."

He snorted, falling back into his chair, shaking his head. "I swear, you're feistier than ever. Come on, babe. Hear me out. I think me taking over the show like this will be even better for you than it will be for me."

I put my spoon back in the bowl and pushed the ice cream to the side, folding my hands in front of me. "Oh, really? It was all just a kindness for me, was it? That's why you decided to spread rumors about me badmouthing everyone on my staff and made up an elaborate story about how I'd stolen your show—to help me out? God, Mike, I don't know what I'd do without your help. Really did a bang-up job."

He just raised his eyebrows, watching me for a minute before he said, "You done?"

"Not remotely," I snapped. "But I know the longer I complain, the longer you'll be here. Say your piece and go, slimeball. Before I call up my security detail, which I *have* because I'm a TV star and I'm not planning on giving that away to you."

He chuckled. "You're so fiery. Now, if you're done with your whole spiel..." He put a hand up. "Let me tell you something. I didn't spread all those rumors about you hating your job. Anyone watching the show can tell you're sick of the damn thing."

"It's creative burnout, and it's natural for a professional."

"Right. No judgment there." He put his hands up defensively. "We all get it. Just a sign to change gears, pursue something new that sets us alight."

When Mike Wallace spouted two-faced bullshit, it was always a bad sign. When he was *right* about something, it was an even worse sign. "And?"

"And so you need a graceful exit. Off to do something else, aside from *Kitchen Rescue*. You're pretty, but I don't think you're made for TV.

You've got to really live for the cameras if that's what you're doing. You need a kitchen to work in, if I know you at all."

I glowered. "Telling me to get out of the spotlight and go back to the kitchen, are we?"

"Don't give me that lip. You know that's not what I'm getting at. Look, I'm telling the truth. You need a change from what you've been doing on *Kitchen Rescue,* but it's hard to get out of a show like that with an established fanbase. So I set up a pretext for you to be the bigger woman by handing it over to someone else, while you can go and pursue *real* cooking, not just fixing up other people's sorry attempts at restaurants."

"I *do* real cooking. I may be on leave from it right now, but I have two restaurant locations that are, last I checked, doing better than yours."

"Ha. Shots fired. Mortal wounds." He brushed back the loose strands of sandy brown hair that fell in his eyes, and he grinned. "I have a proposal. A partnership, me and you. We tie our brands together—"

"I'm refusing already," I said, waving him towards the door. "Leave me alone."

"Hear me out. We strike up a little agreement between our restaurants—"

"I told you, the answer is no."

"—and you let me take over *Kitchen Rescue.* Come on, babe. It's the perfect reversal for your image. Plenty of other people have already signed up with the partnership, and they can speak to how it's helped—*saved* their restaurants at times."

"I don't need anyone to swoop in and *save me,* and even if I did, you'd be my last fucking choice."

"What's the alternative?" he said, leaning in closer and narrowing his eyes. "Letting *Kitchen Rescue* drag itself out like it has been for the last season, and wear out its welcome—wear out *your* welcome—until everyone just looks at you and sees your sad, tired brand image?"

I sighed, swiveling out of the booth and standing up, taking the ice cream with me and walking away. "If you fall into the bay and I never see you again, it'll be too soon. Goodbye, Wallace."

I paused at the counter to slap down a ten-dollar tip, half as a tip and half as an apology for having to witness my and Mike's confrontation. I leaned over to the girl behind the counter, wearing the retro pinstriped uniform, and I slipped in a few words as I passed.

"The ice cream is incredible. Thank you."

And it was, which was some small consolation as I walked back out into the cool night air and back to my car, but it was consolation nonetheless, crisp and sweet lychee on my tongue with a subtle accent of orange.

Kyle was in a rotten mood in the morning.

"What do I look like, a fucking wizard?" he said at one point, shooting me a deadly glare as he leaned over the meeting table. "You gave these same tired 'inspirational' lines in seasons two, three, and four, three fucking times in season four. You really have nothing else to say? Just acting out some kind of routine like you don't give a damn? How am I supposed to make anything halfway decent out of this crap?"

And it was a morning of that, sitting there across from Kyle as he yelled at me and everyone else on his staff, which felt like a hell of a way to wrap a segment.

"I swear to god, Holly Mason," he said, once we were wrapping our meetings, standing at the door on my way out. "We've got one segment left to film this season, and you are going to turn around Cameron's fortunes with fucking *aplomb* or this whole thing is going up in smoke. You hear me?"

I put a hand up. "I hear you. Trust me. I've been hearing you quite loudly all morning."

"Don't think you're in any position to give me that lip. You may have started this show, but I produce it now. And if it comes time to kick you off and give it to Mike Wallace instead, so help me god, at this rate I'll do it."

It left my insides churning the whole time I walked out of the studio, winding down the stairs and heading for the swing doors at the back. Kyle was a man of empty threats, but it wasn't as though every last threat had nothing backing it up. And after Mike cornering me in the ice cream parlor last night, it left me uneasy, which only got worse when I found Tay bickering with one of the production team out in the lot, their hands thrust into the pockets of their ever-present white suit, hunched over and glowering, a look that only intensified when they glanced over at me.

"Tay," I said, taking the detour over to where they waved off the production assistant with a terse word. "You look like you have bad news for me."

"Really starting to feel like that's all I do anymore," they sighed. "Let's head over to the Den. I already ordered ahead. Got your con panna and got my six shots over ice."

"Six shot kind of day, huh?"

"You don't know the half of it." They gestured for me to follow them—Komodo's Den, the team's favorite coffee shop, was just two blocks away, and I stepped up next to them to walk in time as we headed off the lot and onto the sidewalk, under the cloudless sky that was uncharacteristic of an early summer in Port Andrea.

"News so bad you're going to have to wait to tell me until I've gotten my coffee? You know that just stresses me more."

"It's fucking Mike Wallace. Taking a break from harassing restaurant owners to come stick his hooks into our whole production. Makes me want to just gouge my eyes out."

And there it was—my confirmation even sooner than I'd wanted it. My stomach sank. "Should have let me guess. I'd have figured it out."

"Don't tell me he's been bothering you, too?"

"I had the bad luck of running into him in an ice cream parlor last night. Tried to get me to hand over the show."

They paused, glancing over at me. "Ice cream parlor? Your thing now?"

I looked away. "I was craving sugar. I'd just had dinner."

"Went out?"

"Paramour."

They stopped, putting their hands on their hips. "Mason. What a jerk. You went without me, right after I invited you to go with me?"

I turned back to face them, rolling my eyes, but I couldn't help a small smile. "I'm not obligated to bring my agent to dinner. But for the record, I was genuinely planning on not going, and I only changed my mind an hour later on impulse."

"Well, just means we'll have some experience between us when we go next. How was it? Did you meet the owner? You have a knack for meeting the owner."

"Yeah, met the owner. She was waiting tables, actually. Seemed like she was doing it just because there weren't enough diners in to merit bringing in a waiter..."

"And? What was your takeaway?"

I shrugged. "Doomed. Mike has her outmaneuvered and she has no plan. One of those types who are trying to act like they're someone they're not, trying to be cooler than they are, and pretending she has any idea what she's getting into. She's done for."

Tay just raised an eyebrow. "That's pretty harsh coming from you, Kitchen Rescuer."

I looked away, an anxious feeling in my chest. "You told me yourself I'm just losing my drive for that."

"Ah-hah. Getting evasive. I see you, Mason. Somehow this Avery woman has made an impression on you, and you respond to actually *caring* about something by turning and running away."

"And you like to pretend you know me so well."

"It's literally my job, woman. So? What makes her so special?"

I sighed, just fixing my gaze on the opposite side of the street, watching people pass. Wondering what it was they cared about.

Maybe that was what it was. Avery *cared.* She cared more than maybe anyone else I'd met working my career of finding people who didn't know what they were doing, but god did they care. Even among all of them, Avery just *cared.*

And I couldn't fathom that all that much.

"She cute?" Tay said. I shot them a look.

"I'm not about to flirt with her."

"You, ma'am, did not answer the question."

"What does it matter?" I turned back ahead and started walking again, and Tay kept up beside me.

"Been a while since you had a thing for anyone. Maybe a celebrity romance would be just the thing to make a change in your career."

"I am absolutely not about to... romance her, either. She's clearly not sticking around in Port Andrea long."

"Ah, so it's not that she's straight. Very interesting."

I rolled my eyes. "Lay off. I don't need a change, anyway."

They walked around in front of me just before the doorway to Komodo's Den, turning to face me and stopping me on the sidewalk, their hands in their pockets. "That's the thing here, Mason. You absolutely need a change. And I'm not talking about *let's keep an eye out for any opportunities to start taking things in new directions,* I'm talking, you need to have your fucking midlife crisis early, and you're going to have to rebrand yourself *yesterday* if you want to stay on camera."

I stopped, studying them carefully. "Are you sure you haven't had six shots already?"

"As it so happens, I have. But only because I woke up at four this morning and it's been nonstop stress since then. I met with the showrunner. He's thinking of giving it to Mike."

"Are you—" I dropped my arms by my sides. "Gavin is just going to hand off my show? When he was right *there* when I was building the whole damn thing from scratch?"

"Yup. Look, girl, it's bad. Mike's been crawling around in our business for the past week. He's been insinuating himself into the producers' business, he's been making friends where he doesn't belong, and he's been influencing the people on the renewal panel. Apparently, they've been looking over those contracts for the next season, and they're trying to find ways to amend those contracts to put Mike in next season, and have him take over from there. I've been yelling at people all morning to get them to stick to their damn contracts, but all I'm doing is buying time. Look, reality's here, and it's not pretty. Ratings have been falling. We're barely bringing in viewers. Number one complaint, far and away, it's too damn repetitive. No one's looking you up anymore.

Reporting says your name recognition has dropped twenty percent in the past year. That ain't pretty, Mason."

Ain't pretty was an understatement. And— I knew all of that. I knew my ratings had been falling, knew the viewer numbers were declining, and I'd heard the complaints about *repetitive* from a million different people. Apparently I was a one-trick pony, and no one was interested in that trick anymore.

I'd already known. So why didn't I *care?* It had just felt like a distant worry all this time, like I'd deal with it later, but now that it wasn't the show being canceled but the worst person I'd ever dated, Mike Wallace, taking over my spot—after he made up a bunch of shitty rumors to discredit the work I'd put into starting it—

Hell, maybe I owed him. Because now, thanks to his slimy backdoor dealing and his damn *partnership* scheme, I was starting to care about this whole thing, even if it was only as far as that I *refused* to let him take away my damn show.

"I hear you," I said, finally, looking away.

"Yeah, you've been hearing me. And you haven't done a thing about it."

"Right." I shook my head, and I turned my gaze back to Tay, giving them my hardest stare. "Yeah. You're right. I haven't been listening. And frankly, it's because I haven't given much of a damn about the show. I guess the viewers are right. But I sure as hell care about Mike Wallace stealing from me. Let him make his own damn show. So—whatever you've got in mind. I'm listening. Even if it crashes and burns, we'll get the next season and end the show on our terms, instead of letting *him* steal it."

Tay dropped their arms by their sides, looking at me dumbstruck. "What—end the show? That's it? Just because you've gotten bored, all you're going to do is spite Mike Wallace and then you're going to call it quits?"

I pushed past them, towards the door to the Den. "Yeah. Everyone watching knows I'm sick of the damn show. So let's do it. Give me your branding change, and I'll make it. We'll get our last season."

CHAPTER 5

Avery

So, problem is, I'm literally the most useless person alive."

Liv shrugged. "I don't know. I mean, you pay well."

I sighed, shoulders sagging. "I guess I've at least got that going for me."

Maybe it was a little weird to hang out with my own employees, but I didn't really *have* anyone in Port Andrea except for my staff, and— besides, it felt like we were just both in the same position of trying to make sure Paramour didn't crash and burn.

Which was a hard position to be in.

So here we were, enjoying the sun, Liv dressed in a flowy sundress with a stylish scarf and sunglasses, her long blonde hair all flowing, and me in a suit like always. I'd at least put on a casual tee underneath, which was my version of light summer wear.

"I'm guessing your surprise dinner date with Holly Mason didn't go well?"

"Uh—yeah, think *catastrophe* meets *embarrassment* meets *your cat throwing up on your only clean work shirt right before your shift.*"

She whistled low, strolling along next to me, glancing up at the big ground-level fountain we walked past in the center of the plaza—the one that made my heart ache with nostalgia for this old city. "That's pretty bad," she said.

"She essentially told me Paramour was going to fail and then she walked out. I think I said something to piss her off. I think it was my elevator pitch. She asked me why I opened Paramour and I blanked and said I liked food."

She laughed. "Well, it's true. I've seen you eat it every day."

"I'm glad *one* of us finds this funny," I sighed.

"Relax. We'll get coffee."

"Oh. Great. Right. We'll go get coffee, and I'll bury my tears of shame in it."

"Oh, you don't need to cry," she laughed. "It's fine. We all screw things up. Back when I was in college, I procrastinated on every paper, and then when the due date rolled around, I freaked out and promised I'd never do it again, and then what do you know! I'd do it again." She glanced up at me again and stopped, lifting her sunglasses and squinting at me. "Wait. Crap. You're actually crying."

"I'm not. I'm cool. I'm confident." I wiped my eyes. I was definitely crying. "It's just sweat. I'm doing great. I've never been so confident in my damn, useless, good for nothing life."

Liv grimaced. "Yeah, you're, uh, you're not good at lying, Aves."

"I'm *manifesting.*"

"Ain't working."

I sighed, pressing a hand to my forehead. "Can we just—sit down for a second? I'm exhausted."

"Yeah. Of course." Her voice turned more serious, the levity disappearing from her expression. "It's really okay. We'll swing by the coffee shop right on the end, so we don't have to walk far."

I pulled off to the side of the plaza and sat down at one of the patio tables near the line of shops around the perimeter, and I buried my face in my hands. For a while, that was it, just me sitting there sighing and trying not to cry while Liv reached across the table and put a hand on my arm, not saying anything, not judging me. She was a good friend. Employee. That was probably the extent of our relationship.

"Sorry," I rasped.

"No, yeah, it's really okay. I shouldn't be making light of it. I'm sure it's disappointing, and I'm sure it hurts."

"I just feel like an impostor. I *am* an impostor. I don't know what I'm doing. I've never owned a restaurant before. I don't know anything about Port Andrea. I didn't even know Mike Wallace owned the Julius, and I kicked the hornet's nest, and now just like that, one wrong move and I'm dead. Why was I even trying?"

She shrugged. "Because not trying sucks?"

Ugh. That was the long and short of it. "Trying sucks, too," I groaned.

"Yeah, but you'll feel better you did it. For what it's worth, I think it's cool as hell you told Mike Wallace to go fuck himself."

I slumped face first into the table. "It was satisfying, I'll give you that."

"Yeah, I can imagine. I wish I'd been there for it." She shook her head. "Look, you don't need a chance encounter with a celebrity to give your all on this restaurant. You weren't dreaming of opening a restaurant only to have it rescued by someone. You were dreaming of coming here to this old city you loved and giving it your best shot and having no regrets."

"I have a million regrets and a stomach cramp."

"Well, some ibuprofen will help with one of those. Maybe both." She put a hand on my arm again. "I don't think *no regrets* means that you did everything perfectly. I think it means you did your best and it leads you to ultimately being more of the person you want to be."

I sighed, dragging myself back up to my full height. "I'm probably really embarrassing to look at right now."

She shrugged, looking me over. "It's pretty impressive how you manage to cry without messing up your makeup. I get the littlest bit teary-eyed and it's like *bam,* mascara everywhere, raccoon eyes, and somehow my lipstick is on my forehead."

"I've gone on lots of dates to sad movies and had to learn to cry carefully." I sank back into my seat, looking out at the plaza, at the big fountain my ex-girlfriend Cecilia and I had once sat around and shared ice cream, laughing when the water splashed our feet, and I'd thought the world couldn't get more beautiful. "You're right, though," I said, not really even hearing myself. "Even if I royally fuck this up, I'm glad I did it."

"That's the spirit."

I wasn't sure I'd even been talking about the restaurant, though. Because—ultimately—I was glad I met Cecilia. Glad I fell in love, even if she broke my heart into pieces and stomped on the pieces and burned them and dumped the ashes into radioactive waste.

And maybe falling in love with a dream was the same as with a person. And there was nothing wrong with indulging in the love while I had it. Just like I had with that ice cream off of Cecilia's spoon, leaning over to sneak a bite of hers and giggling when she caught me and pulled it away.

Ugh. That didn't mean it wasn't embarrassing, awkward, painful, and disappointing, and it sure didn't make my stomach cramp go away.

"Okay," I said, taking a long breath, and I thumped my chest twice. "Avery Lindt, owner of the critically acclaimed restaurant Paramour in Port Andrea's luxurious Southport district. Me posing on the front cover of Foodie. I look great on the cover."

"You, uh, you sure as hell do."

"You open the magazine. Full spread. No— *foldout* for Paramour. What's it going to say? Big header for some catchy headline on why we're so good."

Liv rolled her eyes. "Probably something cheesy like *redefining fearless*."

"Oh my *god*. Redefining fearless. Olivia Harper. You need a promotion."

"I'm guessing there's no raise associated."

"Yeah, management is flat broke. *Redefining fearless.* It gives me shivers. *Liv.* We're going to redefine fearless. Are you ready for this?"

She shrugged. "Girl, I just wait tables."

"Waiting tables at Paramour is a *legacy.* All right!" I jumped to my feet, fire burning in my chest. "Let's do this thing. I've never been so fired up. I'm going to be in that foldout. And it's going to say *redefining fearless.*"

"I was just saying that to sound like some high-concept bullshit—"

"I don't *care,* I love it," I said, striding ahead. Liv stumbled to catch up. "If that's high-concept bullshit, then put me down as high-concept bullshit. And let's get some high-concept coffee."

"Push the horizons of flavor while we're there?" Liv said, stumbling alongside my longer stride next to me.

"*Olivia.* God, you're good. We're taking that one, too. Pushing the horizons of flavor. No— pushing *boundaries* of flavor. Experimental, dangerous. Mike Wallace wants to brand us as dangerous? Hell, we'll take it. We're boundary-pushing."

"I'm, uh, glad you're happy," Liv said, gesturing off to the side and leading me towards a cute little coffee shop with red-and-brown décor, filled with intricate wood carvings and sculptures, looking entirely too cozy for a place right off Port Andrea's famous Production Corridor. "Here we are. Komodo's Den."

"Am I going to get attacked by a lizard?" I said, pushing open the door, a charmingly oversized brassy bell rang overhead.

"No one's attacking you, girl. It's a coffee shop. Chill out."

I stepped inside, the warmth of the shop and the smell of coffee and croissants enrobing me as Liv followed me in, taking her sunglasses off and slipping them into her handbag. The place was cozy without feeling small, a big space filled with intricate details, warm accents like thick shag rugs and plush sofas, dark walls packed full of wall art with classical ornate frames, maps and sceneries and oil paintings. The scents of vanilla and orange cut through all the coffee and pastries, warming and relaxing.

"Okay," I said, walking up to the counter. "It's cute."

"It was my old best friend Charlie's favorite. If you don't know what to get, try the cinnamon mocha."

"That sounds like an assault on the senses. I'll do a cappuccino."

Behind the counter, a heavy chalkboard hung over the drip machines, big and bold lettering on it spelling out items and prices. I glanced for sizes, only wincing a little at the price, before I asked for a medium cappuccino, my head still buzzing with excitement from picturing myself all prettied up and looking good on Foodie's front cover—buzzing so much I didn't even notice the person standing next to me at the handoff plane wasn't Liv, still ordering behind me, but a man with wild sandy brown hair and a dress shirt buttoned all the way up, a blazer draped over his arm, and a checkered necktie.

And somehow, of all people in the world, I realized I'd run into Mike Wallace again.

He glanced over at me and gave me a sickly little smile, like a conqueror seeing his victims coming to plead mercy. "Hey, Avery. Nice running into you again."

It took me a second to regain my composure, but I put it together and scowled at him. "Hardly. I guess your diarrhea cleared up?"

He laughed good-naturedly. I wanted to punch him in the gut. "Sorry, that's the one place Patterson Butter House will disappoint you. No diarrhea here. So, I'm guessing based on the fact that you and your waiter are both here, and you have basically no one else on your team, Paramour is closing down now?"

I flared my nostrils and turned back behind the counter. "In your dreams, Mike. You'll regret being so nasty about all of this, playing dirty. I've got plenty still up my sleeves I can't wait to show you."

"Avery. Please," he said, his voice more placating now, which was worse. "I don't want things to get ugly here. We're companions, you and me, in the same business, and I don't want to make enemies with a pretty girl like you. That's what I think the real benefit of our partnership system is about—because there's no reason we have to be *enemies* in this market."

"Do I look like I was born yesterday?" I shot, glancing at him out of the corner of my eye. "I know you're the asshole who coordinated the smear campaign on my restaurant."

He put on a look of genuine surprise that would probably have taken me in, if I hadn't already known he was an asshole. "A smear campaign? Who's smearing you? I saw an article about Paramour in the Daily Andrean that came across harshly, but I didn't think…"

"Don't play stupid," I said. "I talked with Holly Mason about it. She knows you all too well."

I was ninety percent bluffing—I had no idea what Holly really had going on, aside from that she wasn't Mike's biggest fan either—but it worked. Mike turned his lips sharply down, into a tight frown. "Holly tracked you down? *Kitchen Rescue* Holly?"

I put on my most obnoxious sneer. "Oh, I'm so glad to know you're already acquainted. She knows what you've been doing. And we all know she's an *actual* expert, not just someone who bought into the market on Daddy's money. We both see clear as day what you're doing."

"Order for Mike," the barista—who was standing four feet from us and doing a great job pretending she wasn't overhearing the conversation—called as she set down a coffee. "Flat white, extra dry, one packet raw sugar."

"Ugh, even your drink order is annoying," I said.

"Funny you should try to be smooth bringing up Holly," he said, taking the coffee without so much as a thank you to the barista, "but it's not going to help you. She's on her way out."

I scowled. "You keep telling yourself that. I'm sure you'd love to think that, since I know she sees what a little rat you are."

He grinned. "You haven't heard? I'm taking over her show, ramping on next season."

Him? Christ. I'd throw a fit. He was lying. I had to believe he was lying. "You wish," I snapped.

"She didn't tell you?" He laughed, shaking his head. "That's a shame. Guess you two aren't as friendly as I thought."

I—frowned. I got to have Holly Mason at Paramour for dinner, but I didn't do anything to keep her. She left seeming like she couldn't stand me. And there was plenty she hadn't told me.

Maybe, when she'd asked if I had any questions for her about the rumors, it was because she knew she *was* getting replaced. Heading out of TV. Leaving the spotlight.

Maybe that was why she didn't give a damn about my restaurant, a hopeless place that needed saving when she was leaving the business of saving restaurants.

Mike *couldn't* replace her. I hated him. I saw his stupid YouTube series. I hated him. I'd write a new complaint to the *Kitchen Rescue* executives every hour until they put Holly back. I *hated* him.

Mike's expression softened. "I don't know what Holly told you, but the restaurant industry can be a dangerous place. When you're all by yourself out there, and especially when you're in a new restaurant as promising as Paramour, you can expect the sharks to come in. If competitors are coming after you, you'll need more than just yourself and your own restaurant to safeguard against it all."

I glowered. "I swear to god, if this is you telling me I need to sign onto your pyramid scheme to keep me safe—is that all this is? Racketeering now?"

"Hey. I'm not writing attack articles about you, Avery," he said, putting a hand up. "But think about it. What are you even going to do about the attacks? You don't have the leverage to respond alone. If you work together with a collective—it's just like a union, joining up to—"

"Don't even think about comparing a labor union to your ratty pyramid scheme," I seethed. "It's a thinly-veiled power grab, and I think now I'm realizing you're attacking Paramour so you can buy it on the cheap."

"Order for Avery," the barista said, setting down my cappuccino. I took it with a grateful smile.

"Thank you so much. It looks amazing."

She smiled back at me. Mike leaned back into my field of vision, giving me a fake-concerned smile.

"I'm not threatening you, Avery. I'm really just concerned. What affects you affects all of us. What do I mean by that? What I mean is that, as a leader in the restaurant industry, I can't stand to see a smaller, new restaurant like yours kicked down and picked on. Even if you don't sign on with us—we're still going to stand up for you. I'm going to look into the source of the smears, see if we can find—"

"You want to *look into the source,* look in a damn mirror, you slimeball," I said, shooting him a look. "I've got my coffee. I'm leaving. Have a rotten day, Mike."

"There's a reviewer for Foodie Magazine coming through soon," he said, which—of all the things in the universe, that was the *one* thing that could have made me stop. I froze on the spot, and he must have sensed his opportunity, because he smiled wider. "Jennifer Allen. And I think we can get her to stop at Paramour."

I stared at him for a second, my head spinning, and—for just a moment, I wondered if it wouldn't be so bad if he bought my restaurant. I'd come out of it with my debts cleared and a little extra for my time, I'd be able to run Paramour and enjoy it as long as I could, and then when Mike ruined it, I'd go home and plan my second try. And if the Foodie reviewer came through... and the smears would stop.

My name would still be associated with it. It had to. Avery Lindt, founder of Paramour. That was just as good as owner, right? I could still see that on the cover of Foodie. Founder and manager.

I opened my mouth, closed it again, and I opened it again and heard myself saying, "You said Jennifer Allen? The one with the famous series of articles in Taiwan?"

"The one and only. She's coming by in three weeks. I think Paramour deserves her attention."

"Jennifer's schedule is booked," a voice said from behind me—the last voice I would have expected—and I jumped when a hand came down on my shoulder. "And it has been for months. Don't make promises you can't keep, *Michael*."

I felt like I was dreaming as I glanced back over my shoulder at where Holly Mason had her hand on my shoulder, and she stepped up to interpose herself between me and Mike. He leaned back, his expression stunned, but not one millionth as stunned as I was.

Dear *lord* she was pretty. She was back in her full makeup and wearing a faux leather jacket that she looked otherworldly hot in, and she reached out and picked up two drinks from the mobile order stand on the handoff plane, and then—she glanced back over her shoulder, hair falling over one shoulder in gorgeous waves, and she gave me a smile that made my knees turn the consistency of wet bread.

"Hey, Avery," she said, and the way she said my name did *things* to me. She glanced back at Mike and said something that did even more things to me, and that was, "Sorry, Mike. She's with me. We're heading out now."

I cast a glance over at Liv, who was watching every bit as stunned as I was, and when I made eye contact with her, she just nodded, mouth hanging open, and shot me thumbs-up with both hands.

Well. Looked like I was with Holly.

CHAPTER 6

Holly

I stopped outside the Den, turning to face Avery. "Sorry for interrupting your chat with Mike," I said. "I hope you didn't mind."

"Uh—not at all," she said, looking me over once quickly, a pink flush in her cheeks.

And I noticed it. Noticed it a little too much, frankly—the way she looked at me, nervous, almost shy. And the way she'd been particularly upfront about dating women.

It wasn't the right headspace, picking up on things like that, but it was hardly my fault. Avery was even more attractive in daylight than she had been in the low lights of Paramour, out here in another neat suit, this one dressed down with a casual tee underneath. She had her hair swept back into a loose ponytail, light and breezy, just a touch of makeup on, mascara and a little blush and bronzer, and she was the picture of innocence—that specific kind of innocence that made her more tempting, especially when the way she looked at me wasn't subtle.

Maybe that was what had prompted me to tell Mike she was *with me,* instead of phrasing it in a less suggestive way. And I doubted that was the branding change Tay was looking for, picking up women in coffee shops.

"I've had… some experience in my life with Mike. He knows how to corner someone and never stop elaborating his sales pitch until they're pressured into a yes. Especially after the shit he's been putting you through, I thought I'd bail you out." I brushed my hair back out of my face, glancing over at Tay's intent, studying expression. "Did he hold you up for anything? I can get you a lift somewhere if you're in a hurry."

"Oh, wow. No, uh—day off today." She shook her head, straightened her back, and straightened her features too—swallowed the butterflies she was getting so visibly I could feel them myself, and gave me a comfortable smile instead. She was a good actor, honestly. Might have been better than me. "I was just out with one of my staff—a friend of mine—to discuss the future of Paramour. Despite everything, we're feeling confident."

And there it was again—that antsy feeling in my chest, same as I'd gotten in Paramour, when Avery had insisted she would just *figure it out as she went*. Like there was any chance for that.

But hell, if I needed a branding change, maybe mindless optimism would be the way.

"Perfect," I said, gesturing to Tay. "This is Tay Atkinson. They're my agent. Tay, this is Avery Lindt, owner of Paramour."

Tay thrust out a hand, giving Avery a firm handshake. "Really an honor to meet you," they said. "You can call me Tay. You cannot call me Taytay. You would be surprised how many people try. I'm an agent based here in Port Andrea, and Holly Mason is secretly my favorite client, even though she's more ornery than sorting grains of rice."

"I can hear you, Tay," I said.

"The honor is all mine," Avery said. "I really owe you both for getting in the way of Mike Wallace. Multiple times, I presume."

"Oh, not me," Tay laughed. "I stay well out of anything to do with that prick. But Holly doesn't seem to have any such luck." They looked between me and Avery, slowly narrowing their eyes—that dangerous look where they were scheming something—before they turned back to Avery. "If you're off today, can I ask you to come back to the studio with us? I'd like to discuss the situation with Mike."

Avery's excellent-actor mask dropped for a second, her mouth falling open, but she composed herself again. "I—would be honored," she said, looking quickly between me and Tay. "If Holly wouldn't mind...?"

There it was again—that something in her eyes in the way she looked at me, just the slightest tilt of her head, the barest parting of her lips, a little flush to her cheeks. For a second, I got the wildest image of how she might react if I put a fingertip to her lower lip.

I shook it off. Maybe I needed a hookup or something. This wasn't like me.

"Not a problem for me," I said, airily as I could manage. "Anything to do with screwing over Wallace, I'm interested."

"Wonderful," Tay said, and they snapped their fingers once before heading towards the entrance to the plaza. "Come on, then. It's only two blocks down."

"Um—" Avery snuck a glance at me, pausing. I glanced back at her, my eyes meeting those shimmery greens, and she swallowed.

"Don't worry about it," I said.

"No, really. Thank you." She looked away. "I... didn't know Jennifer's schedule was booked."

And *that* was what was really eating at her, I realized with a sudden pang. She wasn't frustrated at being held up or angry at Mike's insistence. She must have been boiling in the guilt right now after feeling tempted to give into Mike's bartering, feeling tempted to sell off the restaurant she loved so damn much.

"She's a busy woman," I said, turning back towards Tay and walking.

"Yeah. No kidding. I really admire her work. I guess... getting a review from her would be like a dream come true. Unless it was scathing. Well, even that would be cool."

She was rambling, the poor girl. I walked a few paces before I paused, glancing at where she stopped next to me, looking up and meeting my eyes.

"Don't feel bad," I said, quietly. "Anyone else would have sold a while ago, with Mike directing the kind of coordinated attack he has been."

And just like that, the guilt melted off her face, and she gave me a small, grateful smile instead. "I... thank you. I guess I'm easy to read?"

I laughed, a smile coming on. "I wouldn't say so. I just know how much Paramour means to you."

She flushed and looked down, but before she could say anything, Tay's voice called back, saying, "You coming?"

I gestured after them. "Tay waits for no one," I said.

"I'm getting that impression," she said, falling into step alongside me as we walked through the sunny streets, busy with pedestrians, and into the lot for the studio. Tay led us through the back doors and swiped an access card into an elevator, hitting the 4 button and thrusting their hands in their pockets as they sank back against the wall, looking between us.

"Out with it," I said, and Avery jumped. Tay just smiled wider.

"You sure have a quick turnaround on my requests, huh?" they said, and I gave them a wry smile.

"You say jump, I say how high."

Avery looked between us. "What's, uh...?"

"I told Mason here she needs to change the narrative around her personal brand *yesterday,* take some more risks, and I blink, and the next thing I know, she's running into a building to scoop up a woman and carry her to safety."

Avery lowered her head, but even in the low light of the elevator, standing next to her, I could see her flush. "I really appreciate it," she mumbled. "And all of this. You didn't need to do this for me."

"Mason," Tay said, looking at me. I raised an eyebrow.

"Atkinson?"

They smiled so damn bright the sun probably had to squint. "I think I've had an inspir-Tay-tion."

"I cannot express to you how much I hate when you say that."

"I've seen the smear pieces on your restaurant, Avery," Tay said, as the elevator stopped and the doors opened, and they led us along a quiet hallway and into a meeting room, broad windows showing the view along Production Corridor and out towards the bay. Sleek tables in modern white-and-red stylings ran the length of the room, and a cheap coffee bar with Keurig and all sat along the wall. They gestured for us to sit, and they took a seat at the end of the table, setting their cup of pure concentrated jitters on the table in front of them. "It's ugly. And it's getting worse."

Avery winced. "Yeah. We've had reservations canceled. It hurts."

"And I think I have an idea," Tay said, grinning. "See, truth is, Mason is floundering. Have you seen *Kitchen Rescue?*"

Avery cleared her throat, looking out the window. "Only every episode, uh, at least twice."

"Well then," Tay said, casting a not-so-subtle glance at me, a suggestive eyebrow lift. I rolled my eyes. "You'll know there's talk of having Holly Mason retire and let Mike Wallace take over as the star. Complaints that the show is too tired as it is."

"I've heard them. Er, straight from Mike. But I don't put any stock in rumors," Avery said, same thing she'd said back in Paramour. It was refreshing, frankly, to have someone not come to a meeting with me with every rumor in the world about me stored away on their mental flash drive.

"Smart girl," Tay said. "Except in this case, the rumor's right. Mason and I built the show from scratch, and we found an independent producer to make a pilot ourselves. After six months trying to land it, we finally got a single season—I think mostly just to shut me up," they laughed. "But we took that and kept it going for six seasons now. A seventh is pretty much already a given, but there's a problem. Mike

Wallace is going to be there, unless we do something."

Avery's eyes widened. "You're serious? He *is* taking over next season? He *can't*. Have you seen his YouTube series? He just spends the whole time bragging. I don't think he even notices there's a kitchen around him, I think there's just a mirror behind the camera and he stands there admiring himself aloud for twenty minutes. He seems like the kind of guy who takes a girl to dinner and talks about himself for two hours and then splits the bill."

I felt something like a deep sigh going through me on a spiritual level, the physical pain of reliving my dates with him. Tay raised an eyebrow and glanced over at me.

"Ask Mason," they said. "She dated him."

"Tay," I sighed.

Avery stiffened, eyes going wide, and clasped her hands in her lap. "I am so sorry," she said. "I didn't mean—"

"That is exactly what he did," I said. "I don't know what I was thinking when I agreed to a date."

"Point is," Tay laughed, "he's not replacing her already. She's got contracts for season seven stating she *will* be the lead. But there's no contracts saying there can't also be a secondary lead, and Mike wants the show like a dog wants a hunk of meat. He's been making backroom deals and getting people to look for ways to put him on the show. Now the showrunner wants to make season seven Mason's last season, and phase her out, let Mike take over from eight on."

"Tay, far be it from me to question you," I said, glaring at them, "but is there a reason you're spilling all my tales of personal failure?"

"They can't do that," Avery said, lips drawn in a tight line. "Oh my god. He'll ruin the show."

"Showrunner thinks it can't get much worse," Tay said. "Thinks Mason is too repetitive, that she's like watching reruns. Wants a change of pace. But you, Avery, are the solution."

Avery stared for a second, blinking. It took me that second to figure out what exactly Tay was thinking, and I rounded on them.

"You're telling me we should take on Paramour instead of Cameron's restaurant."

Tay pointed at me. "Winner winner chicken dinner."

"You're doing what?" Avery said, paling. "Oh, wow. I mean... um..."

"How is that supposed to work?" I said, leaning back in my chair. "Paramour is beautiful, clean, well-managed, and the food is delicious."

"Well, *I* wouldn't know that last part, jerk," Tay said. I ignored them.

"The whole point of the show is to turn around wrecks. The viewers want to see something ugly, seemingly unsalvageable. Going into Paramour would be like watching Bear Grylls check into a luxury hotel."

Avery laughed nervously, fussing with her collar. "I don't know if I would say all that about it. I think you could be giving me too much credit."

"So, you're saying the problem is, it's too unlike all the stuff you've been doing," Tay said, their eyebrows raised. They held it there, just taking a long sip of their coffee, while I narrowed my eyes.

"Right. You want something completely different. You want to burn up our contract with

Cameron, take up Paramour, and televise us waging war with the man trying to take over the show."

"Winner winner—"

"Quit it with the chicken dinner," I said. "How the hell am I supposed to fix up Avery's kitchen enough that Mike leaves her alone? Hell, knowing him, if I were in her kitchen, it would probably make him more likely to come by and harass her. It would just be a segment of me sitting at a desk contacting references to trace how many of the smears were bought and paid for, and nobody wants to watch that."

"Come on. Like people don't watch investigative TV. Look, thing about TV—thing about life—you give someone entertainment, and they'll pay attention until it's boring. You give someone a cause, and they're there for good. You wrap up season six saving Paramour from a shady rich asshole building a pyramid scheme, people are going to be livid if that exact shady rich asshole comes on the show to take over right after."

I chewed my cheek. The idea made sense, even though cutting our contract with Cameron made my stomach turn with guilt. But something about it just begged me to turn it down, to find some way to say no.

And what else could it be? It sure as hell wasn't Mike Wallace. I'd have normally jumped at the opportunity to film a segment trying to screw over my least favorite ex, to show publicly just how rotten he was. The only factor left was the distractingly cute brunette across the table from me, looking between me and Tay with nervous glances.

That same feeling that had burned in my stomach when I'd sat in Paramour listening to her talk about how she *would* make it work, when we'd stood outside Komodo's Den and she'd said she had high hopes, it came trickling back into my chest. That feeling almost like...

No two ways about it—it was jealousy. Jealous she cared so damn much about what she did. Jealous of that passion she had. And a little... intimidated.

I didn't have the guts anymore to take a risk like opening an upscale restaurant in a city I didn't live in, let alone the passion. Avery just seemed to radiate the very things I lacked, and the last thing I wanted was to spend too much time on television talking to her, working with her, being close to her.

Especially when she was entirely too attractive, I thought, as I looked across the table at her just as she glanced nervously at me, making eye contact. She pursed her lips, swallowed, and I swear she glanced down at my lips for an instant.

"It doesn't work," I said, suddenly breaking out of my reverie, looking over at Tay. "We're filming for the last segment in the season. By the time it's airing, everything for season seven will be set in stone."

Tay grinned, leaning back in their seat. "That's where my inspir-Tay-tion comes in."

"Tay. I don't need to hear that abomination twice in one day."

"I'm going to '*accidentally*' leak the plan for Paramour to be the season finale. And maybe '*accidentally*' give out some cues to the press when and where we'll be working, and what exactly is going on here."

I stared at them for the longest time, just turning it over in my head, trying to find any way to tell them how ridiculous it was. Of course, Tay didn't usually listen to reason anyway.

"I... I'm not an expert, but I think it makes sense," Avery said, and I looked over at her. She dropped her gaze to the table. "Sorry. I know I'm clearly biased because I *really* don't know how else to deal with Mike Wallace. But I think what Tay is saying makes sense."

I leaned over the table towards her. "Don't know how to deal with him? What happened to all your optimism? Feeling like you could roll with the punches? High hopes for getting yourself out of it?"

She gave me a nervous smile, flicking up to meet my eyes. "Yes. Because it led me to this opportunity. And to you."

And—that wasn't what I'd been expecting. I'd been trying to land a blow right when she left an opening, and instead, she parried and left me with that nervous flutter in my chest.

What, like she'd really been planning this? Maybe she was in with Mike.

Except obviously she wasn't. She was just keeping an optimistic spirit and an open mind, and being ready for whatever opportunities may have come her way. And that was what she meant when she said she was rolling with the punches.

Scrappy spirit. I really had meant it when I said anyone else would have given up under Mike's assault, sold the restaurant and gone on to try again later.

Maybe that was why she gave me those nervous feelings. She really did have me outmatched in a lot of ways.

I looked away. "You say jump," I said, "I say how high. Fine. If Avery is up for it, we'll do it. Can't be worse than the path we're on right now."

Tay clapped their hands together. "That's the spirit. Oh, I'm burning up. This is going to be *good*. This will either be glorious, or crash and burn, and I can't wait to see."

"Sometimes I wonder how I ended up with you as my agent," I sighed.

"No one else would do it. You know that." They waved me off, and they turned to Avery, grinning. "Avery Lindt, it's been an honor getting to meet you. If you'd like to have Paramour on the show, I've got some contracts I can print out and bring you tomorrow to sign. For the rest of today..." They pulled the lid off their coffee cup, downing the rest of it, and they wiped their hand with the back of their mouth. "I've got some leaks to do."

CHAPTER 7

Avery

I was so out of place it was ridiculous.

Holly hung her jacket up on the rack next to the door, and she gestured me to the sofa in front of the massive full-wall window on the thirty-third story overlooking the city into the bay. "I need to run to the bathroom," she said. "Take this makeup off too. Make yourself comfortable."

"Right—yes. Thank you," I blurted, not even sure what I was saying. When Holly slipped out of her heels and headed for the bathroom, I sank listlessly into the sofa, just staring out the window and trying to reconcile the fact that Tay had *actually* sent us off to Holly's penthouse apartment, and I was *actually* sitting in her living room, on her sofa.

I panicked, which meant I pulled out my phone and texted someone. Liv was probably wondering if I was still alive, anyway.

I'm sorry for abandoning you at Komodo's, I typed. *Holly Mason is taking Paramour on her show and now I'm at her apartment and I don't know what's going on.*

The messages ticked as read right away, and Liv started typing. *She took you to her apartment??? Are you banging her or something?*

I think I went so bright-red I might have stained the pristine white sofa. *Not a chance. She's a little out of my league. I don't date people who are out of my league.*

What, she replied, *that's all it takes to convince you not to date Holly? Look, I'm straight, but even I'd let Holly Mason kiss me. Don't look a gift horse in the mouth.*

I scowled. *She's not kissing me. And that isn't the point. I met her agent, and they said Holly is trying to change the media narrative around her before she loses her show, and so they're dropping their contract with the last restaurant planned for the season and they're going to do Paramour instead, and take on Mike Wallace.*

Nice, Liv texted back, and then she started typing again. *Well, sounds like we've got it made? Good on you for manifesting and all that. Maybe I should try it too. What's the stress for?*

I chewed my cheek. This really had been the law of attraction drawing in what I was looking for so damn hard it slapped me upside the head. *Her agent told Holly to bring me back to her apartment so we could talk strategy, but that it was really a publicity stunt, and they'd leak photos of us to the press to push the image of this as a wild, half-cooked scheme thought up in the middle of the night. And now I feel like I have to impress Holly or she'll change her mind on the whole thing, since it was her agent's idea and she seemed reluctant on it.*

Liv was typing for a while before she sent, *Relax, Aves. You're really good. Just be comfortable as best you can, and you'll impress anyone. You do great when you're comfortable.*

I slumped back against the sofa. *How am I supposed to get comfortable in Holly Mason's apartment???*

She sent me a winking emoji, which was the wrong response and also the wrong timing, because that was when the bathroom door shut behind me, and I turned to where Holly strode out from the bathroom dressed in a dark turtleneck and beige pants with a slim black and gold belt, and I had to stop and marvel at how even her lazy at-home clothes looked like something I'd see on a fashion inspo board.

"You look high-strung," she said, shooting me that sexy smirk, and I squirmed. "Not even going to take off your jacket?"

"Oh—right. I forgot I had the jacket on."

She laughed. "I'll pour some wine. That'll help with the nerves. I have an Emiliano Russo vintage, myself. We'll open it just for this."

Yeah, I was definitely not getting comfortable with this. In a good way. Also in a terrible way.

I slipped out of my jacket and Holly took it, hanging it up on the rack by the door, and she gestured me to the kitchen. "Come on," she said. "I'll show you my toys."

Did she *have* to say it like that? "Uh—can't wait," I stammered, stumbling after her into the kitchen.

It was a gorgeous space, not that I expected anything else. The countertops were sleek marble around the edges of the room with a stainless-steel countertop island in the middle, complete with an extensive gas range, and she just had *appliances* for days. I felt like I could have just spent an entire weekend going around testing the gadgets she had, but it wasn't a cluttered feel—mostly because the space was so gargantuan—and the thin, long windows over the counters on one side gave a snapshot of the city below as the sun set further and the lights came on.

"It's beautiful," I said, and she turned and sank back against a counter, giving me a studying look—appraising. I wasn't confident about that appraisal.

"Let's cook something," she said, and I swear, there was this *sultry* quality to her voice as she said it. I blinked.

"Oh," I said. "You're... going to judge me when I cook, aren't you?"

She grinned. "What happened to all that confidence, Avery? I was really coming to like that cheekily confident attitude you have."

I was never, ever ever going to let go of that cheekily confident attitude I had. I was going to fake it the whole way, but I'd never stop faking it.

"I—well, I mean—I'll give it a shot, then," I said, not doing a great job of sounding cool. "What are we going to make?"

"Whatever you want," she said. "I just want to see your style."

That was the worst possible answer. I swallowed hard. "Well... normally we take orders, you know."

"I don't exactly have a menu," she said, smirking. I pursed my lips.

"Fine then. You win. We'll start with salad."

She nodded. "Good choice."

I passed one test. Now all I had to do was pass all the others.

I searched through her refrigerator, which was big enough to live in and immaculately stocked, and it took me a minute of indecision to get the ingredients together for a beet salad. I felt Holly's gaze burning into me from the side as she watched me prep the salad, and I felt like she was making notes on my fingers as I chopped vegetables, which—it was distracting having her pay that much attention to my fingers.

After long enough it felt like my heart was going to explode, I set down the knife and glanced over at her, and I said, "Are you just going to stand there and watch?"

She laughed. "You've seen the show. That's what I do."

"Normally it involves you shaking your head and making faces."

She grinned. "It's for the camera. I have a poker face in real life."

I felt like that was worse than her just shaking her head and making faces.

"Normally it involves you pointing out things I'd be doing wrong, too," I said, turning back to where I was slicing the beets.

"Your knife work is a little sloppy."

I chewed my lip. "I'm a bit nervous."

"Can't work under pressure?"

She said that, but there was a teasing edge to her voice, a playful banter, and instead of just wanting to put on a smile and bluster my way through it, I found myself shooting back. "Would I have a luxury restaurant if I couldn't work under pressure?"

She let out a throaty little laugh that, well— did things to me. "Sure. Anyone with a little money could start a luxury restaurant even if they don't have the skills. Mike Wallace, for example. So tell me, Avery, did you just buy into the market?"

I put on a thin smile. "Pistachios, please. Wherever you keep them. I know you have them."

She laughed, bright and good-natured. "Who told you?" she said, opening a cabinet and pulling down a bag, handing it to me.

"I did not just buy into the market. Contrary to what my—you know, cheekily confident attitude may suggest, I was just a restaurant manager who scrimped and saved and put her car down as collateral on a business loan."

"Ah, the classic dreamer's story. Heard it a million times. I assume you've heard it too, every time I have on the show."

I felt my face burn, and I focused on halving the pistachios and keeping my head down so she wouldn't see. "I have. Yeah. I might have been a little inspired to make it my own story."

She leaned back against the counter, watching me closely. "Inspired by the show? I'm honored."

I was not going to admit to just how much she had inspired me, especially not while this back-and-forth was going on where it felt like she was trying to get in the winning shot. "One of several inspirations," I said, shooting her my best attempt at her smirk. "Don't get too ahead of yourself."

She grinned. "You are something else, Avery. How much longer on our salad? The diner is getting irritable."

I rolled my eyes, smiling. "The diner is in the kitchen talking to me while I cook. That's not standard procedure."

"Touché," she said, pushing off from the counter and opening the refrigerator behind me. "I'll open the wine. Tell me what kind of restaurants you managed."

I glanced back at her, setting down the knife. "You don't normally ask things like that of the restaurant owners."

"And you're special, Avery," she said, making eye contact as she said my name, and—I think she *knew* what that did to me, because when I got that nervous flutter and I think I flushed, too, she smiled. I wondered how much she was doing this to me on purpose and—if she knew exactly how sexy I thought she was. It made me burn with equal parts self-consciousness and desire. "That's the whole point of doing all this, is that this is special. And besides, you yourself are special, aren't you?" she said, raising an eyebrow at me.

I had no idea what made her think that, but I didn't think I wanted to correct her. "Am I? You're the expert."

She smirked. "You're cute when you're giving me sass."

I tossed my hair back over one shoulder. "And that's supposed to convince me to stop giving you sass?"

She raised her eyebrow again, and I got the feeling she knew what *that* did to me, too. "Quite the contrary. Finish that salad, Avery."

I wasn't sure if this was cooking or foreplay, but doing either one with Holly Mason made me equally nervous. I *had* told her I was gay, implicitly. I hadn't meant to, but it just happened. And I swear she never looked at anyone on the show with that look she was giving me. If she was flirting with me, I had no idea how to handle it.

"Balsamic?" I said, deciding the best way out of the situation was to change the subject and hide.

"Avery. You're going to mask the flavor like that?"

"Holly. It's for a glaze."

She laughed, setting down the wine on the counter next to her, and reaching past me to open the cabinet in front of me—leaning in close to me from behind, so close I could feel her loose hairs on the back of my neck and I could smell the faint perfume on her. Fruity and sweet. I wouldn't have expected that. I also wouldn't have expected her to be this deliberately close to me.

"Right in front of you," she murmured, pulling down a bottle of balsamic vinegar. "Let's see your glaze, then."

My heart was beating so wildly out of control, I had to do something that wouldn't require knife work. Making a glaze sounded great. "Thank you kindly," I said, taking the bottle and not-so-accidentally brushing my hand against hers as I did.

"I don't normally shadow people on the show and hand them things as they cook," she said, not moving away from where she stood so close behind me she was all but pinning me against the counter. My pulse raced and I felt a little drunk on the feeling, and I wasn't really paying much attention to what I was saying.

"You also don't pin them up against the counter, as far as I remember," I said, and then immediately regretted it—wondering since when I was even gutsy enough to get my foot that far in my mouth—and Holly stopped, quiet for one agonizing moment where I weighed whether or not to apologize, before she let out a throaty laugh that gave me chills.

"Maybe they don't usually stand between me and where they're asking me to reach for them," she said, still not moving away.

There were a million smart things to say, and instead I said the absolute least smart thing possible, and that was, "And that's supposed to convince me to stop asking you to reach there?"

There was a momentary silence that felt like every muscle fiber in my body was stretched taut, and I knew I shouldn't have, but I glanced back over my shoulder at her and made eye contact—just for one crucial second, dark eyes with irises flared, and I felt a flutter in my chest that was equal parts thrill and terror, and then—

Something buzzed from her pocket, and she jerked back, eyes wide, like she was just as surprised to find herself here as I was, and she turned sharply away as she slipped her phone from her pocket.

"Sorry," she mumbled, swiping to answer the call. "I'll stop looking over your shoulder and distracting you. Hello, Holly speaking," she said, phone to her ear, back to me, and I turned back to where I was trying desperately to remember what was going to be in my glaze.

Christ. It was probably a good thing her phone had rung just then. I had no idea where that had been going, and—my heart would have exploded in my chest if it had continued.

Her phone call only lasted a few minutes, a brief but urgent check-in with staff, but she was quieter the whole rest of the time I cooked, avoiding making eye contact with me. When I served the salad, she sat down across from me at the table and one seat to the side, not looking directly at me, and she poured the wine for us both and handed me a glass even though I was already clearly inebriated on the way it had felt with her nearly pressed up against my back.

Still, she lightened up a little as she ate the salad, slowly working through it, seeming to contemplate every bite. I watched with everything in my body feeling taut.

"If you tell me you hate it, I might cry," I said, and she raised her eyebrows at me.

"What happened to all your cool confidence, Avery?"

I laughed nervously. "I seem to recall you saying honesty was the best policy."

She nodded, looking away. "Honesty's not too bad a policy."

"So, tell me honestly?"

She glanced back at me, studying me for a while, like she could judge my salad based on how I looked, and she narrowed her eyes. "The flavors are disorganized. There's not enough harmony between them."

I forced myself to take it with a listening nod instead of a wince or a groan or crying on the floor like I wanted to. "Thank you," I said, and she laughed.

"No one actually wants to say thank you when they hear criticism."

I put on a smile. "I value criticism. It's an opportunity—"

"Yes, yes, of course it is," she said, putting a hand up. "But let's be real. The people who say that the most are the ones trying the hardest to convince themselves of it."

I froze up a little. She wasn't *wrong,* I figured. Still, seeing my deer-in-the-headlights expression, she just laughed.

"You look so alarmed. Did I call your bluff?" She shook her head, and she looked away. "I just can't stand people pretending to be something they're not. False modesty, bravado, trying to convince ourselves, whatever form it takes, it's all just different forms of lying."

I chewed my lip. Talk about a callout on my whole *will it into being* approach. But a second later, she shook her head.

"Sorry," she said.

"I, uh, didn't really think it would be up to your standards," I said, the words feeling strange in my mouth. There was a nervous feeling in my chest, fluttery and tingly, from being this alarmingly honest. "I feel like an impostor a lot of the time and I don't know how I'm here, even though I've been working in restaurants for the past eight years. But I'd hoped maybe you'd like it."

She pursed her lips, turning back to the salad. "The spinach contradicts everything else here, the pistachios have the wrong mouthfeel, the beets are too sweet, and there isn't enough of the feta to stand up to the other flavors."

I winced. "Right. Yeah. Okay."

"This is the best beet salad I've ever had."

I stopped, my thoughts careening out from under me. "I... wait. I thought you hated it."

She smirked. "It's delicious. I'm telling you how to improve it. Weren't you just saying criticism is an opportunity to improve?"

I blinked slowly, just watching her to see if she burst out laughing or changed tack again. "Aren't you the one who just shut me down for saying that?"

She laughed, picking up her wine glass and offering me a toast. "I suppose I may have been," she said. "Maybe I just feel the need to keep up with that sass of yours, Avery."

This woman was simultaneously the sexiest and the most terrifying thing I had ever seen, and I had no idea how I was going to survive being on a show with her.

"You're doing great," I said, clinking my glass with hers. "Since you like the honesty so much, let me tell you I honestly have no idea how to keep up."

She smirked wider. "I think you'll do fine. Let's finish this salad and see what your main course looks like."

Right. That was terrifying. I smiled. "I'll do my best."

And *that* much at least was true.

CHAPTER 8

Holly

I really couldn't help myself around this woman. Something about her was intoxicating, like she was a fine bottle of vintage Emiliano Russo herself—gorgeous, irresistible, and making me make terrible decisions.

Which probably meant I should have laid off on the literal wine a little bit, but it did pair beautifully with the seared cauliflower steak Avery served for the main course, all artfully plated on a bed of vegetables.

And it was gorgeous, but I couldn't get enough of Avery's cute little pout when I gave her a barbed comment, so I said, "What is this limp asparagus supposed to represent?"

She gave me the cute little pout, sticking her lower lip just the littlest bit out to one side. "I suppose it represents the state of the asparagus you keep in your refrigerator."

I laughed. "Touché. And this glaze? Is it supposed to be this runny?"

"Maybe it's not," she said, "but maybe someone kept distracting me while I was reducing the sauce by asking me every question she could think of about me."

I raised one eyebrow at her. "My. You're blaming me now?"

She tried her best to mirror my eyebrow movement, one eyebrow twitching before both went up in an awkward, entirely-too-cute gesture. "Like there was anyone else asking me questions about my life while I reduced the sauce?"

I really couldn't get enough of her little comments like that. This was going to be a problem. Especially if it led me to pinning her up against the counter again—and the way she'd playfully jabbed at me about it, daring me to *actually* pin her against the counter.

Like I wasn't tempted.

"It smells delicious," I said, settling back into my seat, and Avery shrugged.

"It's all right. A little whiplash never killed anyone."

"Don't tempt me to go harder," I said, taking my fork and knife and slicing into one edge of the caramelized exterior of the cauliflower.

"I get the feeling you don't need much prompting," she said.

I just raised an eyebrow at her, watching her with a steady gaze while I put the cauliflower in my mouth, all too slowly. It had the intended effect, making her flush more than anything I could have said, and she looked out the window at the light drizzle that was coming on over the nighttime view of the city.

And sure enough, just like in her salad, Avery was *good.* The flavors shone, bright and full of character without overly relying anywhere on Maillard browning, which made the sweet and crisp caramelization where she did have it stand out all the better. It was like a game actually trying to figure out *any* way to improve the food. Hard to believe she'd only been in the industry eight years.

She was better than Mike Wallace, and *that* made me feel fantastic.

"You must have been quite the home cook before getting into the restaurant industry."

She laughed, giving me an odd look. "What, because it's so good?"

I smirked, enjoying the way it always made her squirm just a little bit. "I wouldn't be saying that if it were awful, would I?"

She flushed more, looking away. "Well, how should I know? That glaze is so runny, after all."

I laughed under my breath. "Just *so* runny. Ruins this whole experience, and frankly, my whole evening."

She rolled her eyes, smiling. "You're not fooling anyone anymore. You just don't know how to admit to liking something."

"You catch on quickly."

"Would you believe me if I told you I didn't like cooking as a kid?"

I sat up straighter, setting down my utensils and lifting my wine glass. "I'd ask you who forced you to do it day and night, then, but I'd believe you."

"Didn't do it at all. It's funny. My big sister was the one who cooked all the time. She was always looking up recipes and making things to impress our parents, and I never had to cook a thing. When I tried to, it was because my sister twisted my arm into it and I hated every second of it. When she moved out for college, I spent a year subsisting just on prepackaged food."

"Your parents didn't cook?"

"My mom was hopeless in the kitchen," she laughed. "Probably worse than I was. And my dad wasn't at home much."

"So what changed?"

She grinned. "I really wanted a scrambled egg one day, and it didn't taste right. And if there's one thing to know about me, it's that the best way to make me do something is to say I can't do it, so I snuck down into the kitchen one night and went through two dozen eggs trying to make the perfect scrambled egg. I've been trying to perfect it ever since. Still isn't quite right," she said, with a dramatic sigh.

"Your gateway to cooking was a bad scrambled egg," I said.

"My mom was furious when she saw I'd made twenty-four failed scrambled eggs, but I was just there adamantly telling her I *needed* more eggs. One way or another I ended up finding other things to cook that I wanted to get right, and before long, I was cooking everything."

"Did you go to culinary school?"

She laughed. "You'd never guess. Veterinary. I mean, biology to get to veterinary school. I thought I wanted to be a vet because I liked our dog. Turned out I hated biology, and chemistry, and math, and school. I took a gap year to work in a restaurant to save up for tuition, and I found it was a lot more interesting than school."

"If I'm noticing a trend here, it's that you made all your decisions by accidentally wandering into them and deciding to keep them."

She threw her head back and laughed, a bright and clear sound that was not helping me with the obvious attraction. "More or less," she said. "I never think things very far ahead. I never would have imagined when I started working in a kitchen, that I'd end up here, in Holly Mason's penthouse apartment, feeding her a sauce that's so runny it ruined her entire evening."

I licked my lips, tasting the wine on them. "I'd say, actually, my evening is intact. Just barely salvageable."

"Oh, I'm *so* relieved," she said. "Might I ask what did it?"

Primarily, it was the frustratingly adorable brunette sitting across from me, who kept reaching up and twirling her hair idly around her finger. "Who can say?" I said. "Maybe it was this wilty asparagus."

"Oh, you're incorrigible," she laughed, and then she stopped, clasping a hand over her mouth. "I'm sorry. That came out rude."

"Relax. I am incorrigible. Besides, it's cute when you give me sass like that."

She stopped, wide-eyed. I cursed myself inwardly, wondering *when* I would stop inadvertently flirting with her.

"The food is delicious," I said. "The sear is perfect."

She looked away, casting her eyes down, a flush creeping across her cheeks. "Thank you," she said.

I wasn't sure what there was to say, what I could say to try changing the subject further from my helplessness when it came to her. I looked out the window, watching the rain intensify, and I talked more like I was hearing myself from a different room. "The weather is getting bad," I sighed. "If you want to get home safely tonight, we should wrap this up soon."

She looked out the window too, twirling her fingers absently through her hair. "I guess so," she said. "Here I was hoping I'd be able to recover from the catastrophe of my cooking so far with dessert."

"Not with another runny glaze, I hope."

She laughed. "If it's really okay, then let me say it again, because you're incorrigible."

I wondered what it was about a woman insulting me that made me want to keep her around. Avery was just entirely too cute when she did it. "Maybe we can keep dessert on the menu," I said. "It's an important area to evaluate you."

She glanced back at me, eyebrows raised. "My final exam?"

"Don't get ahead of yourself. The last question on your first exam. Of many." I swirled the wine in my glass, watching her carefully. "I'd like to get a sampling of your desserts, as much as you can put them together on the spot. I have a guest bedroom here. You can stay the night."

She blinked fast, and I'd known even before I'd said it I was overstepping, but I didn't take it back. Something about this woman.

"Tay would probably be happy for the extended publicity stunt," I offered, and that did it, Avery taking a deep breath and giving me her best attempt at mirroring my smirk. It was a little lopsided, and more than a little cute.

"Only if I can judge your bedroom décor the same way you judge my cooking."

It made me entirely too happy she was agreeing. I leaned back in my chair and raised an eyebrow, staying cool. "I didn't realize you were a celebrity interior designer."

"And I didn't realize a celebrity chef would keep such wilty asparagus."

I was not going to last long around this woman. With those soft pink lips and her gorgeous green eyes that sparkled whenever she decided to give me cheek, and the pink flush she got when I gave it back, and how strangely hot she was when she sat there across from me and told me I was incorrigible?

I was long gone. And I just had to figure out a way to behave myself for the duration of filming.

We kept trading playful jabs over the rest of the main course, and when we got up for her to make dessert, she laughed and told me to pull my weight and help out, and I would have said no if it had happened a few hours ago, but I found myself going along with it—standing there stirring a pastry cream as she made choux pastry, and I found myself admiring the loose, airy waves of her hair more and more as the rain intensified outside.

When we finished to the tune of eclairs with a red wine chocolate ganache and orange zest pastry cream shared on the sofa in the living room, overlooking the rainy city below us, Avery looked a little lost. She finished her wine and set the glass and the dessert plate down on the end table, sinking into the corner of the sofa, and it took a second before she spoke.

"So, is this the part where I ask for my exam grade?" she said, and I licked my lips.

"I have to admit, the ganache wasn't runny in the slightest."

She rolled her eyes, and I wondered if anyone else looked that good rolling their eyes. "I had a much loftier opinion of you as a chef before this. Now I think the only aspect you can use to describe food is runny or not."

"I assure you I understand more about food than just runniness. I just noticed you were particularly self-conscious about the runniness."

She laughed, meeting my eyes across the sofa. "You were never this difficult with anyone else on the show, you know."

"I do know that. And I already told you, you're special."

She swallowed, looking down, and a soft pink flush crept over her cheeks again. I was just about to change the subject before she said, "I'm glad. Always wanted to be. Special, you know."

I raised an eyebrow. "Is that why you opened a luxury restaurant in one of the most expensive areas of Port Andrea as your first restaurant?"

She didn't give me the cheeky jab back I was expecting, just a nod, still looking down at the sofa between us. "Yeah. I guess so. I saw all these incredible chefs, and I guess on some level I just... wanted to be them. Figured I'd be that amazing if I just pretended I was them. But I went and screwed it up. And you don't even like it when I go around pretending I'm somebody I'm not."

I studied her for a while, feeling almost— sobered, in a way. Because she was a lot more than just a pretty face in my apartment—she was my responsibility, in more ways than one, and I was being remarkably irresponsible.

I looked back out the window and I said, "Frankly, I think that whole *fake it till you make it* mindset is childish and frivolous."

She winced. "Yeah. I have been, um... sort of noticing that mismatch here."

"You really think you can just will something into being by believing in it hard enough? Like you can just want something *really* hard and it'll magically appear?"

"It doesn't sound great when you put it that way," she admitted, looking away.

I sighed, sinking back into the sofa, and I took a sip of my wine, setting it down gently before I spoke. "But I have to admit, it doesn't seem to have failed completely for you so far. And it's not like I don't admire a person who actually has something they care about and focuses on it wholeheartedly."

She glanced up at me, staring at me wide-eyed from the side. "You're... giving me whiplash again," she said. I laughed.

"Maybe. I have a hard time being upfront with my feelings." I sighed, turning to face her, and I said, "I apologize. For earlier. It was unprofessional of me."

She blinked, cheeks reddening again. "Um... complaining the sauce was too runny?"

I laughed, dry, my mind elsewhere. "Very funny, Avery. You know what I mean. Pinning you up against the counter, as you put it."

She coughed hard into her fist and turned away, doing a terrible job of hiding the growing flush on her face. "You—were reaching for the vinegar I asked you to reach..."

"Neither of us buys that pretense," I said, crossing my legs and looking away. "I understand the realities of the situation and how much all of this means to you, and I owe you an apology for inappropriate behavior."

"Um..." She cleared her throat. "What—exactly—are you saying is inappropriate?"

I raised an eyebrow. "You're the oblivious type, aren't you, Avery?"

She flushed. "I've... been told that once or twice or forty times."

"The fact that I find you undeniably attractive and find pretenses for cornering you against a counter?"

She somehow managed to go even redder, dropping her head just about far enough to bury it in her own chest. "Oh. Uh... I... oh."

I looked away. "Just in case you're unaware, your eyes are very expressive, and I can clearly see the way you look at me."

"Oh, god. I'm sorry," she mumbled, wrapping her hair around her finger so tightly I worried about her blood circulation.

"For what?"

"Uh... well. That I was looking at you that way, I guess. I promise I wasn't trying to. I respect you *so* much."

"There's nothing disrespectful about it," I said, and she sank back into the seat, staring pointedly out the window.

"I-I guess. I mean, if you don't think there is. I mean, I don't know why you think I'm..." She cleared her throat.

"Attractive," I finished. She let out a sharp breath.

"Yeah. Yep. That."

"Maybe I just have a thing for runny sauces," I said, looking away, and she sighed.

"Do you realize that sounds like an innuendo?"

I choked. "I—guess I do now."

She glanced over at me, a smile playing on her lips. "Holly," she said. "Was that the first time I caught you off guard?"

I cleared my throat, scratching at my head and looking away. "I did not think that entirely through."

She laughed. "It's... cute when you're caught off-guard like that."

"Don't expect to see it too much. I have an image to uphold." I straightened my back, tried to look a little more put-together again, and I glanced back over and met her eyes across the sofa—and I stopped, frozen there for a second, before she laughed, and I heard myself laugh with her.

"Of course," she said, smiling. "An image."

"I'm a celebrity, you know. Optics are important."

"Mm-hm."

"I see you giving me sass again."

She did her terrible attempt at raising one eyebrow again. "I thought that was what you found so... uh... well... attractive, I mean, maybe, I guess..."

I raised one eyebrow back at her. "You started that sentence with a lot more confidence than you ended it."

"You're pretty far out of my league," she mumbled.

I looked away. "I just wanted to clear the air and apologize."

"Yeah, no. I get that. Thank you. That's, uh—it helps. And, like, I mean, you're not... unattractive. I mean, you're kind of the opposite of that."

"You're adorable when you're flustered."

"I—I mean—it's kind of a relief," she said, taking a sharp breath and putting a hand to her chest. "I mean, all of that. I mean, I guess you know I think you're, uh, very... well... yes. But it wouldn't go well even if... yeah. I mean, I took an indefinite trip to Port Andrea to date a chef before, and it ended up breaking my heart. So I'd be really wary of, uh, you know, doing that same exact thing again, anyway."

I wondered why it felt so much easier to relax now—if it had really been making me that nervous, if this hopeless girl really had that much sway over me. I felt like something tied tight around my chest was loosening. "That girlfriend you mentioned before."

"When I accidentally blurted out something about me being bisexual to the hottest queer woman on television, yep, that happened," she said, dragging her fingers through her hair. "And now I accidentally blurted that I think you're the hottest queer woman on television, so, you know. I'm really doing great over here. Batting a thousand."

That one damn part of me really just wished I could cut off her nervous rambling by leaning over the sofa and kissing her. "I'm happy to be the hottest queer woman on television," I said. "For the record, I'm just off a long string of awful relationships, and when I got out of my last one two months ago, I swore no more of that for a year at least. So you're not the only one with a strict rule not to do this."

She let out a long sigh. "Oh. Right. Okay. Good. So... yeah. Good. I'm sorry about your awful relationships. I'm glad you got out."

I raised an eyebrow. "You don't even know anything about them."

She shrugged. "I know they were awful. And that you're out now. So I'm glad."

She really did have the simplest mindset on things. It was refreshing.

"Dinner was wonderful," I said, sinking back into the sofa. "Thank you for cooking."

"Thank you for not being too harsh with my wilty asparagus that was really your wilty asparagus."

I rolled my eyes, smiling to myself. "If you have nothing better to do, I'm going to put on a movie."

I wondered why I'd even offered—even though I knew the answer clear as day and it was just that I liked to tempt myself with her. She dropped her head, smiling secretly to herself, and she nodded.

"Just no horror," she said.

"Squeamish?"

"I'm more of a romcom girl."

I laughed. "I could not be less surprised. Romcom it is."

Right. I'd been on to something when I'd told her honesty was the best policy. I just had to be upfront with the fact that she was unbearably attractive and how those silly little smiles were so adorable, but that I absolutely could not date her, and this whole thing would work out, no problem. And my feelings wouldn't get in the way for one second.

Right. And I was the queen of France.

CHAPTER 9

Avery

The bed was so comfortable I overslept by at least an hour, and I knew that even without looking at the clock in the morning just by the way I felt like I actually woke up well-rested, which made me panic for a second before I remembered I wasn't scheduled to come into Paramour today until two.

I rolled over in the bed, groaning at just how obscenely comfortable the thing was, and I fumbled off the side of the bed for my phone, nearly falling out of bed in the process. Checking the screen told me it was a little past nine, and I rubbed my forehead, looking around the room.

It was way too pretty to be any room I owned. It took me a minute to make sense of it. The pale white curtains fluttering around the massive window, overlooking basically everything in Port Andrea, the morning sunlight streaming in over all the whites and pale tones of the room...

the massive bed that was too comfortable for its own good.

Right. Holly Mason's apartment. That I'd somehow managed to sleep in, after watching a romcom together with her, cozy on her sofa together with her, after she'd admitted she was attracted to me.

That was a pretty weird dream. Funny how I'd magically teleported to her apartment after waking up so it was almost like the dream had been real, but I knew *that* wasn't true. Magic teleportation made much more sense than Holly thinking I was attractive.

I rolled back over and grabbed my phone again when I heard it buzzing, and I squinted at the screen, idly wondering why I had so many notifications before I swiped it open and saw I had even more notifications than I'd thought. In fact, I didn't think I'd ever seen so many messages on my phone in my life.

My first thought was that I'd slept too long, and I panicked, but then I saw the first message, from Diane, asking me, *did you see you're in the news?* and I relaxed, and then—well, then I read the message a second time, and I panicked again.

I shot up bolt-upright in bed and opened my messages log, my stomach sinking, wondering what the hell Mike Wallace had done now, but the link everyone was sending me—half the staff at Paramour, my friends from back home, and even my brother who I talked to about once a year— had nothing to do with Mike Wallace, and everything to do with Holly Mason.

An article from a bit of a... sleazy rag, but still, an article. With my picture in it, walking together with Holly Mason into her apartment. *Insider leaks report,* the story read, *Kitchen Rescue star Holly Mason is breaking her contract with Jack Cameron's Blue Sail Bar and Grill to take on Paramour, luxury restaurant owned by her girlfriend Avery Lindt.*

I read it about fifteen times before I processed it.

Girlfriend. Girlfriend Avery Lindt. You know—me. As in, the one who was not Holly's girlfriend.

I didn't know if the sudden drop in my stomach when I read it was anger or guilt. *Insider leaks.* They'd been telling the press I was her girlfriend? They were just going to drag me into this, lie to me, lie to everyone, and put on some fake show about me being her girlfriend, just for a cheap shot at changing her image?

But—mostly I felt guilty because I *absolutely* did not deserve to be her girlfriend. And I felt like she would be smeared by association of being my girlfriend. And also because I kind of wished I could be her girlfriend.

My phone was buzzing enough I was starting to think I wouldn't need my vibrator I'd forgotten back at home, only getting more and more messages as more people woke up, saw it. It was getting traction on Twitter and Instagram, too, and my Twitter account with about seventy followers had tripled its follower count already, and gone from zero to a hundred tags. I had some angry-looking DMs and some asking for comments on the story, too. I watched it all for a minute before I just dropped the phone on the bed and jumped to my feet, pulling my pajamas tighter around me—well, Holly's two-piece pajama set she'd loaned me and I'd tried not to think too much about as I changed into it—and stormed out into the living room just as Holly burst into the apartment, flying in through the front door with her face ashen and her lips drawn in a tight line, and she stopped me in the living room.

"Is this what this was about?" she snapped first thing, and I flinched. "Some kind of plan you were whipping up to draw attention to Paramour?"

"What—" My head spun. "What on earth are you talking about? I didn't do anything. You... wait." I shook my head. "You're not suggesting *I'm* the one who leaked rumors about us, are you? You're the one who tracked me down and proposed the whole deal to me!"

"Are you saying *I'm* the one responsible?" She put a hand to her chest, eyes smoldering. "You think I'd go ahead and smear my reputation by propping up some kind of elaborate rumor scheme—"

"Tay said you were looking to change your image," I shot back. "Why shouldn't I think you would? This is a change in your image, isn't it?"

"You think this is the change I wanted? To look like some dilettante who would throw away her contracts just for some..."

"Some what? Some random trashy nobody girl you picked up off the street who you're too good for?"

I didn't know where the outburst came from, but it caught Holly off-guard as much as it caught me. She shook her head, brows furrowed. "I didn't say anything like that."

"Then what *were* you saying?" I didn't even know what *I* was saying. My emotions were leading me like a poltergeist dragging me across the floor by my foot.

"I was *saying*—I don't—" She shook her head harder. "It's not about that. This is obvious publicity for Paramour. How in the world wouldn't I think this is your work?"

"Publicity for Paramour?" I crossed my arms. "You seriously think that little of me? That I'd lie in wait for you to rescue me, set up these kinds of situations, just to get into your apartment and get Paramour famous by association? Like I'm just some floozy of a restauranteur?"

"That's not what I'm saying," she growled.

"Then what are you saying?"

She stopped, squinting at me. I felt suddenly naked, like she was seeing right through me to some embarrassing truth I didn't even know what it was, but—after a second, her shoulders dropped.

"God dammit," she said.

I paused, anxiety churning in my chest, the fire all taken out of me. "What?"

She looked away. "Tay. They weren't sending us back here to spread rumors about us working together to make a scheme to take down Mike Wallace or—whatever they said. They sent us here to snap sleazy pictures and start a rumor we're girlfriends."

And—Christ, she was exactly right. No wonder it had felt like something didn't add up. Holly changing who was going to be on her show wasn't exactly sensational. That wasn't likely to change anyone's narrative.

But throwing it all away for a girl she was supposedly sneaking back to her apartment? And a failing restauranteur, at that?

Ugh. *That* was their inspir-Tay-tion. I was starting to dislike the whole inspir-Tay-tion thing as much as Holly did.

"They really didn't talk to you about it first?" I said, looking away, and she whirled on me.

"Do I *look* like I would do that? I'm a reliable woman. My word is my bond, and that's something I've worked my whole damn career to uphold. We're just yanking the floor out from under Cameron, and that's bad enough, but lying to you about it the whole time—and lying to my entire audience, making it look like I'm throwing it all away just for a random rendezvous? Do you really think I'd be involved in a scheme like that?"

I let my gaze fall to the floor, my stomach turning, a gross feeling like I'd had too much cheap greasy pizza churning inside me. Maybe because I knew she was right. Maybe because she didn't really care that much about me after all, and all I was was just—a random rendezvous, some girl who she was too good for. Just a quick one-night stand she wouldn't do anything of meaning for.

Ugh. I was reading into this in all the wrong ways and caring too damn much about something that shouldn't have mattered.

"Right," I said, finally, a minute later, my voice quiet. "I guess not. Just Tay. And their inspir-Tay-tion."

She snorted, and she looked away, arms folded. "Yeah. For Christ's sake." She rubbed her forehead. "I'm going to go and meet them in person to talk about… what the hell they're doing, and how to take it back. Come with me?"

I kept my gaze fixed the other way, out the window over the city, just focusing on watching the way big clouds drifted in over the water and not thinking about how disgusted Holly seemed with the very concept of someone even mistaking us for girlfriends. I guessed that whole part about her saying she was attracted to me *had* been a dream. Or more likely, the wine. The wine, and trying to make me feel better about having been puppy-dog eyeing her the entire time. She probably regretted it.

"Yeah," I said. "I'll go with you. Right now?"

"Uh," she said, and I looked back at where she was giving me that one-eyebrow-raise that made me feel even more antsy around her. "I think it might feed the rumors more if you go out in public in my pajamas."

I was still wearing her pajamas. Right. My face burned. "Oh. Yeah. You know something? That actually makes a lot of sense."

She gave me a wry smile, and she looked away. "Get back into your actual clothes, and we'll go meet with Tay."

Ugh. I was going to die with shame. And the embarrassment had only just started.

"Yeah, I did that," Tay laughed, once we got into their office and they spun around idly in their office chair on the other side, flipping a few papers back and forth. "I know it's genius, there's no need to tell me."

"Fix it this instant," Holly said, and I had to admit, even though it crushed my soul a little to see her so absolutely livid about the idea of being perceived as my girlfriend, she was also, well, kind of hot when she got angry.

Tay just raised an eyebrow, looking her over. "Fix what? I already fixed pretty much everything, wouldn't you say?"

"I'm not—we're not doing whatever harebrained plan you have that you just ran with without even asking us," Holly said, screwing her face up. I looked down.

Tay put up a hand. "Mason. Relax. What's all this anger for? It's bad for your blood pressure."

"*You* are bad for my blood pressure," Holly seethed.

"It's kind of rude to look that upset about being Avery's girlfriend right in front of her, isn't it?" Tay said, raising both eyebrows, and I think Holly and I both flinched just as hard.

"What—that's not what I—it's not like that," Holly said, looking away, and I waved my hands in front of my face.

"It's not a problem at all," I blurted, face going red. "I mean—she's right. Was this really your plan all along? You were just lying about what you actually had in mind?"

"Sure, yeah," Tay said. "And have you seen the results?"

"What results are you talking about?" Holly said. "I've seen the results on social media. It's exploding right now."

"Exactly," Tay laughed. "You're suddenly the center of attention. And you know what else? None of that attention involves Mike Wallace on your show. Searches of Mike Wallace and *Kitchen Rescue* have gone down to just about zero, and Holly Mason and *girlfriend* has skyrocketed. No one gives a damn about how boring you've gotten on the show anymore."

"What—like all of this is just a stunt for attention?" Holly said, face reddening.

Tay shrugged, leaning back in their seat and glancing out the window, down along Production Corridor and out to the bay. People were strolling on along below, down in the street, just living their lives on the bright sunny morning, as blissful as I'd been just yesterday morning. "Publicity's not bad. But it's not just that. Come on. Look at the bigger picture here, Mason. What's this going to look like on you?"

"It's going to look like I'm a damn flake who—"

"Who actually cares about a human being," Tay said, glancing back at her, one eyebrow raised. "Come on. You're stony. No one wants to interview you. You have the same stiff routine you do on every segment of the show. No one ever talks about you in any personal context."

Holly clenched her fists. "I'm a professional. I don't *want* to air my personal contexts."

"There's a difference between airing all your dirty laundry, and being an approachable human being. You don't exist as a person. Look, you're a great cook, Mason," Tay said, standing up and coming around the desk to stand in front of her, leaning back against the desk, "but lots of people can cook. Hell, I can cook. I made some blueberry muffins the other day, they came out pretty well."

Holly scowled. "I've seen you try to cook. You're horrible. I'll bet your muffins were dry as sandpaper."

Tay's jaw dropped. "You haven't even *seen* my muffins, and you're disparaging them?"

I put a hand up. "Um... the topic at hand?"

"Right," Tay said, waving a hand at me. "Point is, anyone can cook. The challenge here is to be a compelling character while you cook. And you haven't done anything interesting with yourself since you went through hell and high water to get the show on the air. People have gotten bored, because you're not a person, you're just a cook."

Holly screwed up her face, cheeks red, but she didn't say anything. I wanted to shield her from everything that made her feel that way, but unfortunately, in this case, *I* was what made her feel like that.

"With this, you look like you actually give a damn about something other than the kitchen. You've fallen madly in love with this girl, enough to throw away your carefully-laid plans of doing the same thing as always, and you're taking on a giant, throwing your lot in with the underdog for the sake of love. And people care about that."

"People are furious with me," Holly growled. "And they should be. They think I'm just dropping a hardworking restaurant owner for the sake of some girl."

"Hey," Tay said, hands on their hips. "There you go again, right in front of Avery. She's not just *some girl.* She's a hardworking restaurant owner too. What's the problem?"

Holly flinched, and she pursed her lips. I looked away.

"It's really okay," I said. "I mean, you don't need to worry about me here. The situation at hand is a little more urgent."

"No, I..." Holly rubbed her forehead. "I'm sorry. I'm speaking out of turn. I don't mean it like that."

I pursed my lips, looking down at the floor, heart thrumming unevenly. It wasn't the time or place to talk about it, and I really didn't even know how to bring it up, so, like a mature adult, I ignored it.

"Sure, some people are mad," Tay said. "But that's proof you're doing something people care about. Some people are furious. Some people think it's amazing. Some people are just interested in seeing what the hell happens now that stony old Holly Mason who hasn't publicly dated anyone ever is now throwing away everything she's been doing on her show to take *down* a restaurant instead, for the sake of someone she's in love with. It's compelling. People care."

Holly was quiet for a long time before she said, quietly, "But it's not true. I can't just lie to all my viewers. Put on something fake."

"You don't need to *say* Avery's your girlfriend. Just let the rumors do their thing."

"*You* told them she is," Holly snapped.

"As an anonymous insider leak. Those things happen. Look, if you want to throw me under the bus and admit it was just your agent spreading rumors, by all means, go for it. But do it *after* all this is through. And just because you're not Avery's girlfriend doesn't mean you can't care about her. That's what this is really about."

Holly sighed, but she didn't say anything.

I looked down. "I guess at this point, it's probably more harm than good to try clearing up the misconception, anyway," I said.

"That may also be true," Tay laughed. "I knew Mason would never go along with it, so I kind of just did it while you were asleep so you wouldn't know it was happening until too late to turn it back." They shot me a flawless grin. "Sorry."

I cleared my throat, looking away. "How did you even know I'm, uh...?"

"Don't worry about that," Tay said with a wink. "I just know things."

That was the number one way to make me worry about that. I gave them a very, very fake smile.

"I hope you know I'm furious with you right now, Tay," Holly said, her voice small. Tay sighed.

"The sacrifices I make for you, Mason."

"Sacrifice my ass," Holly muttered. Tay raised their eyebrows.

"No, you can keep that. I know you work on it plenty with your gym routine, and I'm sure your new girlfriend appreciates it."

I choked. I mean—it wasn't that I *didn't* appreciate... well. I looked away. "I didn't know people usually had such... close relationships with their agents," I mumbled. Tay laughed.

"Yeah, we're a bit of a special case," they said. "I'm guessing the little *I hate you so much* means you're going along with it, though?"

Holly sighed. "What choice do I have? Guess you're right it's going to be good for my image. Even if it's going to make me look like a flake and a liar when I announce it's all a fake."

"You can just have a quiet little fake-breakup too afterwards. People break up all the time. Trust me," Tay said, shrugging. "I'm a pro."

"If it keeps Mike Wallace off the show," Holly said.

Tay grinned. "He's your villain now. He'll never be the protagonist."

"The only consolation I'm getting here." Holly shook her head. "Fine. I'm ready to do whatever the hell you're putting us up to. If Avery is, too."

I clasped my hands at my waist, looking down, suddenly forgetting completely how to act professional. "I, uh—I mean—yeah. I guess." I took a long, shaky breath. "It's a lot easier for me. It's easy publicity for Paramour. I just feel bad for giving Holly such a hard time, but I'm... grateful for the opportunity it gives our team at Paramour."

"*So* glad to hear it," Tay laughed, clapping their hands together. "Now, I've got those papers for you to sign right here, Avery. And I've got a boxing class booked for Mason in half an hour at Stella's Gym."

Holly stopped, blinking fast. "A boxing class?"

"You mentioned looking for an upper-body workout, and I thought you'd want to punch something right about now."

Holly just stared for the longest time, and I had to try not to laugh.

Tay really did know her well. I just had to hope they had *any* idea what they were doing with this whole thing.

CHAPTER 10

Holly

I didn't see Avery for the next couple of days, as we prepared for filming, and we both kept in touch sparingly. I liked to think it was to let us both focus on getting the work we needed done before we started filming, but I knew it was just me getting angry.

Mostly just angry with myself. I knew I'd taken it out on Avery unfairly. I'd just seen red when I found out what was happening—just like Mike leading me on and then instantly turning around and using our relationship for his publicity stunt, back when I'd made the mistake of dating him. Thought I'd been ridiculous enough to fall for the same trick again, even without dating someone this time, and I'd snapped at her.

Even a few days later, as I greeted Kyle and the others on my way up towards Paramour for the shooting, I hadn't figured out what I'd been trying to say to her. *Just for some... some what?* I didn't like to think of what I'd been trying to dismiss Avery as in that moment.

But she was as professional as could be when she greeted me in the kitchen of Paramour, which was a little busier now with the drive all the rumors about us had brought in. And she looked even better than I remembered, wearing a pantsuit with a red plaid tie that was a little too eye-catching.

"Hi, Holly," she said, once I got into the kitchen, cameras setting up. "I met with Kyle. He's a bit... overbearing."

I laughed. I was glad to know I wasn't the only target of her sass on this team. "That's the kindest way of putting it. Did he talk you through everything?"

"Yes. I'm prepared. Um—" She flushed, looking down, her professionalism breaking and that cute little brunette who had gotten me drunk on her in my apartment the other day showing through. "He told me to, er... play up the rumor, I guess. He's a fan of it."

I wrinkled my nose. "He told me I was going down in flames for doing it. Sounds like he likes you better."

"Maybe he just figures it's a terrible idea, but if we're doing it, we should lean into it," she said, still avoiding my gaze.

"Probably." I looked away. "Right. So, not-so-accidental hand brushes, glances full of meaning..."

"Right. Yeah." She cleared her throat, fussing with a spice rack on the counter in front of her. "Sorry."

I paused. "Sorry for what?"

"Just... the whole situation," she mumbled. "This wouldn't have happened if I hadn't antagonized Mike Wallace. You wouldn't have been pulled into this."

"I'm not—that's not it," I said, frowning. "I mean—it's good for my image, ultimately. Or, well, it's good for the goal of getting him to leave me alone, and to keep him from taking over the show."

"Yeah. I mean, I guess so."

Dammit. She wouldn't even look at me. The guilty feeling squirmed in my gut, and I didn't even know where it was coming from.

"The first episode starts with our meeting," I said, straightening my back, brushing the thoughts away, "and it's supposed to look like the first time we meet. Obviously, it never is, I always meet with the owners before to talk things over, but we act the part for the show. You and I are going to also act it, but we're going to make it obvious we're acting it. Charged looks, lingering handshake. Got it? Make it look like we're doing a bad job of pretending we're not..." I stumbled a little on the word. "Girlfriends."

"Yeah. Totally. I got it. I can do that."

"Good. One minute for Mack to get her staff in here and we'll start with the first takes right away."

And the first takes went well—Avery was just as good on camera as I'd expected, flicking like a light switch into her more professional self, back straightened, a confident and easy look on her face as she played casual like she was working in the kitchen when I came in and she looked up, striding to meet me and giving me a handshake that felt just a little *too* personal.

"It's such an honor to meet you," she said, looking me right in the eyes with what was definitely a charged stare—exactly what I'd asked for, and yet here I was, getting nervous over it. I remembered suddenly the way she'd smelled so close to me in my apartment, when I was leaning right past her to reach for the cabinet. "I've heard so much about you—I'm such a fan of the show."

"It's an honor to meet *you,*" I said, putting just a little something… extra in my voice, in the way I met her gaze. Her eyes widened just a hair, the slightest change in her expression, and I could tell she was thankfully just as nervous as I was, and not at all over the cameras rolling. Perfect acting. Or maybe not acting. "Paramour is a beautiful restaurant, and I'm looking forward to getting to the root of what's going on here."

"Of course," she said, lingering on my hand. She was too damn good at this. "I really appreciate all of this."

"Let's get right to it," I said, looking around the kitchen, but keeping my gaze on Avery out of the corner of my vision—I wasn't sure how much of it was for the cameras and how much of it was because of that wide-eyed look she was giving me, just a flash of vulnerability there. "Show me around, give me the tour."

"You got it," she said, gesturing for me to follow her, and I brushed my hand against hers as I walked with her.

She one-upped me by curling her pinky finger around the edge of my hand with just the slightest little gesture, and I couldn't get my mind off of it the whole rest of the time we were filming, not even when I had plenty of distractions to take my mind off it—the way Avery snuck glances at me out of the corner of her eye when we were working side-by-side and she thought I wouldn't see, the way she'd gaze at me when I was off-camera and she was talking to a member of her staff.

God, I had it bad for her. Bad enough Tay squinted at me as I was wrapping up, stepping off towards the back and out of the way of everyone in the kitchen to wash my hands.

"I think I'm starting to see why you were so opposed to the whole pretend-girlfriends arrangement," they said. I sighed.

"Because I don't want to lie to my fans."

"Uh-huh. Sure. Totally believe you." Tay winked. "You're actually into her, aren't you?"

"You really don't know how to mind your own business, do you?"

Tay dropped their arms by their sides. "You literally pay me not to mind my own business."

"Ugh. Touché. Look, we already talked about it," I said, heading for the back door, eager to get out of the heat of the back of house. "We acknowledged there's some mutual attraction, but it's not convenient for either one of us to pursue it. And we were satisfied with that, until you came along with your..." I waved at them. "All of this."

"Surprisingly mature of you to just talk about it like that," they said, stepping outside with me as the cloudy sky rumbled with thunder somewhere far off.

"I'm thirty-two years old. I know how to talk about my feelings."

"Real likely," they said. "More importantly, I booked dinner for the two of you."

I paused. "You did what," I deadpanned.

"Booked dinner. You know, food. Evening food." They mimed eating. I wanted to push them over.

"Tay, I know what dinner is. What the hell do you mean, you—"

"For crying out loud, calm down, woman. You're dating her. Not-so-secretly. Of course you're going to go out to dinner with her. And of course I've already leaked the location to some people with cameras."

I rubbed my forehead. "You certainly don't take half-measures."

"And I take pride in that. Rosco's Point. It's under partnership with Mike Wallace, so you can do double duty there and do a little research. See if you can meet the owner and get a little insight onto what kind of tactics Mike pulled on them, see if you can get them to appear on the show."

I straightened my back, the sick feeling in my stomach dissipating. That was work. I could do that. "Good thinking," I said. "We'll canvas

Wallace's restaurants and see if we can find some common threads. Other people having bad things mysteriously just happen when they don't sign up."

"And you'll make heart eyes at your girlfriend."

I slumped again. "Right. And that. Tay, cut me some slack."

"Go on and hurry over to the studio, you," they said, patting my shoulder. "I picked out a very sexy little dress for you that will leave no doubt it's a date. Got one for Avery, too. And I'm sure you won't even have to act the reaction."

I stepped in front of them on the pavement, still wet from the rain earlier, and turned to face them. "Tay, you know I'm not going to *actually* date her, right? I feel like this is predicated on us becoming a real thing."

They put their hands up. "Get with or don't get with whoever you want," they said, but the vague, dismissive tone in their voice was a clear giveaway.

"I'm *not* doing anything with Avery. I refuse to be in the same position with her as I was with

Mike. I couldn't stand it, and it wouldn't be fair to her. She was very clear she's not dating an Andrean chef again, too."

"Oh, hit a nerve with that, did we?" they said, raising an eyebrow.

"It's none of your business. And you can't argue it is this time, because I pay you to mind *my* business, not Avery's. I get you're helping Paramour significantly, but I will not let you invade Avery's private life and give her trouble. Understand?"

Tay pursed their lips, but they gave me a smart salute and said, "Yes, ma'am. She can keep her privacy." They paused. "But you're still getting dinner. Get a move on."

And it wasn't all that bad. Rosco's Point was a beautiful steakhouse by the pier, under the lighthouse, and when I pulled up to the restaurant, I saw not only was the place gorgeous—the cape was swathed in the faint mists brought on by the drizzling rain, and with the sun setting over the water, it cast everything in a pale glow—but so was the brunette standing by the side of the building in a red dress that, sure enough, left no doubt it was a date.

Avery turned when I stepped out of my car and stopped at the sight of me, eyes wide, before she looked away, a flush creeping into her cheeks. And as much as I loved when she got professional and acted like she was capable and in charge of everything in the kitchen, I couldn't get enough of this shy, awkward Avery who got flushed at the sight of me in a dress.

"Avery," I said, stepping up next to her. "You're looking good."

"Thanks. I think that might be more a compliment for the clothes and makeup people who made me look good."

I smirked, leaning against the wall of the restaurant. "You looked plenty good in my pajamas."

"Jesus," she said, taking a sharp breath and looking away. "I mean, they were some really nice pajamas. How much did they even cost? Three hundred dollars?"

I laughed. "Never wore silk pajamas before? They're not that expensive."

She shrugged. "I usually rock oversized Goodwill couture to bed, myself, but sure thing, miss *oh-you-must-not-own-silk-pajamas*."

"Sassy as ever tonight," I said. "Shall we get inside so you can give me cheek somewhere dry?"

The restaurant was gorgeous on the inside, too—I'd been once before, a beautiful rustic theme with wood paneling on the walls and a massive fireplace the host led us to, and Avery looked around nervously as she sat.

"I'm more used to saving up for two weeks to afford a dinner in a place like this," she said.

"I've been there," I laughed, and she stopped, cocking her head at me.

"You're kidding. You weren't born rich and famous and attractive?"

"Contrary to what you may think, no. About your most average blue-collar family possible. Mother worked at the drugstore, father did window installation, and we were the most unremarkable people on the block."

She laughed, a hand over her mouth. "So the great Holly Mason has humble origins. Is that why you like being sassed? Keeps you humble?"

I raised an eyebrow and let it sit in the pause just to watch the way she lost her cool, chewing her lip and flushing, before I said, "Maybe. Probably more that I like being treated like an actual human being."

She sank back into her seat just as the waitress came out, and I ordered a glass of chianti, Avery passing on wine and getting sparkling water. Once we were left alone with drinks, she glanced out the window and said, "I guess when you don't grow up around fame and all that, it feels weird."

"That would be an understatement. People acting like I'm a mythical creature..."

She laughed. "I'll be the first to admit I'm intimidated by you, though. I mean, you're talented and you're pretty. Two areas where I'm iffy at best."

I raised an eyebrow, and I waited for her to take a sip of her water before I said, "Do you think I pin unattractive women to counters?" and I watched the way she choked on her water.

"Oh, uh," she wheezed, face red, for—I assumed—multiple reasons. "I mean, maybe you don't."

"You're so easy to fluster. It's adorable."

"I'm glad you enjoy it," she laughed nervously, looking away again. "You think anyone got a picture of that?"

"Don't worry about people taking pictures. Just focus on dinner and look natural."

She sighed, sinking back into her seat. "It's hard to look natural when I know there are people looking to take a picture of me."

I smiled wanly. "You get used to it. In the meantime, conversation is a good distraction." I set down my menu and looked her over. "So, is this what you had in mind when you were trying to manifest something? Having dinner with— what was it—the hottest queer woman on television?"

"Okay. Yeah. You're not going to let that go. I guess I wouldn't, if I were in your position." She twirled her hair around her finger while she babbled, looking out the window, a nervous smile on her face. "It really wasn't. I'm so nervous I feel like I'm going to die. But—by that I mean—I'm okay. I'm fine."

"You're not fine."

She closed her eyes. "I'm faking it in hopes of making it."

I laughed, leaning back in my seat. "Have you always been like that? Manifesting everything in your life?"

"Oh, not really. I was a pretty moody little kid. Didn't really get excited about much, didn't really have any big dreams or anything."

That was the exact opposite of her now. Sounded more like me. I looked away. "Hard to picture. What changed?"

She cleared her throat. "Er, well. I'm not totally open about this kind of thing, but you'll keep it between us, right?"

That was another thing she could do that I couldn't—share private things in private conversation, like normal people were supposed to do. I envied that. "Of course," I said. "I'll protect your dark secrets."

She laughed, a lopsided smile spreading over her face. "I did not say a word about dark secrets. Projecting much, Holly Mason?"

"Do I look like I carry dark secrets, Avery Lindt?"

"A little. You've got that brooding energy."

I rolled my eyes, smiling. "Tell me what you wanted to say."

She scratched the back of her head. "I'm trans, actually. That has something to do with it. When I started transitioning and saw myself as a woman, I sort of realized I could really bring about whatever kind of change I wanted, if I just believed in it."

That was a bit more... sincere than I think I'd been expecting. I couldn't make a sarcastic comment about that. I nodded slowly before I said, "That makes sense."

"Yeah. I mean, if I can grow boobs, I can do anything." She rubbed her forehead. "God, why am I talking to Holly Mason about my boobs?"

I tried to suppress a smile. I failed. "You have to understand how tempted I am to comment on them," I said, laughter bubbling under my voice.

"I know. I kind of put that out there. I have no one but myself to blame." She straightened, clearing her throat, putting on her professional face again. "Ignoring all of... uh, that... point is, after I started transitioning, I felt like it was so satisfying seeing something about me become the way I wanted, I just wanted to find the next one."

"And that was becoming a restauranteur on Foodie Magazine."

"It took me a little while to get there, but yes. That's the goal." Her smile faltered. "Er... if Paramour survives. Otherwise, the goal is getting another car back home, to replace the collateral."

And there, *back home,* was the reason not to get too attached to her—to not let myself feel all of this wild-eyed attraction for her. She wasn't around here. She was here on a dream voyage, and she was only staying on a tenuous connection that could have broken at any time.

And it could all end as swiftly as the ridiculous time I'd spent together with *Mike Wallace,* of all people.

I had to manifest some very level-headed feelings about her, and fake it till I made it.

"I think Paramour will do well," I said, my voice low, subdued. "You're an excellent cook, and the restaurant is beautiful. The whole experience there is memorable."

"Sometimes I wonder if I should have just let Mike buy it, after all," she sighed, sinking back into the seat. "I'd have gone on being the manager, and how good would that have looked on my resume? I'd have been able to get some amazing management jobs, and eventually open a restaurant again with more clue what I was doing."

"And you'd have spent the whole time wondering what could have been if you'd stuck with your dreams," I said. "Because Paramour is your dream. And your dreams are important to you."

She chewed her lip, staring out the window. "Yeah. Useless daydreamer over here. Head in the clouds."

"Avery," I said, quietly, and she looked across the booth at me. I reached out and laid a hand on top of hers on the table, not really sure what was driving me, but just... not wanting to see her look that sad anymore. "Hey. Look."

She blinked fast, cheeks slowly flushing pink. "I... yes?"

I didn't know what I was supposed to say. This wasn't my strong suit. I *was* normally the type to just brood. I'd lied to Tay in their office the other day—I wasn't trying to keep my personal life to myself, I didn't *have* a personal life. I didn't know who I *was*, off of the camera.

But I knew I didn't want Avery to look that defeated.

"Someone needs to dream," I said. "The world never changes without people who dream. Don't you ever say you're useless, Avery."

She stared at me for a second, eyes wide, but she didn't get to say anything before the sound of shoes clicking towards us pulled my attention away, and I sat back to look at where a young blonde woman in a smart jacket and glasses approached with a smile, saying, "Holly Mason? It's an honor to meet you."

Avery stiffened, sitting up rigid as a flagpole, but the woman, striding over to offer me a smile I could only describe as *sophisticated,* was just fixated on me. I just smiled.

"You must be the manager?" I said. "It's wonderful to meet you, too. The restaurant is beautiful."

"Thank you," she said, standing next to Avery but without even looking at her, just keeping her eyes on me. "Although our sponsor makes most of the decisions about the design and arrangement, for the most part, our assigned sponsorship liaison gives me free reign with the decisions. The previous manager set me up for success, at any rate."

And here we were, already getting down to the meat and potatoes. I smiled wider. "You must mean the sponsorship with Mike Wallace and the Julius?" I said, politely as I could, and she put on a thin smile that seemed more defensive than anything else.

"It's not as though Mike himself is here owning the entire restaurant. It's less a sponsorship with him and more of a collaboration of restaurants in the area, sticking up for one another. It's a beautiful arrangement."

I had to wonder about that. "This is actually relevant to something I've been looking into lately," I said. "Do you think I could get an interview with you at some point?"

She put on a clearly fake smile. "I'm afraid my schedule is quite busy. The restaurant has been doing so well under the sponsorship, there's been quite a bit of work on my plate."

Seemed like she'd bought into the whole thing hook, line and sinker. "Well, if you ever change your mind or want to talk about the sponsorship to a wider audience, feel free to contact my agent Tay. I'll give you their email address."

She smiled wider. "It's an honor, Miss Mason. I'll be taking care of you tonight. And your friend…"

She turned, looking at Avery and freezing in the exact same way Avery froze at her. The two of them stared for a second before she said, her voice incredulous, "*Avery?*"

Avery cleared her throat, loudly. "Hi… Cecilia. It's, uh, been a while."

CHAPTER 11

Avery

Today was a rollercoaster, except it was the kind of rollercoaster where you reached the bottom of the hill and the track just ended and you launched off a fucking cliff, because suddenly there I was sitting in the booth with my ex-girlfriend standing there just up to her *ears* in her own success, having achieved my dream that I'd failed at, by taking the exact opportunity that I'd spat on.

Holly looked between us, her brow furrowed, confused, but I didn't really have it in me to explain right now. Cecilia squinted at me, studying me, and I hated it so much I just wanted to pull my skin off so she'd stop looking at me and seeing what a failure I was.

"God, you look different," she said, finally. "Or maybe I just forgot what you looked like."

My heart was already broken again just seeing her, and then saying something like that was just stomping the pieces with a steel boot. I smiled thinly. "I mean, it's been five years now, hasn't it? A lot happens in five years..."

"It certainly does," she said, arching her eyebrows at me. "Taking over Rosco's Point and making it more successful than ever before, somehow. I'm quite proud of my work over the past few years."

And judging by the engagement ring on her finger, she wasn't the only one proud of her work. I was really trying hard not to look at it, but it certainly looked... expensive.

"You should be," I said, looking around, putting on a smile. "Rosco's Point was always a beautiful place, but you really made it shine, didn't you? Holly and I have been talking plenty about restaurants ever since she came to mine and we got to be friends, but yours definitely stands out."

The shots of *my restaurant* and Holly Mason being my friend seemed to land, because she furrowed her brow. "You and Holly Mason are friends?" she laughed, looking between us. "You certainly picked up the pace in the past five years, Avery. And you're running a restaurant?"

"She is," Holly said, giving me a studying stare. "It's a beautiful luxury restaurant by the water."

I felt like I could have melted. Holly sticking up for me in front of my much-more-successful ex would have been enough to make me fall for her on the spot, if it weren't for the glaring reminder of why I did *not* date people who were a million times better than me standing right in front of me.

Cecilia looked back at me before she laughed lightly. "And when you say you and Holly are friends, that just means you need her help on the show, right? For that beautiful luxury restaurant by the water?"

I flushed. I hated when she called me out on some way I'd screwed up. She'd done that a lot before. "I—well—"

"That's a yes," Cecilia laughed. "And... I think I might have heard something about that, actually. Something about someone having a restaurant so bad Holly needed to cut her contract with someone else to rescue them urgently? I think it *was* supposed to be some luxury restaurant in Southport."

I swallowed, my throat dry, searching for anything to say. Cecilia just stared at me, her smile growing wider, an expression like a cat playing with a mouse in front of her.

"Ah, my poor, sweet little Aves. You always did take on a little too much at once. Opening up an entire luxury restaurant in Southport without any idea what you were doing? No marketing strategy?" She shook her head. "You should see if Mike Wallace at the Julius can help you with that."

I chewed my lip, tempted to just blurt out *Mike Wallace is a sleaze running a pyramid scheme that's going to bite you in the ass, and Holly Mason thinks I'm attractive, so there,* but that wouldn't have worked out very well, so I just smiled thinly. "Mike actually gave me an offer," I said. "I turned it down. I still have every faith I can turn around Paramour's fortunes. But I guess you need a little security and stability when you're probably engaged to another girl who makes half as much as you do?"

She laughed, smiling wider, shaking her head. "I'm glad to see you're still so attentive to the details, but it actually so happens Harriett Browder makes a bit more than I do," she said, pushing meaning into the name like I was supposed to know it. At my blank stare, she raised an eyebrow. "Don't know her, I assume? Runs the executive office of Salins, the payments company here? Maybe I can bring her to that lovely little luxury restaurant of yours sometime," she said, glancing back to Holly, her expression instantly changing, sweet and polite now. I sank like a deflated balloon, hating the feeling like I was just some speck of grime to wipe away before talking to the actual important person here, but it was true, wasn't it? "It really is a small world," Cecilia said. "Aves lucky enough to get to meet Holly Mason herself. I am a big fan, you know. I'll ask for your autograph, but only if that's okay."

Holly gave her a polite smile back and said, "That should be all right. Thank you, Cecilia. I think we're ready to order."

I wasn't. I'd lost my appetite. But I asked for a small salad, burning under Cecilia's gaze, and I listened to the clicking of her shoes once she took our menus and walked away until I felt like I could have sunk through the floorboards and into my grave.

Holly studied me for a while before she said, "I'm assuming she's—"

"Yeah."

She looked away. "I apologize. You could have told me she ran this place. I would absolutely have vetoed Tay picking it."

I fussed with my napkin, staring down at the floor. Now I just saw my beautiful tailored dress as a sign I was trying too hard to be feminine, my open-toe heels weird on my feet, like every part of me was gross. "I didn't know," I mumbled. "I haven't seen her in, er... a while. She was helping run Skyward Lounge when we, um... broke up."

"I'm sorry." She looked away, avoiding my gaze, and I wondered if she did regret getting stuck with me. Seeing me humiliated by my ex probably put out whatever attraction she somehow had for me, if me being trans hadn't already done that in. "We could just go."

"I'm not going to just run away. It's really fine." I picked my fingernail at the corner of the seat cushion. "Do you know Harriett Browder?"

"I do. Her company specializes in payment services for restaurants and restaurant suppliers, so she runs in our circles."

I kicked at the floor. "She's pretty successful, huh?"

"I suppose," Holly said, her voice hesitant.

And I left it at that, because clearly whatever I said was just going to dig me deeper into the hole I'd climbed into.

Our conversation was subdued, Holly clearly not really wanting to talk to me anymore, and me not wanting to make her talk to me if she didn't want to, until Cecilia came back out with our appetizers that I was sure would be the only thing I could eat.

"The stuffed mushrooms for Miss Mason," she said, setting the plate down for Holly, almost a reverent tone in her voice, until she turned to me and said, "And here's you, Aves," dropping the salad down in front of me. My meal even looked sadder than Holly's, just a bunch of limp greens and a watery dressing. I wondered if she ordered it screwed up on purpose.

"Thank you," I said. "It looks delicious."

She smiled wider at me. "No need to be surprised by it. I'm sure you serve salad at—what was it? Paramour?"

"To no one's great surprise, we do," I said, still not looking her in the eye. "But they've always been my favorite."

"Ah, yes. I'd forgotten about that. You always did talk about salad this, raw vegetable snacks that. Always trying to keep in good shape. So much more diligent than me always just eating whatever I feel like."

Even that was obvious mockery, because she was a million times prettier than me no matter how much salad I ate and how many different face masks I used. I just shrugged. "I mean, Sweet Dreams was always a good visit together."

"And you'd get low-fat sherbet," she laughed. "So responsible. I'd forgotten all about those days. It was fun, in its way." She turned back to Holly and said, "Miss Mason, please, let me know if there's anything I can do to make your visit more comfortable. I hope your food is wonderful."

A minute after Cecilia left and neither of us touched our food, Holly leaned in closer and dropped her voice. "She's very clearly trying too hard to be happy about the partnership. I think we could ask around with the staff and see what the real story is."

I scratched my head. "Yeah, I, um... I guess so."

She paused, pursing her lips. "On a day Cecilia isn't in. Obviously."

I laughed drily. "That would be ideal, wouldn't it?"

"I'm sorry for—"

"No, it's really okay." I looked away. "I mean, she's right. I've always tried too hard. Just trying to be... you know. Something I'm not."

She studied me, and I looked out the window.

"Sorry," I said. "Just forget I said all of that."

"That's not about your gender, is it?"

"What?" I turned back to her, my thoughts thrown into disarray. "Oh. No. Not at all. That's about the only thing about me that feels real anymore, I guess. God, I don't know why I'm talking about this with Holly Mason."

"Quit that," she said, and I frowned.

"Quit—what?"

"Saying my name like that. Like I'm some mythical figure." She reached a hand across the table and laid it over my hand again, and my heart jumped in just the same way when she did it a minute ago. "I'm just the woman sitting across from you at the table. Talk about whatever you'd talk about with any other woman sitting across the table."

I felt a nervous thump in my heart, and I let my gaze fall to the floor. "I mean, if it weren't for you being Holly Mason, we wouldn't be here. This is a business meeting. And I'm *really* okay. I'm just a little bit messed up after seeing—you know, her—but I'm really okay. I promise."

She stared for a while longer before she sighed, sinking back into her seat and looking out the window. "Right," she said, her voice distant.

"Well, I'm not going to pressure you into talking about anything. Let's eat, and we can get out of here. I don't think I have much appetite for the main course."

I didn't even have much appetite for the appetizer. I picked at it, eating limp forkfuls of wet lettuce, and managed to get about a third of it down before I gave up around the same time Holly finished the mushrooms and flagged down a different waiter.

"Sorry. Could we get the check now? It's a bit of a hurry."

I watched her as the waiter left to the back, before I glanced back out the window. "You didn't have to do that. I know how to talk to—you know, her. We could have—"

"I know. But she annoys me." She gave me a sardonic smile. "And if she saw me again, she'd probably ask for my autograph before I left, and I don't really want to give her my autograph."

I tried to give her that one-eyebrow-raise, but as usual, I think I messed it up. "So popular and famous that you need to ration out your autographs?"

She laughed. "There's sassy Avery again. No, she just pisses me off."

I'd... never really heard anyone criticize Cecilia before, honestly. The criticisms were always why she was dating me. I blinked. "Did she do something wrong?"

"I have some personal vendettas against petty exes. It's pretty clear she was trying to make you feel bad."

I cleared my throat, looking down at the floor. "Well... I mean, I would have felt bad meeting her no matter what. I was hoping if I ever saw her again, I'd be really successful and I wouldn't still look like a loser in comparison. I don't know. I guess I wanted to win the breakup. That's silly, I know."

She smiled. "Make her jealous and regret letting you go?"

I snorted. "I wouldn't go that far. But at least not look like I'm nothing without her."

She kept studying me the whole time the waiter brought back our check, until we were heading back towards the front door, and I thought we were going to get out of the building without another word, but that was when Cecilia called after us, "Oh, Miss Mason!" and Holly's face fell.

"Sorry to run," Holly said, glancing back at where Cecilia looked a little lost, confused and disappointed, but putting on a smile. Ugh. It messed with my head looking at her, those pretty green eyes that had been my whole world for one glorious moment in time where I'd been punching well above my weight. "But thank you for the mushrooms. They were lovely."

Cecilia didn't even look at me the slightest fraction, and it hurt more, I think, than if she'd been degrading me to my face. She just smiled and said, "Well, of course. If there's anything we can do to improve the experience, or convince you to come back—"

"No, I don't think that's likely," Holly said, raising an eyebrow at her. "Anyone who talks to Avery like you do, I have no interest in seeing again. Goodbye, Cecilia."

I think the only person who looked more like she'd been slapped upside the head than Cecilia right now was me. My eyes went wide, but

I tried to keep my cool as Cecilia looked between the two of us, jaw hanging open.

Christ, Holly was hot when she was sticking up for me.

I gave Cecilia the best smile I could, and I said, "It was nice seeing you again, Cecilia. I'm sure under your leadership, Rosco's will survive even once your onboarding period with Mike expires and you're left on your own."

The way Cecilia twitched would have been the most satisfying thing in of itself, but then my heart jumped into my mouth when Holly looped her arm around mine, and she gestured me back to the door. "Let's go, Avery."

"Wait," Cecilia said, paling. "Are you two—I didn't mean to—"

But I couldn't really process what she was saying, or anything else in the world other than the feeling of Holly's arm linked with mine as she led me out the door and into the covered front patio, where the rain was pouring around us now. She glanced back one more time before she muttered as she dropped my arm, "Should have given her more of a piece of my mind."

My head spun. "I—you really didn't need to—"

She laughed, brushing her hair back from her face. "Need to? Avery, you misunderstand. That was me trying my best to hold myself back. The way she was about shoving that ring in your face, making smug little comments about you? I hope Harriett calls off the engagement and sends her an invoice for the ring."

Jesus. For one breathless minute, I wondered if this was what dating Holly Mason would actually be like. Who said Andrean chefs were all bad?

But—right. If anything, that was proof dating Holly would be disastrous. If dating someone as out of my league as Cecilia had been bad, I couldn't imagine Holly.

"I wouldn't want to wish that on anyone," I said, turning away and fussing with my hair. "But I'm not saying I'd be sad if it happened."

"And if you just so happened to accidentally bake a cake to celebrate it?" she said, and I snorted.

"It's a distinct possibility. And I'd call you over to have some."

She licked her lips, and *that* gave me knots in my stomach enough I'd need a mythical future king to undo them. "I'd be there. Forget the dinner assignment. Let's just go get a crepe from the stand on Talman Street and call it a night."

That sounded like a great night.

CHAPTER 12

Holly

Filming with Avery was, dare I say it, *fun*. It had been a while since I ventured to describe a filming as fun, but there was just something about that infectious smile, that cute little laugh, and the way she would give me those quirking smiles and sassy comments even on recordings and adlib them in scripted scenes—and underneath it all, the intimacy of her sharing something as personal as being trans with me over dinner—it just felt like there was a connection between us. I couldn't get enough of filming together with her.

The next few days flew past, and linking arms to get her slimy ex-girlfriend jealous wasn't the last little gesture we did. I'd spot people I knew or people I thought looked like they recognized me while Avery and I were on one of our Tay-assigned outings, and I'd slip a hand down to the small of her back just to tempt someone to snap the photo. The way she flushed, eyes going wide, made it too damn tempting for myself, too. When we went to a confectionary store Mike reportedly had his eyes on, I felt like someone was watching us intently, so I pushed one of my cream puffs up against Avery's lips to watch the way she swallowed hard and bit her lip just a little before she opened her mouth and let me feed her the pastry, wiping a little bit of whipped cream off her lower lip after.

"It's pretty good, right?" I said, and Avery seemed to struggle with the English language for a minute, which was so adorable I desperately wanted to see what else I could do to her.

"It's—delicious. I mean, uh... the vanilla in the cream is really fresh and clear, and the flavor is so simple but so good."

I put the whipped cream I'd wiped from her lip in my mouth, just to watch the way she went even wider-eyed, and I nodded. "You're right about the vanilla. I didn't notice. You've got a good mouth."

She sputtered. I think I realized about then that I was doing it at least as much for myself as for the cameras.

And I had to hand it to Tay, they were right about the rumor. It spread hot and fast, especially with Cecilia telling everyone that Avery had done something to suck up to me enough I agreed to be girlfriends—I really could not stand that Cecilia woman—and with the way Tay kept assigning us places to go around town together, almost like a tour schedule just to make sure people saw us places.

Avery's friend and one of her only staff, Liv, flagged me down at one point while I was on break from shooting at Paramour, and she said, "Hey— just to be clear—*are* you two girlfriends, or not? Avery's my friend and she's being coy about it."

I arched an eyebrow at her and I said, "We are certainly girls who are friendly with each other."

"Ugh, you're both coy. You so are a thing," she said, throwing her hands in the air and storming back to the kitchen.

I had to wonder, though, as I sat across from Avery at one restaurant after another, talking to staff at different restaurants and the owners where we could meet them to try to piece together a common thread, watching the way Avery leaned in with an intent expression on her face but would still smile and laugh to disarm someone we were talking to, make them comfortable enough to answer questions—there was something just in the way she carried herself, and I had to wonder what it would be like if we *were* a thing.

"You're thinking about Avery," Tay said at one point while I was thinking that exact thing, sitting in the studio with them and going over reports. I frowned.

"I'm paying attention."

"To the thoughts of making out with Avery in your head?"

I rubbed my forehead. "You're my agent. Be more professional."

"I'm your friend from a million and one years ago who just so happens to be your agent now. Take a chill pill. Get the stick out of your butt. Put a chill suppository up there instead."

"We've just been getting along well, and I'm glad it's her we're doing all this with. And..." I looked away, cleared my throat. "I still think the whole thing with starting a rumor about us dating was a horrible idea, and I'm still angry at you, but urgently getting Paramour on the show was a good call. I've been hearing so much more new interest, but honestly, it's been fun, too."

"Yeah, because you think Avery's hot."

I scowled. "I do not."

They gave me an inquisitive look. "Don't you?"

Well—I did. "That's not the point. It's been entertaining trying to track down what we can between all of Mike's restaurants. It feels different and new, and I've been enjoying it. Nice knowing he's probably livid about it too."

"Found anything?"

"All the owners in the partnership are uncomfortably enthusiastic about how helpful it's been. They're all intent on convincing other people to sign on, too, but the line cooks and the servers generally agree nothing really changed except that the owners spend a lot of time meeting with the sponsorship liaisons. It has all the trappings of something more like a multi-level marketing scheme."

"I'm impressed you managed to pick all of that up while gazing lovingly at your girlfriend."

I sighed. "Tay, are you even paying attention?"

They grinned. "Yes ma'am. The footage of your outings and the interviews with Libby and Kisha are great. Kyle's actually seemed *happy* for once in his sad life, piecing together the episodes with this. I think he's enjoying it, too."

"Never done a segment this unscripted," I said. "I was worried how he'd fare. But I guess all I have to do is make sure Avery and I take down the big boss Mike Wallace in the final episode."

"About that," they said. "You might run into him for a midpoint episode. Run-in with the bad guy to up tension. He's attending the Swanson Charity Dinner, and you're invited."

I chewed my lip. "They're inviting me again? I told them I wasn't interested."

"Well, some anonymous agent of yours may have told them you've changed your mind."

I rubbed my temples. "I swear to god, Tay."

"Relax. It's for the show." They put a hand up. "I've talked a little with the guys behind it, they were pretty crotchety but they got sick of me asking a billion times so they gave in. They're not letting us film in there still, but they agreed to bring their own videographer in and let us look over the footage and decide if there's any we want to use for the show. I think it'll make for good television, especially seeing you and Mike run into each other."

I wrinkled my nose. "This is supposed to be you convincing me to go? By telling me you're going to record my interactions with my ex and put them on TV?"

"Please?" They clasped their hands together at their chest, and I sighed.

"Ugh. Fine. I can go, if it's just confronting Mike and not dealing with anything else."

They grinned. "Some anonymous agent of yours may have told the organizers you're bringing your girlfriend."

"Jesus Christ, Tay," I groaned, sinking back in my chair. "Just like that? Now you're making it official that we're supposedly girlfriends?"

"Just to the organizers. Don't worry. It's nothing public." They winked. "But given it's a bit more of a private event, you can certainly enjoy the time there with Avery."

"Once this show is wrapped up fully, I'm going to thank you for all your work as my agent, end our contract, and then as your friend, I will strangle you to death."

They grinned. "I'll change my name and book a flight to another continent to get away on the last day of the contract. Always wanted to see Australia. Plenty of outback to hide in."

"Fine. I'll go. I'm sure Avery will be interested, too, if it means we can confront Mike Wallace about all of this directly together. But don't think I'm happy about this."

"Love it. I can't wait to see the action unfold."

I could absolutely have waited. The time until then passed too quickly.

But for all my complaining, seeing Avery in the dress they put her in made it all worth it.

"Hey," I said, looking her over as she stepped out of the limousine outside of the hotel we were meeting at. "You look amazing."

And she *did*, wearing a black dress with an asymmetrical cut at the hem, and the V-neckline drew my attention to some things we resolutely did not talk about, the gentle fit around the waist accentuating her hips. But she just put her hand on one of those hips and gave me what was, by now, a slightly better-practiced one-eyebrow raise, and she said, "Look who's talking. And besides, compliment Kacey in wardrobe, not me."

"I can give credit to both. But Kacey gets paid to do that, whereas you seem to be beautiful for everyone else's benefit."

She laughed, rolling her eyes, but a slight flush crept over her cheeks. "Well, whatever beauty is supposedly there, it's for my sake, too. I very specifically chose to look like this, you know."

"Fair enough," I said, following her inside, past the door guard, who just nodded at the sight of me. When we got into the elevator, she chewed her cheek, looking away.

"I hope it's not weird or too personal if I talk about being trans."

She had no idea how happy it made me just to have someone share something personal with me. I shook my head, playing it cool. "I'm happy you told me. I understand it isn't always easy to open up about."

"Thanks," she mumbled, kicking idly at the floor.

"I don't have anything interesting to open up with to make it even. I'd say I'm bisexual, but you know that."

She laughed. "I mean, I kind of noticed. I scrolled to the Personal Life section on your Wikipedia page."

An antsy feeling settled into my stomach, thinking of Avery looking up things about me before we met. At times I couldn't help myself wanting to just invite her back to my apartment, tell her I wasn't interested in faking it anymore and to just let me kiss her already, but it was moments like that that reminded me why I couldn't.

I'd had enough experiences with people just looking to date the girl on TV. Sometimes it was for the thrill of it, sometimes it was to impress their friends, sometimes it was to get industry secrets from me, and sometimes—in the case of men, I found—to make themselves feel good by trying to explain TV or cooking to me.

And Avery seemed different, but hell, didn't I say that about all of them? *She's not like the others, he's not like the others.* I'd say it time and again, and every time, a month in at most, they'd be one of the others I'd say the next person wasn't like.

"Something's bothering you," Avery said, turning to face me. "Do you want me to talk about something else?"

I hadn't realized I'd zoned out. "I played lacrosse in college."

She blinked. "What?"

"Just thinking of things you wouldn't have guessed about me."

"Lacrosse?" She laughed. "Oh, wow. I really can't see it."

"It was pretty fun. I had a crush on the girls' varsity team captain."

She covered up a laugh. "That's the most classic queer-girl-in-college thing I've ever heard."

"That's an honor, right?"

"Oh, absolutely." Her eyes sparkled, looking like an angel, and I had to look away so I didn't think things like that.

"Here's our floor. Look sharp," I said.

"I don't know how to look sharp."

"Look couple-y."

"Oh, god. I don't know how to do that with someone so out of my league, either."

"I am not out of your league. Just link arms with me or something."

"What?" She turned to me, her face scrunched up.

"I said, link arms. Come on."

"I mean—" she started, but she stopped when the elevator slowed to a halt and I slipped my arm around hers, walking out into the low lights of the event reception arm-in-arm with her, and heads turned as we strode in together, looking more like a couple with her than with anyone I'd ever *actually* dated.

Not that I didn't want to date Avery.

But I was resolutely *not* thinking that.

CHAPTER 13

Holly

A very flushed at the attention as we strode into the reception hall, all heads turning to look at us, but she stumbled along with me, putting on a rehearsed movie-star smile and drawing her shoulders back, nodding at anyone who came close.

And god, she looked so good on my arm like this.

It was busier than I remembered, four years ago and the last time I'd been here. I only recognized a fraction of the people here—the faces of the Port Andrea area's culinary scene had changed while I was spinning my wheels, and all of a sudden I was flooded with the keen sensation that I'd been wasting my time all along.

Avery leaned a little closer to me and she mumbled, "Everyone here is so pretty. And they look talented. I feel like an impostor."

"Ninety percent of the people in this room don't have a clue what they're doing and are just posturing."

"*I'm* one of those ninety percent. Fake it till you make it is literally my motto."

"Holly," a woman's voice said from the side, and I turned to where Kimberly Grove, a tall, older Black woman I hadn't seen in forever, swept out from the crowd to give me a quick kiss on either cheek. "Oh, goodness. It's been... what, two years? More, isn't it?"

"Two years four months," I said, nodding. "You look as beautiful as ever."

"Oh, you flatter me. Please keep doing so. My husband doesn't do it nearly enough." She nodded. "Two years, four months. That's right. It's gotten to be June already somehow, heavens above. Happy Pride, speaking of. And to your... girlfriend?"

I fumbled as Kimberly glanced over at Avery, who was struggling to keep that professional demeanor. Maintaining plausible deniability about us was hard when someone just walked up and asked. "Avery Lindt here is my current show partner and a... very good friend of mine."

"Ah, a *very good friend,*" Kimberly said with a sly smile. "Good to meet you, Avery. I'm Kimberly. My husband and I run a company that helped Holly start up her restaurant back when she was fresh and bright-eyed and full of hopes and dreams."

Avery just smiled. "Holly's really wonderful to work with. It's been such a delight to film with her."

Kimberly raised both eyebrows, eyes wide. "I don't think she's normally so close with the people on her show. Anything to do, perhaps, with why she's back after so long with her head buried to work on her show?"

Avery inched closer to my side, and part of me ached to just take her and pull her closer. "Mine's a bit of a special case," she said. "We're really here to see Mike Wallace."

Kimberly laughed drily. "Oh, there's some history there, I'll give you that. Well, I don't want to keep you too long, but—Holly, if I may, could I just steal you for a moment?" she said, before glancing over at Avery. "Avery? You won't mind if I take your, ahem, *very good friend?*"

Avery laughed, but there was so much nervousness under her expression as she let go of me and stepped back. It was only then that I realized how attuned I was to the emotions she was hiding, and I wondered if that was a bad sign. "Of course," she said. "I wouldn't want to get in the way of reunions, now that I've dragged Holly back out of hiding."

"I was not in hiding. I was literally on television. That is the opposite of hiding."

Kimberly laughed, putting a hand on my arm and guiding me towards her, down a side hallway and towards a room on the wings. "Come, come now. My husband will be so disappointed if he finds out you showed up and he didn't get to meet you!"

And so it was that my *just a moment* with Kimberly turned into meeting her husband again over a plate of hors d'oeuvres, which turned into meeting her husband's friend, who wanted to tell me all about his new startup, which led to him introducing me to his business partner, who wanted to tell me all about their clients, and standing there faking a smile and wondering if Avery was still alive back in the reception, I remembered why I'd avoided this event so long.

It was all tolerable, barely, until Kimberly's husband's friend's business partner's first client introduced me to his friend, who, by some sort of providence with a dark sense of humor, turned out to be Mike Wallace himself, standing and talking with a woman who barely looked twenty years old while he sipped champagne from a flute. All I could think was how utterly tasteless he was to go straight for the champagne the moment the event started.

He looked up across the table at me as his friend introduced me, saying, "Mike, I wanted you to meet my friend Holly, she works in—"

"Oh, we're acquainted," Mike said, raising an eyebrow. He gave the woman he was with a wink, getting a stomach-turning giggle from her before he walked around the table and gestured to another room in the wings. "Hey, babe. I was hoping I'd run into you here. Talk somewhere a little more private?"

"No," I said. "We can talk right here."

He chuckled. "Always full of spunk, Hol. All right. We can talk here. But I don't want to hold up Jordan. Go tell Elsie I told her hi," he said, waving his friend who'd *introduced* me to Mike away, before he turned to me, his eyebrow raised. "What's this about this girl you've got, huh?"

"What it *is* about Avery is none of your business," I said. "What do you want?"

"Just wanted to see an old friend, you know?" He leaned back against the table, giving me an obnoxious grin. "Not to mention someone who's been a little more than just an old friend..."

"I am not your friend, I was not your friend, and I regret every second of what we did."

He grinned wider. "Didn't seem to regret it then, babe. So," he said, his expression getting more serious now, "what's this about, Hol? I've been hearing from all my sponsored restaurants you've been harassing them on some personal crusade together with that cute little sidepiece hanging off your arm."

My throat tightened. "Don't talk about her like she's just an object, Mike. Her name is Avery, and she's an excellent chef."

"Can't be that great, if she landed herself on your show, and urgently enough you had to kick someone off, at that." He shook his head, smile disappearing. "Are you serious, Holly? Are you going to be so petty about me getting your show, you have to break your contracts to make some kind of story arc about me being the bad guy, even if it's going to sink your show? If you want to throw it away that badly, why not just hand it over?"

"I am not throwing away the show. I'm doing what I envision with it. And helping Avery against you and your ridiculous pyramid scheme is one hell of a noble cause." I folded my arms. "And don't pretend I don't know why you're upset. You've become irrelevant, except as the evil mastermind. No one's talking about you taking over the show anymore. The rumors of you being the show's original creator have died off, and the only talk of you and *Kitchen Rescue* is how we're confronting you. You're intimidated, now that

Avery and I are investigating your pyramid scheme."

He scoffed. "Now that you've got a hot little girl you're flaunting around Port Andrea, more like. That's not exactly like you, is it, babyface? You were always a little more private. Stubbornly refused to talk about us, anyway, and about everyone else, far as I can tell. What changed?"

I pursed my lips tight enough they hurt. "Maybe I just actually care about Avery."

"That's a laugh," he said. "Just falling head over heels for the girl and needing to throw away your plans for the show, let all your chances with it burn up so you can get into her pants?"

"*Mike.* What is it that makes you think you don't owe her basic human respect? Because she's a woman? Because I care for her?"

He gave me a sudden pitying look. "Oh, babe. They put you up to it, didn't they? It all makes sense, now that I think about it. I'm so sorry, Hol. I understand now why you've grown to hate the show so much. They decide every little thing you do, and now you have to go along with this notion of pretending to be Avery Lindt's girlfriend just to make your show more interesting. That must be so demeaning. And now having to come out here and get mad at me for your little girlfriend's sake, just because they're afraid of someone else taking over the show…"

I felt sick to my stomach. It churned like I'd eaten something rotten. And *yes,* they had put me up to it—*yes,* I was pretending to be Avery's girlfriend—*yes,* I was basically being paid to care about Mike's sponsorship scheme that I hadn't given a damn about before, but it still made me want to punch him.

"Answer the question, Mike. Why do you think you can just dismiss Avery as some—"

"Relax, babe," he said, pushing off from the table and coming towards me, backing me into a table. "You always know you can be real with me. Tell me how you're really feeling. You don't have to pretend anything about you and that chick. Don't worry. I'll keep your secret." He winked. "And any other secrets you want to make with me here."

I was positively going to be sick. "Get out of my face, Mike."

"Look, babe. I think we can make something amazing together. I want to relieve you of the burden of that show for both of our sakes. Just say the word and all the pressure will go away, and we can do whatever we like." He dropped his voice to a breathy whisper and leaned in. "I'll even drop everything against Paramour."

I was a hair's breadth away from punching him in the jaw when I heard from next to me, coming up around the table, the sweetest sound in the universe—Avery's voice, her heels clicking as she rounded the table towards me.

"Excuse me," she said, putting on a smile but with a look underneath it like she was ready to throw a punch, her voice a few decibels too loud for her regular levels. "Hi, Mike. Been a minute since I saw your slimy face in my restaurant. I'm going to need you to get out of my girlfriend's face."

My heart jumped, instantly doing a count of how many people were in the room—how many people must have heard it—but I felt like I could breathe again as Mike backed away, looking between us with a sardonic smile.

"And here's the girl in question," Mike said, raising an eyebrow. "Pleasure to see you again—"

He stopped when Avery stepped in between me and him, into his personal bubble and backing him up, leaning away. She took another step towards him, and I watched disbelieving.

"The pleasure is *all* mine, Mister Wallace," Avery said, the fake smile in her voice getting more and more transparently fake. "The pleasure of seeing you again, and getting to tell you *exactly* what's on my mind this time. I hate your show, you're a self-centered asshole, your sponsorship scheme is going to collapse around you, and your checkered ties look horrendous. Get out of my girlfriend's face this instant."

My jaw fell open. "Avery, it's okay," I said, putting a hand on her shoulder. "Come on. Let's just go. We don't need to start anything."

Mike looked between us, confusion written all across his face. "You're sure taking all this seriously," he laughed. "Come on. Relax. I was just having a chat with an old friend of mine."

She snorted. "Old friend," she said. "You can hit on my girlfriend over my cold, dead body."

He rolled his eyes, his smile disappearing. "Studio pay you to act this way, or you're just doing this to get exposure for Paramour?"

Avery laughed, brushed her hair back, and she said, "Go fuck yourself."

I think part of me fell in love with Avery on the spot.

I could have stood here all day and watched Avery tell off Mike, but I wasn't keen on having him shout to everyone in attendance that we were faking it. I put my hand back on Avery's shoulder. "We don't need to bother with him, Avery," I said, and she whirled on me, her eyes burning with— something.

"Yeah," she said, a second later. "Don't need to bother with *anyone* who tries to take you for themselves."

I swallowed. "Relax, Avery. No one's taking me away from you."

She chewed her lip, looked down at my mouth, and back up to make eye contact before she said, "Good."

And before I could say another word, she took me by the collar of my shirt, and she pulled me into a kiss.

There were so many reasons I knew *not* to kiss Avery Lindt. She wasn't around here—tied back to someplace else, outside of Port Andrea. She'd come here resolving not to date someone exactly like me. I'd sworn never to date someone who had a restaurant to benefit from my celebrity status.

But the number one reason not to kiss Avery was because I had a feeling it would be the best damn kiss I'd ever had, and god *dammit*, I'd been completely right.

She tugged me into her and pressed her lips against mine, a feeling like a burning match dropped into lighter fluid, feeling how she moved her lips against mine—the desperate way she moved, crashing her lips against me, like she just couldn't take holding back for one more second, and god, it was such a wild turn-on the way she couldn't.

I should have played it cool. Quick kiss. Acting the part. Pull away. How the fuck was I supposed to do that? I *needed* to kiss Avery. And I did—moved my lips against hers, nipping at her bottom lip, letting my hands fall to her hips and backing her up against the table, pulling her flush against me, every millimeter between us too damn far. She moaned against my lips, and it sent heat straight to my core.

Jesus. I could have taken her on this fucking table right this instant if it weren't for all the people around us. I almost didn't care about the people. The way she gripped me, desperate for this, needy whining against my lips, it just lit me up with desire.

There was no way I was ever going to stop kissing Avery. Not now, not ever.

God dammit. I blamed Mike for this.

CHAPTER 14

Avery

Holly didn't talk to me for the whole rest of the event, leaving me to stew in feeling like the worst human being on planet earth for totally losing myself and kissing her like my life depended on it.

Ugh. I wouldn't have felt so guilty if I hadn't enjoyed the kiss so much. But the way she kissed me back was just... I wondered if it was possible to die from arousal. There was no way it was possible, because if so, I'd have dropped dead.

So I just felt dirty and gross and awful the whole time we went around the rest of the event, Holly barely even so much as *looking* at me, let alone speaking beyond simple formalities in front of other people, and we left maybe ten minutes later, the moment the first speaker finished on stage and told us to sit down and eat, and I stumbled along after her.

"Holly, listen—" I started, once the elevator doors closed behind us, but she turned away, not looking at me.

"Thank you for helping with Mike," she said, her voice clipped. "You should not have... done that, though."

I looked down at the floor. "Yeah. You're right. I'm really, really sorry. I don't know why I did it. I understand if you're mad and hate me or whatever, but—I didn't want to screw up your time here, you know."

"I didn't want to come here, anyway," she muttered. "Just had to swing by, talk to Mike, look like I'm your girlfriend. Check, check, check. Done. We're leaving. You don't have to leave with me."

I paused. "Do you—want me to go back up? Or just wait and—let you leave alone?"

She spun her bangle idly around her wrist. "No. I changed my mind. Come with me. I need to talk to you. Somewhere private."

I paused. "Private...?"

"To talk about what we do now. Somewhere without paparazzi."

Oh, god. She was going to murder me. "Oh... right. Yeah. Okay. Where to?"

"I drove myself here. We'll go back to my penthouse."

Under different circumstances, I would have loved to kiss Holly and have her take me back to her apartment. But—I was not supposed to be thinking that right now. I kicked myself, hanging my head. "Of course," I said. "I'm ready to discuss the consequences of what happens from here."

And she didn't say another word, just leading me to her car and driving back, gripping her steering wheel so tightly her knuckles turned white, eyes straight ahead with a focus like she was trying to bore a hole in the road. When we parked at her apartment tower, I stumbled along following her inside, and into the elevator for the long ride up, which was even more painful than the long ride down from the dinner event.

She didn't even take off her heels when we got inside, just sinking back against the wall and putting a hand to her forehead. "Avery," she rasped, sounding tired. "Why'd you kiss me?"

I looked away. "I-I don't know. I mean, I do know. Mike was leaning up in your face and I couldn't stand him doing that to you. And... well." I dragged my fingers through my hair, looking away, out the full-wall window over the city. "And because I'm really, really attracted to you. That's also part of it. That's the biggest part of it. I'm really sorry."

"You *really* should not have kissed me."

"I know. I—don't want it to get in the way of the show, your image—"

"They brought a videographer in. They captured that kiss in ultra-high definition. And you didn't hold back."

My mind circulated through all possible responses and picked the worst one imaginable. "What, and you did? If that was you holding back, I can't imagine what it's like when you let loose."

"Christ," she sighed, dragging her hand down over her face. "How the hell am I supposed to do this, Avery?"

I chewed my cheek. "I guess we should see if Tay—"

"Not the damn *show,* Avery." She took a step closer, her irises flared, heels clicking on the floor, and she dropped her voice into a low, throaty murmur as she backed me against the wall and said, "How the hell am I supposed to keep myself from kissing you again now that I know it's that fucking good?"

My stomach dropped. "That—wasn't exactly where I was expecting that to go," I said, my breath coming faster, lungs straining to remember how to breathe.

"Yeah, I'd say all of this came from left field, Avery. You just sweeping in and telling off Mike in the way no one else ever would, standing up for me, laughing in his face and telling him to fuck himself, and then you turn around and kiss me like I've never been kissed before?"

Suddenly, I wasn't sure what Holly had brought me back to her apartment for. I got nervous flutters in every part of my body. "You can't blame me. *You* came sweeping in and told off Cecilia like no one else ever would, stood up for me, and—well, you didn't kiss me, so, yeah,

I'll give you that," I said, just nervous babbling as heat flooded my face.

"And I'll be damned if I didn't want to," she said, putting a hand on my shoulder and trailing her fingertips down my bare arm, and I shuddered to my very core. The deep red lipstick she had on was suddenly the only thing I could look at. "No one has stood up for me like that before, Avery. I wanted to kiss you then and there, even before you did. And thinking about it makes me just want to take you against this wall."

Something dropped in my core. My heart raced and my breath came short as I paused, and I said, "And... that's supposed to convince me to stop standing up for you like that?"

"For Christ's sake, Avery," she growled, trailing her hand back up my arm and across my collar, pausing with long, graceful fingertips on the base of my neck. My whole body thrummed with need, breathing hard, looking up into her eyes. "I'm not supposed to be with you. I made a promise."

"R-right. I did, too." But I was having a hard time remembering what the promise even was right now. "We should... just... cool off."

"I don't want to cool off, Avery," she murmured, trailing her fingertips up to caress my jaw, tilt my head up towards hers, and heat shot through me. "Just once. Just for tonight. I don't care about logic, or reason. I need you tonight."

I swallowed. "I, uh... you really think we'll manage to make it just once, do you?"

She smirked. "Giving me sass now, Avery?"

"I thought you found it attractive."

"God, I really do," she growled, and she shoved her hips up against mine, pressed me back against the wall, and she kissed me.

I'd thought kissing her at the dinner felt good. I mean—truth be told, I'd thought it was the best thing anyone had ever felt. But here we were, and now I was finding out that had nothing on this, Holly shoving me up against the wall, slipping her hand back into my hair and holding me, and pressing her lips up against mine, parting and tilting her head, taking my lips slipping in between hers. I groaned, my hands falling to her hips, and she responded with a hungry growl, shoving me harder up against the wall, which shot arousal through me like fire along gasoline.

I slipped my hands around to her back, gripping onto her, and she responded by sliding down to kiss my neck, sending shivers through to every part of me, including the desperate aching between my legs. When she ran her tongue up along my neck, back towards my chin, I let out a long, low moan.

"Oh, Holly," I groaned.

"God, I need to hear you say that again." She reached around, under my dress, which—I only just remembered I was supposed to return to the studio after the dinner, but—they'd get it back eventually—

She slipped a hand along my thigh, and I arched my body into her, away from the wall. She pressed me back into the wall again, dragging her hand up, hiking the hem of my dress up, and pressed her lips back to mine as she teased me, higher up my inner thigh until I felt like I was about to burst, and stopping right before my panties. I whimpered when she dropped my skirt back down, but it cut off into a gasp when she grabbed me, roughly, by the hips.

She pulled me away from the wall and, still kissing me, backed me across the apartment floor, awkward and stumbling in my heels walking backwards with Holly's lips pressed to mine, sucking on my bottom lip, until she pushed me onto the sofa, pressing me against the back and leaning over me to keep kissing me. My hands kept exploring over her body, moving from her hips up to her upper back and down along her sides again, until she had me on my back on the sofa and she was on top of me, straddling me, my heels kicked off, and she sat up to pull her dress up over her head.

"Oh my god, Holly," I gasped, looking at her there in just a bra and panties.

"Yours too," she said, her voice deep, husky, growling. An order. I bit my lip, desire and need quivering inside me, and I submitted as she undid the ties on the back of my dress and pulled it up, over my head, dropping it onto the floor, leaving me in my underwear below her. She leaned over me, a hungry look in her eyes as she dragged her hands up along my bare stomach, up towards my bra, where she fondled one cup in either hand, and I arched my back into her.

I opened my mouth to let out a long groan, and she cut it off by bending down and kissing me, pressing her mouth to mine in a hot, wet, open-mouth kiss. She spread her legs wider to press her hips against me, straddling me tight enough I could feel her wetness seeping through her panties, and the tiny fraction of presence of mind I had left marveled at how I'd made Holly Mason wet.

She pulled away to hover just over where I could feel I was red-faced and panting, gripping tightly at the smooth, toned skin of her hips, and she bit her lip, eyes half-lidded. "Tonight, you belong to me. Completely. Do you understand?"

I swallowed, hard. "Does that mean no sass? Won't you get bored?"

She laughed, a deep and throaty sound. "Don't pretend I don't know you want to bottom for me. Be a good girl and let me do what I want with you."

I felt like I melted hearing that, every part of me lighting up with the blissful pleasure of obedience. I bit my lip and nodded. "Whatever you want."

"Good girl. Bra, off. Now."

I arched my back to let her slip her hands underneath me, unclasping my bra and slipping it off of me, flinging it aside. She licked her lips, looking me over before she bent down and took one nipple in her mouth, and I gasped and slipped my hand up to her hair, holding her and digging my fingers into her scalp as I felt her tongue work around the tip of my nipple, sucking lightly.

"God, Holly," I groaned.

She didn't slow down for a second, taking my nipple until she dragged her tongue across my breasts and over to the other, sucking on it and leaving me melting under her. She slipped down my body, kissing and licking her way across my stomach until she knelt between my panties, and I propped myself up on my elbows to watch, breathless, my hair mussed and falling in my face, as she leaned in closer, her mouth to my panties, looking up into my eyes, and dragged her tongue up along the front of them.

It was lightning through my body, and I collapsed, sounds escaping my mouth. I hooked my legs around her without trying to, and she didn't let up, licking me through my panties, teasing, so good it felt like I could die but not enough at the same time. The sensation of her tongue through the fabric of my panties, her fingers on my thighs, on my nipples, it went on and on and on until I arched my back in desperation, thrusting my hips up into her.

"Holly, please—*please*," I gasped.

"Be a good girl and tell me exactly what you want," she said, voice throaty. "And don't you dare look away from me."

Christ. I struggled with my breathing long enough to look back down, down at the deliriously hot sight that was Holly in between my legs, my panties wet from her tongue. I bit my tongue. "Please—take my panties off and... and..."

She raised one eyebrow at me. *God*, it was sexy when she did that normally. This was another universe. "And what, Avery? What happened to all that confidence?"

I groaned. "Anything. Please. Whatever you want to do with me."

"Desperate little girl for me, aren't you?" She sat up and wiped her mouth with the back of her hand. "Stand up. Take your panties off."

I struggled to regain enough control of my limbs to get up to my feet, and then, hands shaking, tug my panties down, dropping them to the floor, feeling the cool air on the blazing heat of my center. She stood up with me, looked me over, bit her lip, and the desire in her eyes as she looked at me just threatened to burn me up.

"Good girl," she said, standing up with me and pulling me into another kiss, reaching in between my legs and brushing her fingertips over my folds. It lit me up like a firework, every part of me igniting, and I broke away from the kiss without meaning to, rolling my head back and groaning. My moaning wavered when she moved down and kissed my neck instead, sucking on it just a little harder.

She kept going until she put her hands on my hips and walked me backwards again, kissing me the whole way until she pinned me up against the door to her bedroom, pushing it open and stumbling inside with me, kissing me while she kicked the door shut, and she shoved me backwards onto the bed, where I fell into a sit and sank back on my hands, looking breathlessly at Holly standing there in a black lace bra and panties with her heels still on, and I didn't think I had a thing for that, but that was *definitely* doing it for me.

She bit her lip as she looked down at me, that hungry expression making fire spread through me, and she took in a long breath before she said, "I want to fuck you into the bed with a strap-on," which—well—my heart wasn't ready to hear those words in that order. I swallowed, hard.

"Yes. Please." I squirmed, looking away, feeling my face burning. "Um—I don't, you know, get... wet, though..."

She laughed, tilting my chin up with her fingers. "Do you think I'm a stranger to lube, Avery?"

I let out a sharp breath. "Well, to tell you the truth, I'd never stopped to think about whether or not you're a stranger to it. Did you stop to think about—"

She put a finger to my lips, and I stopped talking. She smirked. "I may have ended up thinking some things about you, Avery."

Christ. The way she said my name—especially with a statement like that—just made heat plummet in my core. "I... want to help you fulfill all your fantasies."

"Good girl." She opened a bedside drawer, pulled out a harness, and I watched breathless as she slipped it on over the lace of her panties, fitting a dildo into it, and then just seemed to relish standing there over me in her lingerie and strap, watching the way I squirmed. "On your back," she said, finally.

"Holly," I whimpered, obliging, falling onto my back, gripping the sheets as she climbed on top of me, reaching up and gripping the hair on the side of my head as she just hovered over me.

"Tell me what you need, Avery."

I bit my lip, hard. "I-I need you inside me."

She licked her lips, smiling. "Good girl."

She put the lube first on me directly, rubbing it on my clit, around my entrance, reaching down and teasing around my shape with her fingers, until I was desperate and aching and gripping the sheets tightly, gasping for breath, begging her in small, panted breaths, "please, please, please." I breathed hard once she pulled her hand away, applying the lube to her strap instead, holding eye contact with me the whole time, hungry, ready to take me.

She reached down to spread my legs wider, and then to guide the tip of her strap against me, teasing my entrance. I let out a desperate moan as she pushed inside, slowly, spreading me wide, filling me up deeper and deeper, until her hips pressed into mine, and she just paused there for a second—and then she shifted her hips, grinding against me, inside me, and I pressed my head back into the mattress and let out a long, wavering moan.

"Oh my god, Holly, yes, please," I gasped, my breath ragged, gripping the sheets. She gave me that ridiculously sexy smirk that only looked hotter with her hair falling messily down over me to one side, pinning me down like this, and she pulled out, slowly, until it was only the tip left inside me. She watched me squirm, watched the way I gasped, and then—in one swift motion, thrust back inside me, filling me up again, lighting up every nerve in my body, until I felt like I could have come apart.

"You take it so well," she murmured, pulling out and thrusting back into me again. I let out loud, obscene gasps with every movement inside me—I couldn't control them, couldn't control myself. I really tried to, but the feeling of Holly filling me up, thrusting into me, I couldn't control anything in my body anymore. I hooked my legs around her, moving my hips in time with hers, thrusting up to take her so fucking deep inside me it felt like she filled up every inch of my body, felt like she was going to just fucking break me, and I *needed* it, needed all of it.

"Hard—harder," I gasped. "Please, please, please."

She laughed that deep, throaty laugh, and she licked her lips once before she murmured, "Such a dirty girl for me."

I just nodded, mouth open, gasping for breath, struggling to hold eye contact. I lost it when she fucked into me harder, gripping my hair tight on the side of my head, and I arched my head back into the mattress and groaned.

"Don't look away," she growled, pushing me back to meet her eyes. "I want to watch you come for me."

I gasped out a breathless *yes* again and again, just ready to go along with anything if it meant she would keep thrusting inside of me, filling me up like this. It didn't take me long, anyway—with the way she built up speed and power, slamming in and out, I felt the pleasure building up higher and higher in me until it threatened to spill over, like a pot boiling over, and my *god* I needed to let it all go.

"Please," I gasped, voice cracking. "Holly, please, *please*, I need to—I need to—"

"Say it for me," she growled, gripping my hair tighter. My body flamed with need.

"I—I need to come, Holly, please—"

"Good girl," she said, licking her lips and thrusting in harder, faster. "Come for me."

I gave in, let go, let loose, and I felt it flooding over me with a desperate feeling of release. It flooded through me as I arched my back and cried out, and that sensation like my whole body was coming undone spread out through every inch of me.

And—god, if I thought kissing Holly was unlike anything with anyone else, then having an orgasm with Holly was indescribable. The feeling of her thrusting into me and grinding inside of me while I came just made me lose control, completely, gripping her tight with my legs and digging my fingernails into the sheets, letting out a desperate moan as it felt like every muscle in my body released everything it ever felt.

When I collapsed, breathing hard, I felt like my whole body had been reset, and I had to figure out how to move so much as a finger. I sank into the mattress underneath her, gasping, trying to regain some semblance of breath, feeling sweat sheening on every inch of my body, and all I could think was that Holly—eyes sparkling, that satisfied smile both the sexiest and the most beautiful thing I'd ever seen—she was an angel, descended from heaven, to fuck me right out of this mortal plane.

"You look good when you come," she said.

"Wow," I sputtered. "Oh my god. That was the hardest I've ever come in my life."

She licked her lips. "I'm not done with you tonight. You're going to come harder the next time."

I—wasn't complaining.

CHAPTER 15

Holly

I'd never woken up feeling so good in my life, and when I stepped out of the bedroom and into the kitchen, early morning sunlight streaming through the windows, I was faced with a beautiful reminder of why I did wake up feeling so good, and that was Avery wearing my silk two-piece pajama top and a pair of panties, standing in the kitchen with her back to me, humming while she cooked.

And god, she had some great legs.

It took her a minute to notice I was there, leaning against the wall and watching her, and she turned and glanced over her shoulder, beaming at me with her hair mussed and her face absolute blissful perfection.

"Holly," she said, voice crackling. "Hey. Good morning. I'm making scrambled eggs."

"Ah," I laughed, coming up towards her and leaning against the counter, looking at the double boiler she had set up, stirring a batch of eggs on top. "The legendary dish I've heard so much about."

She laughed, turning back to the eggs. "I have to impress you somehow."

"I was plenty impressed with lots of things about you last night," I said, and she sputtered, nearly dropping the spatula. I loved the way she flushed pink for me.

"I, uh—"

"Very impressed how good you are taking a strap in your mouth."

"Jesus," she said, putting a hand over her face, turning away, and she cleared her throat loudly. I had to admire her dedication, still stirring the eggs with her other hand. "Planning on just going around talking about that all the time?"

"Do I look like an exhibitionist, Avery?"

She shrugged. "You have a massive, full-wall window. I don't know how many people you might have fucked like that in front of it."

I grinned, reaching out and flicking her hair back from her face. "Are *you* an exhibitionist, seeing things like that just from me having a window? Or are you a voyeur? Which side of the window are you on, Avery?"

"I see you're very invested in knowing about my sexual preferences now," she said, glancing at me from the corner of her eye, and I raised an eyebrow.

"Who could blame me? I quite enjoyed what I found out last night."

She cleared her throat, looking away again, and turned off the stove, plating the eggs along with seared mushrooms and grape tomatoes, and she handed one plate to me. "Coffee?"

"I think I'll have tea this morning."

So we ended up sitting down together, across from each other, with a pot of English breakfast tea and Avery's legendary eggs, and we spent maybe half an hour talking about everything other than the topic at hand—including my very emphatic tasting of Avery's scrambled eggs—before I let it slip.

"I sometimes like to dress them up," Avery said, a forkful of food on her way to her mouth, and I raised an eyebrow.

"I sometimes like to undress you, but that works, too," I said, and she fumbled and nearly dropped the food on her lap. I laughed. "You okay there, Avery?"

She looked away, setting the food back down. "Doing great," she mumbled. "Um... Holly. What exactly happens now?"

I raised an eyebrow. "Now that I've talked about undressing you?"

"Now that you've—well—done it." She cleared her throat, still avoiding my gaze. "Is that it? Like you said? Just one night?"

I—stopped. I had said that. I'd had a whole list of reasons not to be like this with Avery, and right now, I was having a hard time remembering any of it.

"That was the plan," I said, every part of my voice laced with reservations.

"It was. And, uh... what's the expression?"

"Even the best-laid plans?"

"Something like that." She scratched the back of her head, still not looking at me. I laughed.

"You're shy, aren't you, Avery?" I said. "If you regret it, we can pretend that didn't happen."

"I—I don't think there's any pretending that," she mumbled, fussing with her napkin. "It definitely happened. And I don't regret it. My concern is more about, uh, you know. If we'll actually be able to make it a one-time thing."

I leaned back. "What makes you think we can't?"

"Well, this morning, you've talked about undressing me, about the sexual preferences you found about me last night, the way I, er, well... had something in my mouth."

"My strap."

"That'd be the thing, yeah," she said, rubbing the back of her neck, looking out the window. "And I think if I asked you for balsamic vinegar again, we'd end up having sex again, and I'm not entirely upset about that outcome."

I chewed my lip. There were plenty of responsible choices I could have made here. Ways to let go of all of this smoothly and cleanly, and just let that one night with Avery be an incredible memory. But right now, none of them quite seemed feasible.

"You're saying you want to have sex again," I said, and she made a sound I didn't know humans could.

"I—well—I'm not saying I *don't* want that," she said, flushing pink. I laughed.

"You're so cute," I said.

"Just—you know. You said you can't date me. Long string of awful relationships, and all that. You were trying not to date."

That really wasn't the reason I couldn't date her, but it was the one I'd given her. How was I supposed to just out and say *I don't trust you're not trying to use me for my fame?* If she was, she'd just play it off. If she wasn't, then that'd be an awful thing to say to her.

But—she was right. That, and several other reasons, I could not get into a relationship with her. But...

"We wouldn't have to date," I said, and she whipped her head over to look at me, brow furrowed.

"Hold on. You're not suggesting a friends-with-benefits situation."

I licked my lips. "Why not?" I said. "You told me you can't date me, either. Why not just have the thing we both want, without the part neither of us can do?"

"But—but—" She stammered, mouth moving a lot more than she was talking. "I... I've never done that before."

"It's not rocket science. We'd be just like we have been, except also like we were last night."

She drew a long, shaky breath before looking out the window. "I'm not... um. Wow. What about exclusivity?"

I raised an eyebrow. "My. Didn't realize you were sleeping around with so many other people, that was the worry."

"That—don't be difficult with me, Holly Mason," she said, screwing up her face in the cutest way possible. I laughed.

"Do you want it to be exclusive?" I said, trying to sound casual about it, but it made my heart race, wishing, *praying* she would say yes, because—now that I'd put the thought out there, I hated the idea of Avery sleeping with anyone other than me.

Which, logically, would be a clear sign this was too fraught with various feelings to pursue it. But logically, there was no way Avery and I *weren't* having sex again. We were just preparing for the inevitable.

"I, uh... what's the difference between exclusive friends-with-benefits and dating?"

I raised an eyebrow. "Doesn't have to be exclusive. Won't bother me if it is. I've been avoiding that scene for a while."

"Okay. I mean, me too. I mean... I wasn't super into it to begin with. It's a little scary for a trans girl anyway." She scratched her head, looking away. "So I guess it doesn't matter a lot."

I think she and I both knew it mattered a *lot,* and we were explicitly not addressing it. "What if we just say it's not exclusive, but anyone else, we clear it with one another first?"

"That just sounds like polyamorous dating."

I laughed. "Do you want to, or not?"

She sighed, sinking back in her seat, picking at the corner of her chair arm. "Well, I mean, yeah, I want to. Of course I want to. Have you seen you? I mean... yeah."

"Great," I said, licking my lips. "We'll do it. Let's lay down the base rules, then."

"Base rules?" She glanced up at me, eyes wide.

"Of course. These things get messy easily otherwise." I held up a finger. "Exclusivity is one. Kissing is two," I said, holding up a second finger.

She furrowed her brow. "Kissing?"

"I know very well you're familiar with the concept, Avery."

She blushed, looking down. I couldn't get enough of that.

"Keep it separate," I said. "No kissing outside of sex."

"Ohh. Right." She nodded. "Yeah. That makes sense. And then... in public?"

I snorted. "Well, you grabbed me and made out with me on the floor of the charity dinner, so I think that ship has sailed. No more of the will-they-or-won't-they. In the public eye, we're girlfriends."

She flushed, looking down. "So, I guess, exception to the kissing rule for on camera or anything."

"Oh, of course. Never had to kiss someone for the camera before?"

She scrunched up her face. "No," she said, as I stood up and walked around the table towards her. "Have *you?* I don't remember you getting that friendly with any of the owners on *Kitchen Rescue.*"

"I haven't," I laughed. "But no one better to start with than you," I said, standing over her in the chair, before I sank onto her lap. She went bright red, pupils dilating, leaning back, but she met me when I leaned in and kissed her on the lips again. It felt like a sigh of relief deep inside me every time our lips met, and I needed it to never stop.

"Uh," she said, once I'd pulled away just enough the tip of my nose still brushed hers, and she glanced down out of the corner of her eye at the floor. "I'm pretty sure you just said no kissing outside of sex."

"I did," I said, kissing her again. She swallowed hard, eyes going wider. "And that's supposed to convince me to stop kissing you?"

She blinked, eyes going wide. "I... would certainly hope not."

"Good," I said, and I pulled her into another kiss as deep, sensual, fiery as the one in the charity dinner, unbuttoning that silk pajama top, and god, I was long gone.

We barely even got out of the apartment in time for Avery to make her scheduled shift at Paramour, and when we went out for dinner again after that, Tay not-so-accidentally leaked the location of our dinner date to the gossip rags, who showed up ahead of us with microphones and cameras in our faces.

But this time, when someone shouted the question on if I had any comment on my and Avery's relationship, I just pulled Avery closer to my side and kissed her on the cheek before shoving through the crowd to get into the restaurant.

Conditioned like Pavlov's dog, though, even kissing her on the cheek got me turned on. And it was hard sitting there across the table from her watching her mouth while she ate, and thinking about all the things she'd done with that mouth last night, and wondering if it would be too passe to just take her to the women's restroom and have her there.

Needless to say, when we got back to my apartment that night, we didn't even make it away from the front door before I ripped her clothes off, dropped my panties to the floor, and had her on her knees in front of me to give me what I'd needed all day long.

All in all, the filming arrangement was turning out to be quite... agreeable, I thought, as I lay in bed that night looking over at Avery curled up naked next to me, sleeping softly with her hair falling in perfect little waves over her face, one strand fluttering in each soft exhalation through her lips, and I brushed it out of the way before I laid a soft kiss on her lips.

We were still naked. We'd just had sex. That counted as not kissing outside of sex.

I knew if I was trying to convince myself, I was already screwed, but I was going to do my damnedest.

CHAPTER 16

Avery

I t's been a minute," Liv said, standing up from where she was waiting at the subway terminal, wearing a graphic tee and faded jeans that both looked a size too big, but worn deliberately that way. "You look better these days, you know, Aves."

I smiled lightly. She didn't need to know it was because I'd spent the past two weeks having sex with Holly in every possible place, including just yesterday when we'd been shooting at Paramour and Kyle gave us a thirty-minute break, and Holly locked us in my back office and took me over my desk. "Things have been pretty good," I said.

"Yeah. Paramour's picking up. It's been weird having new staff. I'm like... this was supposed to be our skeleton crew to go down on the ship with, and now we're sailing normally again? Who are these strangers coming into our little disaster kitchen?"

I strained my smile a little. "Liv, I'm standing right here."

"Yeah, and you'd be the first to admit it was a disaster kitchen," she said, jerking her head towards the plaza, full of foot traffic on a rare sunny day in July, kids playing in the ground-level fountain, people picking up ice cream and cold drinks from stalls along the edges or the two-story installation in the center, the few restaurants lucky enough to have this space packed with outdoor seating right now. "Come on. Komodo is waiting. I need to actually have you try the cinnamon mocha this time, instead of running off with a hot celebrity to go bang her."

I stumbled, missing my footing. "That's not at all what happened," I said.

"You've quit being coy about it and admitted you're girlfriends," she said, shoving her hands in her pockets and strolling on ahead of me a little ways. "People bang their girlfriends. No surprises there. I'm not asking for details, don't worry."

"Okay, but—" I started, my face hot, picturing entirely too much of the ways Holly *did* bang me. "I didn't leave Komodo's with her to, uh…"

"Yeah, yeah." She waved me off, and it was only then that I realized she was avoiding looking at me, a sort of weight about her. "Save it for the jury. I know celebrities lead exciting lives."

I pursed my lips, walking alongside her. "She's just an ordinary human being, you know."

"Yeah, right," she snorted. "And I'm a sea sponge."

I paused. "I don't think you're a sea sponge."

"Eh. I'm clingy and full of holes, and the whole world just sees me as a tool."

I blinked. "I, uh… Liv, are you okay?"

She let out a long sigh through her lips, shoulders dropping. "Totally fine. What makes you think anything else?"

"Um… everything."

"Yeah, whatever. Just let me get coffee. That'll help."

"All right," I said. "But if you need to talk, I'm here for you."

"You'll just tell me to manifest a happier existence," she sighed, heading up towards the doors with the windows stuffed full of knickknacks that led to Komodo's Den.

"I'm not one-dimensional," I said.

But she didn't reply, just pulling open the door and heading inside ahead of me. The line was long, but it moved along quickly, and Liv only had to shove her hands in her pockets and look moody for a little while before she got up to the counter and ordered her cinnamon mocha, and I butted in to ask for a chai latte too and put down my card. Liv looked at me like I'd stabbed her.

"I can pay for my own coffee," she said.

"I've had a celebrity turning around my fortunes. I'm not quite as broke anymore. Come on. It's my thanks for all your great work lately."

She pouted, but she didn't argue. I tapped the screen on the register for a generous tip, and it was only once we got to the handoff plane that Liv mumbled, "You ever just feel like you don't know what you're doing with your life?"

I softened, leaning against the counter and looking at her. "Plenty of times. It's a rough feeling."

"Yeah?" She arched her eyebrows at me. "I mean, you know. Aside from worrying about Paramour failing?"

I laughed drily. "Let me worry about that again once Holly is done working with us and I'm back on my own again."

She frowned. "You're girlfriends. She's not going to leave you high and dry. You've got it made over there," she said, a touch of bitterness in her voice.

"I, uh... let's talk about this somewhere a little more private," I said. She gave me a strange look, but she didn't argue, just taking the cinnamon mocha from the barista and heading outside ahead of me.

"And order for Avery," the barista said, a girl who actually managed to rock pink hair, setting down my chai latte. "Avery Lindt, right?"

Oh my god. I was getting recognized in public. I beamed. "That's me. Fan of Holly's?"

She grinned. "Not at all. But my best friend is, and she won't shut up about how cute you and Holly are."

I deflated just a little. "Here I was hoping maybe I was getting recognized by fans. I guess maybe that's still a step away."

When I got outside, Liv just arched her eyebrows at me, slurping her mocha. "Took you long enough," I said.

"Would you believe me if I said the barista wanted an autograph?"

She rolled her eyes. "Course I would. You're all famous and successful and popular now."

"She actually didn't care about me at all, she just wanted the autograph for her friend. It wounded my pride just a little."

"Just manifest the fans recognizing you on the street."

I laughed. "You say that like I don't already do it. Come on," I said, leading her to an overhang strung with ivy, in the shade near a little indie bookstore that was quiet right now, and I sat down with her in the corner of the plaza well away from everyone before I said, "Don't tell anyone, but Holly and I actually aren't dating."

She frowned at me, cocking her head. "What are you talking about? I've seen it all over everything. And everyone at Paramour is talking about it all the time, how we're busy now because of your famous girlfriend."

"Yeah, uh... it's a long story and it starts with inspir-Tay-tion."

She blinked. "It starts with what," she deadpanned.

So I explained how it was Tay had gotten us both to agree to a pretend relationship, how they'd set it all up to not only draw attention to Paramour, but to revitalize Holly's image. And Liv just watched, her expression more confused by the second, until she just shook her head.

"I don't get it," she said. "There's no faking the way you two are looking at each other."

I cleared my throat, looking away. "Yeah, well, see, the thing is, we actually did already like each other."

"What?" She squinted. "Then why not just *actually* date?"

"Holly's not interested in a relationship," I sighed, looking away, picking at the sleeve around my chai latte. "She's had a lot of bad relationships, and she's just kind of... done with them for a while."

"That's not how it works at all. Look, I know you'll think I'm just a kid and all, but you're being ridiculous. You don't just turn off your feelings."

"I think there's something more to it, too," I said. "She... well. She's had some bad experiences with people taking advantage of her celebrity status. And I obviously have a lot to gain from it, so she really can't date me."

"You two are ridiculous," she said, shaking her head. I scowled.

"Excuse me. *I'm* ridiculous. She's amazing and smart and talented and really, really out of my league."

"Ugh, you even sound like a lovesick teenager."

"You're barely any older than a teenager yourself," I said, a hand on my hip.

"I'm twenty-two! You're only six years older than me!"

"Still barely any older than a teenager."

She huffed, looking away. "You two are going to end up kissing or something sometime soon. I can see it in the way you two gaze at each other."

I cleared my throat. "We, uh... did, you know."

"Yeah, for TV. I mean for real, for real."

"No, I mean... for real, for real. We kind of did." I fussed with the corner of the table. "It's... well, it's complicated. But we're not girlfriends."

I took a sip just as Liv said, "Don't tell me you just agreed to be fuck-buddies or something," and I spat my drink back into my cup.

"I—" I said, face going red. "That's—a crude way of describing it."

"Oh my god. You're kidding. Do you know how bad an idea that is?"

"*Yes,* I know how bad an idea it is," I said, putting my drink down, and it seemed to catch her off-guard. "How would I not know? But what am I supposed to do, make Holly Mason herself actually fall for me? I'm just... just a failing restauranteur."

She stared at me for the longest time, and I sighed, letting my gaze fall to the ground.

"Sorry," I said. "I offered to talk to you about what's bothering you, and I ended up dumping on you about my feelings for a girl a million miles out of my league."

"Who fucks you," she said, and I choked.

"I—well—you're very upfront about these things," I said, scratching my neck, looking away.

"Is this you trying to make me feel better about being a walking disaster?" she said, and I shrugged.

"I guess that's where it came from. Point is, there's not a soul alive who's never struggling. I don't want you to feel like you're alone. You can share whatever's on your mind with me. I admitted to how stupid I am, getting into something with Holly that's obviously going to blow up in my face, so whatever's bothering you, you can admit to."

She laughed awkwardly, looking away and staring out at the plaza. "I think you'd get pissed off if I told you what was really on my mind."

"Pissed off isn't exactly a setting on my dial," I said.

"Everyone's got that setting. It just takes some work to get it there."

I chewed my lip. "I mean, I got pissed off at Mike. But... I think he's kind of the exception. I don't think you're going to get the dial there."

"I was the one who wrote all those articles about Paramour."

I blinked. "Er... come again?"

"Yeah. Mike's guy paid me pretty well, and I figured Paramour wasn't going to last either way, so what was the harm?"

I just sat there for a minute, my head spinning, staring at her.

Well. That was pretty rude of her. But honestly, I wasn't pissed off so much as feeling my head spin with the fact that I had the missing piece in the whole investigation right here—Liv, with all the contracts and paper trails to show she was paid off by the people from the Julius to write smear articles against Paramour and publish them under different names for different blogs— and she was my *friend*. I couldn't just ask her to come out in front of everyone and say *hey world, I'm the asshole*. She'd just been trying to get by.

She sighed. "I'm fired, aren't I?"

"What? Oh. No. You're really good at your job. You'd be expensive to replace." I shook my head. "Seriously? You were the one writing the articles, and then you would go strolling with me in places like this and talk about *hey it's cool, I'm sure Paramour will be okay?*"

"Yeah, I know. I'm a piece of shit. I felt bad about it when I was doing it, but... like I said, I figured it wouldn't do any good if I turned it down. He'd just get the next guy to do it. Dominic, probably. He'd be happy to write smears for cash."

I crossed my arms. "*You* made up that thing about roaches? And... wait. You said the waiters are all assholes in one."

She grinned. "It's mostly just me and Diane, and if I'm being totally honest, she can be kind of asshole-ish at times."

"Diane is sweet. She's just... blunt. And *I* wait tables sometimes."

She squinted. "I expected you to be screaming at me, not... getting huffy."

"I'm not an asshole. I try my best to be nice. You take that back."

"*That's* what's bothering you? I was lying in everything I said in those. I just wanted money, okay? And I didn't even use it for anything good. I got some more cash and it felt like blood money, and I just wanted it gone. Went to some concerts. My friends and I went down to the Sea and Stars Song Contest finale to watch Emmy Montford sing Katy Perry. I bought some new clothes. Got rid of all the new money pretty quick. Then I felt even worse about it. Like, what am I even doing with my life? I justified it to myself being like *yeah, fuck the system, screw over my boss, workers' revolution,* but it wasn't a workers' revolution, you're just some girl trying to run a restaurant and you pay me way better than I'd get anywhere else just because you think your employees should be comfortable, and all I did was sabotage your dream restaurant for a quick buck."

I sighed. "Liv, I'm not mad."

"What the hell? You should be. I'm the one who fucked over your restaurant."

"That was Mike who did. And besides, those smear pieces going wide ended up bringing Holly to my restaurant. I should be thanking you."

Her mouth fell open, arms dropping by her sides. "Are you fucking serious? Jesus, your dial really doesn't have pissed-off on it. Who broke your dial?"

I laughed. "It was just always like that. Plus, you know the stereotype of the angry trans woman. I guess I just wanted to avoid that, and I forgot how to feel angry."

She paused. "Wait. Are you trans?"

"Yeah. There you go. Your little secret for mine. Now we're even."

She put her hands up. "What the hell? Your secret is cool as hell. Mine is awful and mean. You can't compare being trans to all of that."

"I know, I know." I put my hands up. "I'm trying to learn how to tell people about it. Holly's kind of the only person outside of my old life who knows. Now you do, too. To show we're still friends."

She blinked fast. "So... the real reason you wanted to leave everything behind, start a new life in a different city where no one knew you, it was because you wanted to start a life where no one knew you're trans?"

"Pretty much, yeah. Something like that."

Liv stared at me for the longest time before she sank back in her seat with a long sigh, slurping at her cinnamon mocha. "Damn," she said. "You know, I kind of envy that. Sometimes I just want to go back and start my whole life over, you know?"

I laughed. "Yeah, I get that."

"I swear, I thought I knew what I was doing. I wanted to go into film. I moved to Port Andrea to go to uni at UPA, study film and production, but all I did was bounce around between a million different things I sucked at and got bored of before a semester was done. Then bills getting tight, I dropped out to just focus on working and getting a little cash to help get me through school, but I haven't wanted to go back. Why bother if there's nothing I want to learn, nothing I want to study, nothing I want to do with my life? I'm just spinning my wheels miles away from any roads."

I nodded, slowly. "Yeah. It's hard, when you feel like your life's stalled out."

"Ugh, stop being so damn empathetic. It's annoying."

I paused. "I, uh… it is?"

"No. I mean, not really. I'm just grouchy and get annoyed over everything." She rubbed her forehead. "So what now? If you're not going to fire me, what'll it be? Dock my wages? Publicly shame me? Aw, you probably want me to appear on the damn show and admit to how I'm the one who fucked everything over, don't you?"

I swallowed. "Well… Holly and her team would probably want you to. But I'm not going to make you."

"Why the fuck not? I'm your missing piece. Here's your lead, right here." She looked down. "It's the least I can do for fucking everything up."

"Well… for one, because I don't think that would look good on your resume. I don't want to screw you over like that."

"I swear, you are the weirdest boss I've ever had."

I laughed. "I'll take that as a compliment. You can come out with it to the whole team if you want to, but I won't make that choice for you."

"Thanks," she mumbled, sliding the sleeve up and down her cup idly, her head down. "Aves, what am I supposed to do?"

"Just in general? With your life?"

"Yeah. Something like that, I guess. I just... I kind of thought you were full of shit at first, with all your *manifest a better reality* bullcrap. I was just along for the ride to get some good pay while I watched you crash and burn."

I blinked. "That's... candid."

"But I guess I was wrong. You turned it all into a good thing, somehow, even when I fucked things over. You transitioned into the right gender, started a new life in a city you loved, opened your dream restaurant, got in with a celebrity, kept the place afloat when it was falling apart, and you even get to fuck Holly Mason."

Well, she generally fucked me. I kept that to myself and ignored the last part altogether. "I've gotten lucky," I said, looking away.

"Yeah, but you know, you've just been so full of hope throughout the whole process. And you *enjoyed* everything along the way. And I was expecting that hope to blow up in your face and to see cynicism was way better so that nothing can disappoint you, but you were just always unfazed. Now I'm starting to think *I've* been the one full of bullcrap, acting like the world is all out to get me and I have to make myself miserable so nothing else makes me miserable." She picked at her fingernails, studying the window of the bookshop intently. "Teach me how to manifest too. You should lead classes or something."

I laughed. "Sounds like you've already been doing it. You were looking for a way to work for a while, get some money while you figured out what you want in life. Here you are, getting work experience, some money, really drilling into what you want in life."

I expected another flippant answer, but she didn't say anything, just staring off into the distance. I softened my voice, leaning in towards her.

"You would be amazed what can change in five years. Hey, you'd be amazed what can change in one year. You can start your life over any time you want to."

"Sounds like some kind of bullshit mission statement you'd find in a self-help book."

"Yeah, it probably does," I said. "But sometimes, we don't need specific, practical advice. We need to return to the innocence of having no preconceived notions, of seeing the whole entire world, and realizing we can do—and be—whatever we want. Sometimes you need a lofty statement to realize you can do lofty things."

She gave me a dry smile. "Like redefining fearless?"

I clapped my hands together. "Oh my god. I got so caught up in Holly Mason and everything that day, I forgot all about redefining fearless."

"Guess you already did. You redefined fearless as banging Holly Mason."

I laughed. "Liv, I think you're doing fine just the way you are. Not many people realize as young as you have that they're not sure of their trajectory in life. Lots of people go their whole lives without noticing they're living it."

She chewed her cheek. "That just sounds like another empty statement."

"That just sounds like more cynicism."

She laughed, shaking her head. "You know? I guess maybe it does. Maybe I need to make the conscious decision to quit doing that." She paused. "You can start your life over any time you want to, huh?"

"Absolutely. I've done it three times. Once went great, transitioning and picking up a new name. Once was fun and ended terribly, coming here to date Cecilia. And this latest one has been pretty messy, but... I'm really happy I did. And I think I'm still going to do it plenty more in the future."

"Sounds like bullshit, but that's probably the cynicism talking." She sank back in her seat, giving me a lopsided smile. "Yeah. You know something? I guess I'll try that. See about... starting my life over. Redefine fearless myself. Manifest a happier life for me."

I grinned. "I think you're going to do well. And I still think I'm going to look great on the cover of Foodie Magazine, by the way."

She laughed. "I can't believe you're not doing anything about me writing the smears."

"I think with every major experience, we can either grow from it, or we can wither. I'd prefer to help make it the former."

"You are a never-ending font of lofty statements. Yes, and I'm going to choose every morning to decide anew who I'm going to be."

"You know... not to get even more obnoxious on you, but I think that probably came from somewhere," I said. "Anything coming right to your mind like that is probably important to you on some level."

She stopped, frowning, furrowing her brow. "What? What did I even say?"

"You're going to choose every morning to decide anew who you're going to be."

"Damn, that sounds cheesy." She scratched her head. "Yeah. Sure. What the hell. Gives me something to believe in. It's, uh... been a while since I had that."

I smiled, sinking back in my seat. "We all need something to believe in."

"Yeah, there's an airy-sounding statement that I actually agree with. Going all this time not believing in anything has sucked. Probably better to get my hopes up believing in something and be let down than to never believe at all."

"I'll toast to that," I said, lifting my cup, and she tapped hers to mine.

And she was right—it was *so* much better to get my hopes up believing in something, even if I was going to be let down.

I'd been doing it all my life, and I wasn't about to stop now.

CHAPTER 17

Holly

Have fun with your shift," I said, giving Avery's hand a squeeze before I let go. Holding hands in public was one part of our pretend relationship I didn't want to let go of.

"Oh, a blast," she laughed, tossing her hair back. "I look okay, right?" She fussed with the collar of her blazer, and I pulled her hands away from it.

"You look amazing. You always have." I gestured to the front of Paramour, even though I just wanted to stay here with Avery and treasure that wide-eyed look she gave me. "Get a move on. Your fans are waiting."

"I'm not the one with fans, missy," she laughed, but she stepped back, heading up for the front door. "I'll see you tonight!"

"See you," I called after her, and once she was out of view, I turned away, sighing heavily to myself.

God, I was awful at not developing feelings. I'd always been, but keeping my feelings for Avery in check was the hardest of all.

I checked my phone. I was supposed to be back at the studio at three, which gave me an hour to find lunch, and before I knew it, I was on the subway and off again at Florence Station, heading into the boho sandwich place to get an avant-garde sandwich called the Lucid Dream, which tasted entirely too good for the sheer number of bizarre ingredients in it. I didn't want to be a hipster, but as I sat under the strings of flowering vines strung along the ceiling, I bit into my sandwich, and I found myself in hippie dream land.

I was halfway through my sandwich, though, when a voice I *hated* hearing came ringing in my ears, and I winced.

"Babe," Mike's voice said, coming around the corner and leaning over my table. The red blazer he was wearing today was the epitome of awful, and with the checkered necktie, he looked like if an Escher drawing sprang to life as an awful man with pretty eyes. "Look at you, sitting all alone in a hipster sandwich shop for a sad, lonely lunch. Where's your cute little girlfriend?"

I rubbed my forehead. "God, how are you so annoying in so few words? Avery's at work. I'm grabbing lunch before mine. Go get to your own job."

"You know it only encourages me when you give me sass, Hol." He dropped down in the seat across from me, and I wrinkled my nose.

"Did I invite you to sit with me?"

"This will be quick," he said, leaning across the counter. "How are things with that girl?"

I rolled my eyes. "It can't be quick enough. I'm trying to eat, and I have no interest in talking to you."

He frowned suddenly, sharply. "Don't play games with me, Hol. You and your side chick have been awful for my image. What's the big idea here?"

"You ran a secret smear campaign against Paramour. And your partnership thing is a pyramid scheme designed to kill your competition and net you some profit in the meantime."

"I'll have you know, I lose quite a bit of money buying out and supporting all these places."

"And your asset value? Your market share here?" I shook my head. "At first I thought you just wanted Paramour for its profit potential. I see now you wanted it because you knew people would talk about it, and you wanted that to be yours. I'm beginning to think you don't even *care* about money. You just want attention."

"I don't want the attention you and the Paramour girl have been giving me."

"Will you just *say her name?* It's infuriating the way you won't even give her the dignity of her own name."

He grinned, and he said it, drawing out each syllable. "A-ver-y. Poor, heartbroken Avery Lindt. She's probably really falling for you, isn't she? I saw the way she got so upset when I was talking to you at the charity dinner."

"Mike, I'm not going to talk about her with you. Leave me alone."

"I'll give you a time and date you and your arm warmer girlfriend can meet me." He raised an eyebrow. "That's what you want, isn't it? For the show."

"Great. Let's hear it."

He grinned. "Let me finish talking first. The least you can do for an old friend, right, Holly?"

It made me shudder a little when he said my name. I rolled my eyes. "Fine," I said. "Say your piece and then tell me the time and place."

"What are you doing after this?"

I scowled. "Work. I told you. Back to the studio."

He shook his head. "After this segment. This season. Filming never goes on this long for you. Kyle must be royally pissed. You *have* to be wrapping soon. What comes after?"

That was a great question. I had no idea. "None of your business."

"Don't you want the date and time?" he said, grinning. I wanted to strangle the rat.

"Fine. Honest answer? I don't have plans. It depends on what happens with this segment. If it all goes well? Maybe I'll try exploring new things I can do on *Kitchen Rescue,* without you. If it goes up in flames? I'll wrap it up next season. Without you."

"Ah-ah. I've got a contract with old man Gavin."

"Tay read it. Don't think you can slip anything by us."

"Atkinson's not bad," he said, brushing his hair back from his face. "But unfortunately for you and them both, I'm better."

"That's my answer. Now yours. Time and place, Mister Wallace."

"Ooh, now she's really frosty," he laughed. "I'm not done yet. The real question I wanted to ask here... Hol. What are you doing with the poor Paramour girl? Are you just going to drop her as soon as the segment's over?"

I pursed my lips. This was a topic too difficult even to get into with Avery. It definitely wasn't something I was getting into with *Mike*. "We're girlfriends," I said, a nervous flutter in my chest even though I knew it was a lie. "We won't be filming together, but we'll still be girlfriends."

"I already know that's a lie, babe, and you know I do."

I glared, frustration spiking suddenly in my chest. "For Christ's sake, stop calling me *babe.* We dated for two months, four years ago."

"I know enough about how Atkinson works to see what's been going on. Your personal image was sad and worn-out. You needed a change. Pretend you're fucking the Paramour girl and take her on the show, so all everyone can talk about is whether or not you can just throw someone off the show to put your girlfriend on, and then once everyone's paying attention to you, you say something awful about me, so that way no one wants me on the show."

"I care about Paramour," I said, my voice low. "And the main reason it was struggling was because of you. So naturally, if I'm trying to bring some life back to Paramour—"

"There was no one there to begin with," he snapped. "Not a soul to be seen. I didn't *need* to do anything to bring it down. I gave her one shot at helping her, and she spat in my eye. You want to ask me why I don't give her the dignity of her name, maybe it's because she acts like she's so much better than me just because she's got a huge fucking ego and a miserable, failing restaurant."

"Mike—" I started, anger churning in my stomach.

"Don't try arguing. It was a failing restaurant, and it will be a failing restaurant once you leave. Won't it? You're not changing anything there. You're attracting people to the restaurant because the show is ongoing there. The moment you leave, this whole high she's been riding is going down harder than she's been on you to get you to agree to all this."

"Mike Wallace, I swear to—"

"So you fuck her, you get her hopes up, both about you and about her restaurant, and then you dash both. But who cares? You've moved on by then. Just like always. Don't give a damn. How many people's hopes have you gotten up, and then left them alone in the dust? Poor, sad little Avery. But at least you got what you wanted."

"Time and place," I said. "I'm calling my security."

He snorted. "Don't like being called out? Shoreline Blues, this Saturday, eight o'clock. Bring your little sidepiece."

I stood up, leaving my sandwich unfinished on my plate, and I stormed away, not even glancing back at him, not even with a goodbye. He didn't deserve that dignity.

God, I hated that man.

"Hey," I said, but my heart wasn't really in it as Avery beamed at me with that beautiful, cheery smile, stepping into my apartment.

"Howdy, stranger," she said, crouching to get her shoes off. "I need to tell you all about the new line cook. He's ridiculous. I mean, not in a bad way. He used to work in a Formula One pit crew—"

I pinned her up against the door the moment she stood back up, and I kissed her, crashing my lips into hers. She let out a muffled squeak, and then tentatively, she dropped her hands to my hips and cradled them, held me, but when I pulled away, she had an apprehensive look on her face.

"Can we?" I said, and she chewed her cheek. Guilt turned in my stomach. "Sorry."

"No, it's, uh, it's good, it's really good, just, uh... are you sure *you're* into it? You look like something's bothering you."

I sighed, hard, rubbing my forehead. "Yeah. I'm all right. Just... give me something to vent my frustrations on."

"Okay... if you're sure," she said, dropping her hands back to my hips, but she still looked uncertain. Uncomfortable. I was making her uncomfortable, and I hated it. "But we can stop at any time. You remember the safe word, right?"

"Yeah. I do." I kissed her again, and after a minute, she got into it, too, hot and sensual, nipping at her lip, slipping her out of her blazer, dropping it to the floor. Unbuttoning her shirt, walking her back towards the bedroom, stepping out of my pants, kissing her up against the bedroom door, shoving her inside and pushing her onto the bed and kneeling to pull her pants off, Avery kicking to help me get them off.

"God, Holly," she groaned when I got her pants off and stood up to take off my bra. I loved the way she looked at my breasts, just so mesmerized by me and...

Somewhere after I'd gotten her panties off but before I'd gotten out of mine, something gave way in me, and I collapsed on the bed next to her, sighing hard.

"Hold on," I said. "Wait. Slow down. Just a minute."

She responded immediately, propping herself up on her elbow to face me, expression serious. "Okay. We can stop. Or pause. Are you okay?"

"Yeah. I'm fine. Just a second." I rubbed my forehead. "Christ. I hate him."

"Uh..." She blinked fast. "Dare I ask who? I didn't think we had company."

"Ha, ha." Even the bad joke made me feel a little better, and I swatted at her playfully. "Sorry. I thought I needed to just fuck you senseless to make myself feel better, but I just feel guilty doing it."

"It's okay. Maybe you can fuck me senseless after talking about it."

I laughed. "I'm guessing you're keen on it?"

"Ugh, I'm exhausted from work, and exhilarated from it too. I'm just pent-up and nothing would be better than getting fucked senseless right now. But no pressure. Only if you're *really* into it."

"Yeah. Maybe in a minute." I dropped onto my back, just staring up at the ceiling, and a minute later, I said, "I found a time and place to run into Mike Wallace. We'll meet him together and see if we can get him to agree to an interview on the show."

"Oh... cool," she said, but slowly, she sank back down next to me, shifted closer, and ran her fingers through my hair, which—I'd found out in the past few weeks, being intimate with Avery, that precise feeling was the one thing that could calm me down when nothing else could, her slender fingertips trailing along my scalp. "I'm guessing you got it from the horse's mouth. And the horse harassed you."

"I *wish*," I sighed, hard, rubbing my temple. "He harassed *you.* Said some of the worst things about you. I just... I couldn't stand it. And I couldn't even correct him, tell him properly he was wrong about you, because it felt inconvenient to me at the time." I snorted. "Inconvenient to me. What a great friend I am."

She just studied me for a minute, eyes wide, before she said, carefully, "What did he... say?"

I frowned sharply. "It doesn't matter. I'm not going to repeat it back to you."

She looked away. "It's not because it's true, is it?"

"Avery," I said, sitting up. "No. It's because he's spiteful and petty and making things up. And I don't want to give his words the dignity of repeating them."

She rolled onto her back, staring out the window. "Yeah. Okay."

Ugh. Dammit. Why'd I even say anything? I sighed heavily, pinching the bridge of my nose. "Look, if you really want to hear it that badly, I'll tell you, but I don't want you to think they're true."

"I just feel like I already know what they are, and I doubt he's that far off-base."

I dropped back down in the bed next to her, just staring at the ceiling, remembering my whole conversation with him.

Maybe I was also worried he was right. Worried that I was making Avery hope for something she couldn't have, and then pulling it all away. Getting close to her and then leaving, just like I always had with everyone.

"Apparently," I said, "you *really* hit a nerve when you insulted him at Paramour. He told me he won't even say your name, always just calling you my *sidepiece* or something, because you insulted his ego when you turned him down."

"Really?" She glanced over at me, eyes wide. "Just because I hoped the butter gave him diarrhea?"

"I'd... forgotten you'd said that. Yeah, basically. I think the real reason he's been waging a campaign against you isn't even about the partnership, I think it's about his ego."

"So what, he said I was mean?"

I laughed drily. "Well, he said you had a big ego, which is a projection if I've ever heard one. But mostly he just said you were a failed restauranteur and Paramour would collapse as soon as I left, but—" I rolled over on my side to face her. "You know I'm not going to let that happen."

"What?" She frowned. "Holly, I... you're already taking me on your show to save me once, you can't keep holding my hand forever. You don't owe me that. I need to do this myself at some point."

"I..." My head swam uselessly. "I know. And I'm not saying you would fail without me. But— I'll be there. And I don't want to see Paramour fall through."

"It's really okay. You've done enough." She trailed her fingers through my hair again, but this time there was something wistful about it. "If Paramour fails after you go, then that's just how it was meant to be, you know? Not my time yet. My time will come, after I've had a chance to recover my losses."

But she *couldn't*, and—and I was telling myself ardently it wasn't because I didn't want her leaving Port Andrea. I chewed my lip. "I know all that. I know. You have a good mindset. And you're right, that even if it did fail, it would just mean it wasn't your time yet."

She raised her eyebrows. "But something's bothering you."

"Christ, Avery, I don't want to let you down," I sighed, slumping onto my back again, slinging an arm over my forehead. "That's what it really is, isn't it? Guess it's just about me in the end."

"Holly..." Avery shifted in closer to me, working her fingers back through my hair again, her expression soft. "You're not letting me down. No matter what happens, all of this has been amazing, and I'm really grateful."

"Is it something I'm doing wrong?" I said. "No one really comes close to me. It's always arm's distance. At first, I was stuck-up and full of myself, and I thought it was because my ambition put people off. Then when I owned a restaurant, I thought it was that people were intimidated. Then when I started filming, I thought it was because people only saw me as a celebrity. But then... then you come along, and you're not afraid of dreaming big, you're not intimidated at all, and you just see me as a human being. As a woman. But still, no matter how much you show you're willing to come close to me, I... I think *I'm* the one keeping arm's distance, Avery."

She just nodded along with me, nonjudgmental, stroking my hair, and I couldn't bear the thought of losing this. Christ, this wasn't friends-with-benefits. What was I doing?

But Avery nodded and she said, "Are you afraid other people will hurt you? That they'll get your expectations up and disappoint you?"

"Yeah. Afraid other people are just out to take advantage of me, and... yet somehow I'm afraid of you, too."

She smiled a little wider. "I'm pretty scary. I did kendo in college."

I blinked, and I turned to face her. "Did... did you really?"

"Yeah. It was fun. Nothing to take out your frustration with math classes—you know, existing—than swinging a sword and yelling."

"You surprise me every day," I laughed, sinking back into myself. "It's not that you're scary, Avery. Not that at all. I don't think it's ever been that people are scary. I think I'm scared of myself."

She raised her eyebrows. "What do you mean?"

Ugh. What the hell was I doing? Dumping my insecurities on her was only making me more attached. Avery had been right—there was zero difference between this and being girlfriends. And I *wanted* to be her girlfriend.

This was a professional relationship that happened to also involve us fucking, and the sex was *wonderful*. I wasn't going to do anything to jeopardize that.

I sat up, and I shook my head. "Forget it. It's all a bunch of nonsense and I'm getting my head up in a way because Mike spouted off on me. I just need to distract myself. Probably by tying you to the bed and making you come."

She went wide-eyed and flushed, but she sat up with me and put her hands on my arms, looking me in the eye. "Look," she said. "I would *love* for you to do, uh, pretty much exactly that. But not if you're just using it to change the subject. I'm here. I'm listening. I'm not afraid."

I sighed, shaking my head.

Christ, I was going to fall in love with this woman if I didn't do something about it.

"It is what it is," I said, looking away. "I'm not... I don't know how I'd talk about it."

She looked down. "All right."

"But..." I cleared my throat. "Maybe... maybe another time. I appreciate you being there for me."

The words felt weird to get out and it sat strangely in my stomach, but the way Avery lit up made it all worth it. She beamed, brushing my hair back from my face. "Sounds good," she said. "I'm always listening."

"Thank you," I said. "I mean... genuinely. I'm grateful."

She laughed. "It's the absolute least I can do for you."

I wondered how it was she could just be so... good. I was wondering that, just staring at her, until I found myself leaning in and planting a kiss on her lips, and she sighed into it, pulling me into her.

Crap. This was the wrong kind of kissing. This was *I care about you* kissing. That was outside the contract.

Not that I had any qualms about making it *I want to fuck you* kissing.

I pulled away, feeling my eyes smoldering, and I laid a hand at her collar and said, "So, *now* I can tie you down and make you come?"

She bit her lip. "If you want to. Anything you want."

There was the flush of heat between my legs. That was the correct response. Seemed like my body had finally gotten over its hangups.

"Good girl," I said, and I pulled her into another kiss, laying her down on her back, the kiss getting hotter the longer it went on, hands traveling over one another's bodies. She moaned against my lips, and I loved seeing the way she squirmed for me, so desperate to do whatever I ordered, and I could absolutely have thought of worse arrangements.

I moved to the side just long enough to get the bondage tape from the drawer by the bed, and I pinned her down again, lifting her hands over her head. The way her eyes flared, that green seeming to get darker with arousal, just filled me with ideas of what exactly I wanted to do with her.

I strapped her hands together over her head to the headboard, and I got in between her legs, shoving them wider. She gasped, spreading them wide for me, and I strapped her ankles to the bedframe, too, just to watch the way she gasped for breath, her face stained pink as she tugged lightly against her restraints.

She looked so damn good spread out and tied down for me.

I trailed my fingertips lightly along her stomach, watching the way she arched her back into the soft, teasing touch—down towards her pussy, back up again, and down again to glide along the line of her hips just above where she needed me, before I slipped both my hands along her thighs and lowered myself closer to her center.

"God, Holly," she groaned.

"You're not going to look away," I said, hovering my mouth just above her pussy. "You're going to watch me eat you out until you come."

"Oh, Holly. Yes. Please. Whatever you want."

I licked my lips, and I sank into her, teasing my tongue up along her folds. She tugged against the restraints, gasping for breath, and then she collapsed against them breathing hard as I settled in and pressed my lips up against her, teasing my tongue around her entrance.

I couldn't get enough of watching the way she squirmed, seeing her struggle against the restraints, struggling to look down at me, biting her lip, face red, as I held steady eye contact with her the whole while.

I added a wand vibrator eventually, alternating between my mouth and the vibrator on her, going harder and then softer to work her slowly closer to the edge without going too far. I got to enjoy plenty of her gasping and straining under me before she cried out, "Holly, *please*," and I knew she was close. I licked my lips, trailing two fingers lazily over her clit.

"Please what, Avery?"

"Please—I need to come—"

"Do you?" I laughed, slipping in to tease her with my tongue again, just until the way she arched her hips told me she was about to come—and pulling away, hovering over her pussy, biting my lip at the way she cried out and arched her body towards me.

"God, Holly, please, please, please—"

"You'll come when I give you permission. Do you understand?"

"Oh, Holly," she groaned, face going redder, but she nodded. "Please. I'll do anything. Whatever you want."

And she did—lay there and took it all for me while I licked at her, got her so close her whole body shuddered at the lightest touch of my tongue, and just grazed my touch over her. When she sank back down, gasping for breath and pleading for me to let her come, I took her back against my mouth, licking and sucking until she was close again, and going again and again, switching between my mouth and the vibrator. I teased the vibrator around the line of her hips and along the insides of her thighs when she was close, and the desperate pleading that didn't even sound like words anymore from Avery was everything.

It was after ages of that, when her eyes were clouded over and her whole body glistened with a sheen of sweat, her whole face red, and she didn't seem to be capable of using words anymore, that I held her on the edge, counting down from ten, agonizingly slowly, and pressed the vibrator up against the folds of her pussy when I hit zero, telling her, "Come for me, Avery."

She let go and pressed back into the bed, letting out a long cry of desperate pleasure, and the way the orgasm seemed to take her away from this entire universe—I couldn't get enough of seeing her like that, especially as it went on, and on, and on, moaning and thrashing her body against the restraints until she collapsed, breathless, and looking more satisfied than I'd ever seen another human being.

"Good girl," I said, unstrapping the tape from her ankles and her wrists, and she tried to move but didn't seem to have much in her aside from rolling her head to meet me as I lay down on top of her and kissed her.

"Jesus Christ," she panted, a few seconds later, once she seemed to have words again. "How... how in the world... did you try telling me you were *less interesting in person?*"

I laughed. I *had* said that, hadn't I? "Well," I said, "I guess you bring out the best in me."

CHAPTER 18

Avery

Shall we?" Holly said, offering her hand to help me out of the car, and I took it with my heart doing weird things in my chest as she helped me up and shut the door behind me, leaning in to plant a swift kiss on my cheek.

God, I wanted so badly to be Holly's *actual* girlfriend. Not her fake-girlfriend, not her friend-with-benefits, but all of this for real.

Shoreline Blues, a seafood restaurant on the water, was packed with people, a live performance in the patio seating area, where the warm summer breeze blew in over the bay. The sun was nearly done setting, and the temperate night air along with the smell of brine and seafood, it all felt so vivid it etched in my mind, a memory I knew I'd have forever, no matter what happened with Holly.

From the corner of my eye, I spotted Mack, the tiny redhead who directed Holly's camera crew, shoot us a thumbs-up. Seemed like we were in position.

"Let's," I said, looping my arm with Holly's and, when I somehow found it in me to be gutsy, sidling up against her side and leaning my head against her. "It's beautiful here. I've never been."

"You'll like it. Reminds me of Paramour's style a little. Everything is very simple with a focus on immaculate execution."

"And do you like it?"

She kissed the top of my head and said, "I like it because you're here," which nearly killed me on the spot.

Dammit. Did this *have* to be acting?

I laughed and said, "That's not fair. I should have said that to you first."

"Beat you to it," she hummed, as she led me up to the front doors with the porthole style windows and pulled them open for me, the sound of chatter and music louder as we got inside. In the open kitchen, I saw a dozen cooks moving fast, all expertly, seasoned staff. I admired the way they handled a rush while Holly turned to the hostess and said, "Reservation for Mason. Can you tell Mike Wallace that Holly and Avery are here?"

"Oh..." The hostess looked thrown, but she put on a smile and nodded. "Of course, ma'am. Your table is right this way."

We got outdoor seating, which seemed to be a luxury right now, right during the change between performers on the stage. Mack and her team set up in the corner, just past the little wood railing with the overgrown trellis, and I pretended they weren't there, like I'd gotten good at doing over all this time filming.

"Nervous?" Holly said, and I busied myself with getting my napkin in my lap, looking out over the water.

"Maybe just a little. We're filming for the last episode right now, aren't we?"

"That's the plan. Bringing everything we've found and confronting Mike Wallace. That's not here, though. First, we need to get him to agree to a formal appearance on TV. We'll never get him to sign anything to release the footage if we ambush him here."

"But what on earth would make him want to agree? He's safer staying on the sidelines."

She brushed her hair back, her expression turning more serious, and I admired, as always, how sexy she was when she did that. "So we make it in his interest. I don't think he's thinking in terms of dollars and cents. I think he's thinking in terms of his ego."

I chewed my lip. "So... what? We make it look like we're a couple of fumbling losers and ask him to show down with us on TV, so he can show us up and look like the winner?"

"That's what I'm thinking. He likes to consider himself magnanimous, so he should be easy to persuade. And we'll promise to give him the footage, too, so he doesn't have to worry we'll just not run it if we get shown up in the interview." She paused. "And then we just have to find a way to actually get a leg up over him in the interview. Nothing we've found is conclusive. Sure, walks like a duck, talks like a duck, it's obvious to anyone looking what's going on, but we don't have any irrefutable proof his partnership is a scam and that he sabotaged Paramour."

Well... Liv had the proof. But I couldn't ask her to do that. I chewed my cheek. "Right... well, we're not trying to change his mind, just trying to win over the viewers."

"Right."

"Attention, everyone!" a voice called from behind Holly, and I glanced up to the stage, where a woman with a fiery red pixie cut and colorful tattoos stood at the front of what looked like a punk band. It took me a second to recognize I'd actually seen her before—Carrie Simmons, lead singer of *Junior Funk,* what I assumed was the band on stage. "We've got some special guests in the audience today who I'm personally a big fan of, so I wanted to start by asking Holly Mason and Avery Lindt if they want to join me up here on stage?"

I stiffened, looking up at where Carrie was looking right at our table, and back to Holly, who just gave me a lopsided smile.

"It happens, Avery. Let's not let them down," she said, standing up and offering me a hand.

People clapped for us, including Carrie and the rest of her band, as Holly led me by the hand up onto the stage in front of everyone, and once we got up in front of Carrie, she pulled me closer into her side and I just about melted into her.

Before I'd come back to Port Andrea, I hadn't even *dreamed* of anything like this. Everything felt too good to be true, like a happy dream I was waiting for the unhappy waking-up from.

But I was going to at least enjoy the dream.

"Big ups to you two with everything you're doing," Carrie said. "I've been following everything on social and I've never been so excited for a season of *Kitchen Rescue*. I think you're the lifeblood of Port Andrea, Holly, and I'm booked for a reservation at Paramour and I cannot *wait*."

I didn't know how to handle this kind of situation. Normally, I'd ask myself *what would X cool person do in this position,* but maybe Holly was right, and honesty was the best policy. So I clasped my hands together at my chest and I said, "I'm going to be honest, Paramour is my first restaurant, and I don't know what I'm doing. I don't have a clue how I got to this point, but I *have* been told I know how to make a pretty good beet salad, so give that a try?"

Holly laughed, looking over at me with her eyes twinkling, looking so radiant illuminated by the little fairy lights strung around the trellises and around the stage, in her deep purple dress, and I wondered if it was too much to just want to fall into her arms here.

"Look, I'm gonna be honest with you, too, Avery," Carrie said, shrugging, "I don't know what I'm doing, either. I think we all just kind of stumble into our places in life. But I *have* been told I know how to do a pretty killer guitar riff on *All the Ways into the Night*, so what do you say we'll play you that one and you guys at Paramour can make me a beet salad, and we'll keep doing our thing?"

Holly and I each gave Carrie a quick hug and a kiss on either cheek, and she whispered something to Holly about maybe an autograph later, and from her girlfriend too, and I'd never felt as warm and bubbly in my life as when Holly led me back down the two steps off the stage and into the little area cleared in front of the stage, where she took me by either hand and said, "I think we'd better oblige them a dance?"

"Oh. Wow. I don't know how to dance."

She laughed. "Relax, Avie. Just follow my steps."

I blinked fast. "Avie?"

"I can't keep calling you the whole thing forever," she said, starting a simple dance with me in front as the drummer kicked in the start of the song. "Unless that's no good? I've heard people call you Aves, but I want one that's special."

How in the world was I supposed to not fall in love with her? *How?* How was this friends-with-benefits arrangement simultaneously the most wonderful and the most painful thing to ever happen to me?

"I've never heard it before," I said, carefully, stumbling to keep up with her dance. "But... it is special, and it makes me think of you now, so, I... happen to quite like it now."

She let her eyes flutter shut naturally, just breathing in the warm night air, still moving fluidly with the song, and she smiled wider before she said, "I do, too. Cute name for a cute girl who's full of sass."

"Oh yeah. That was the reason you were attracted to me."

She cracked an eyelid open. "Were?"

I just grinned, shaking my head, and I must have lost myself for a second in there, because I leaned in and planted a quick peck on her lips.

I spent the rest of that dance wondering if it was okay. We'd talked about kisses in public. Little quick ones when necessary to make it look like we were together, that was okay. And Mack had the cameras rolling. I was sure she'd gotten that kiss, and I was sure it looked great in her footage.

But the problem was that I hadn't been thinking any of that when I'd kissed her. I'd just been thinking she was the best thing to ever happen to me.

We were halfway through the main course when a shadow darkened our table, and Holly's expression with it, as I glanced up and saw Mike Wallace in a well-tailored brown jacket striding towards us, a sardonic smile on his face, and he spoke before either of us, saying, "I invited you to come and meet me here, not to give a speech on my stage and schmooze with the performers I scheduled here."

Holly raised an eyebrow at him, her nose wrinkling. "And you thought it was a good idea to schedule a fan of ours at the same time you told us to be here, then?"

He waved her off. "That was Jane who did the scheduling. Think I might have to have a chat with her. Well, wasn't too bad. Hey, Hol. Nice seeing you here."

I frowned, but Holly outright glared. "And my girlfriend, *Avery*," she said, which made me instantly fluttery again. He raised an eyebrow, smirking, but he didn't look at me.

"Yes, I saw her too. So, you two are here to talk to me, I'm assuming, not just for our excellent food."

"Let us interview you on the show," I said, mostly just hoping to make him actually look at me.

He glanced over at me, one eyebrow raised, and said, "Very tempting offer. Is there literally anything in it for me?"

Holly leaned in towards him. "The fact that if you turn it down, everyone is going to know you're afraid to actually talk to us about the accusations?"

"Our people don't follow mindless gossip," he said. "We prefer to focus on real issues."

Holly shook her head. "Only you could describe a pyramid scheme as *mindless gossip.* On the contrary, plenty of Andreans who take their food seriously care quite a bit. You told me yourself it's been bad for your image. This is your chance to come on television and set it right."

"Give you the chance to edit the footage and make me look bad?" He shook his head. "I'll do it on one condition."

"Tell me," Holly said.

He grinned. "The show. Season seven. I'll be there."

Holly's jaw dropped. My stomach did, too. "You're not serious," Holly said. "You want us to let you on the show after we tell the whole world you're a sham running a pyramid scheme?"

"After we interview, I think you mean," he said. "I have nothing to hide. And I don't think what will happen on that interview will keep me from getting on the show. I'll clear up the record, and I'll be on in the next season to set it straight and get the show back on track with something a little more exciting."

"Are you kidding?" I blurted, surprising everyone and most of all me. "You're just trying to be *that* blatant? You're obviously bluffing with this. You want to be on the show, so you're not going to do anything that's going to make the finale of the season before fall flat. You want the opportunity to go on and not only show your supposed innocence, but to try taking over a show in a good state. You want the damn interview and we all know it, you're just trying to see what else you can get in the deal."

Mike just laughed. "You sure are talking like you know a lot about bargaining, especially given how bad you were at bargaining in Paramour."

"Oh, I wasn't bargaining," I said, rising halfway from my seat. "I was telling you to get *lost* and the only reason I'm not doing that again now is because we're doing this for the sake of all the restaurants caught in your scam."

"I'm terrified," he said, flatly, turning back to Holly. "Anyway, Hol. Babe—"

"Stop *talking around me*," I said, standing up the rest of the way, drawing attention from the tables around us. "And quit calling my girlfriend *babe*. I don't know if you've noticed, but she's mine."

He gestured me back to my seat. "Sit down, would you? You're causing a scene."

"Avery," Holly said, expression pleading, "it's okay. Don't let him rile you up. It's what he wants."

I gritted my teeth, but I sank back into my seat. I'd told Liv I didn't *have* pissed off on my dial, but once again, this man was the exception. "Seriously, stop with the *babe* thing, though."

"I've been telling him to for years," Holly said. "Mike. How's this. We'll give you access to all the same footage. And then—"

"So you can use your bigger platform to shut me down?" He laughed. "I don't think so. What leverage would I have compared to whatever you wanted to do with it?"

"If you really think you're the one in the right here," Holly started, but Mike put a hand in her personal space to cut her off. I'd never wanted to slap someone's hand away before, but hey, first time for everything.

"Let's be rational negotiators," he said. "Leave the emotions out of this. You need this, urgently. Kyle is running out of time for filming. Gavin wants the damn season done already. Me, I've got all the time in the world. Looks like I'm the one with the power."

Holly screwed up her face. "You're the one who wants on the show. *We're* the ones in the—"

"I've been thinking," he said, grinning. "If I just leave you hanging and deny you the space, and it leaves the season to end on a dead note, you won't get renewed for season eight. But then I can strike up a little deal with Gavin and make it a switch to me instead. The old man's really come around to my way of thinking, you know?

So—I really don't need you after all, Hol. I just need to watch you fail."

"It's not going to just fall off a cliff like that," Holly said, jaw tensed. "If we can't wrap it up this season, then we lead into doing it next season. And if I have to spend a whole damn season investigating your shady organization, so help me god, Mike Wallace, I'll do it."

"Not if Gavin says otherwise," he said, smile widening more and more. "You should have a look sometime. I've helped him through drafting up a few more contracts for the next season... you know. To prevent this kind of random excursion in the future."

"What?" Holly paled. "I—when have you even been *meeting* with Gavin?"

"The guy owes me a favor. We meet when I want to."

If I didn't know any better, I'd say Mike had blackmail on Holly's showrunner. I felt sick even thinking about how much control he must have had through the rest of the production team.

He really had just been driving at this for *years.* He dated Holly to get her secrets about cooking, restaurant management, everything, and dropped her to the side. And then over the past few years, he'd just been constantly hounding her day and night about this damn show—spreading rumors about it, about her, making deals behind the scenes. Years of wearing her down, trying to steal what she'd built.

The guy probably thought he was entitled to it. I could *not* stand entitled men.

Hell, the reason Holly had a reputation as icy and hating her show, he was probably behind that, too. He was probably behind all of it, the more I thought about it.

Just ready to spend years dedicated solely to undoing the legacy of a woman who he knew was so much more than he could ever be.

Ugh. I hated Mike Wallace.

"We'll do it live," I said, barely even hearing myself. Mike turned to me, brow furrowed, and Holly just gave me a wide-eyed look. "The interview. We'll broadcast it live. And neither of us can edit it to look nice. Only the raw truth of the situation, and people can make of it what they will. And we'll see whose side they take."

"Avery," Holly said, concern creeping into her expression.

"Live? You want to host it live? Where?" He laughed, shaking his head. "So you can broadcast it and then, if it goes badly, cover it up with the actual show itself?"

"Your choice if you want to be there or not," I said. "We'll go to the Julius, and we'll shoot live. We'll either talk to you about it there, or one of your staff. Your call."

He glared at me. "You really like to think yourself important enough to throw your weight around, don't you?"

"You know what?" I straightened my back, put my chin up a little, and I said, "As a matter of fact, I do. I'm sure we'll see you there, Mike."

Holly, who still had her brows knotted in an anxious look, broke into a small smile. Mike scowled at me.

"Aren't you just a charmer," he said. "Name the time and date, and I'll see what to do about you filming live in my restaurant. And I hope you enjoy the rest of your dinner, you two *lovely* ladies."

After I gave him the time and date, he left, muttering something about me and storming away. I sank back into my seat, adrenaline still racing through me, and it was only when I realized Holly was still giving me that anxious look that I deflated.

"Sorry," I said. "That was a terrible idea, wasn't it?"

"It wouldn't have been my first choice," she said, as diplomatic an answer as any, and I looked down. "But it's what got us the interview, so we're running with it. I'll tell Kyle and Tay and everyone else as soon as possible, and we'll do what we can to prepare."

Which meant, if we screwed up, it was my fault, but—hey. Law of attraction. If I focused all my thoughts on success, we were guaranteed to make it.

I mean, mostly guaranteed.

CHAPTER 19

Holly

"Thanks for helping," Avery said, shutting down the lights and turning to me. "I know still helping in the restaurant is outside of your contract at this point, and I really appreciate it."

"It's all part of the show," I said, tossing my apron in the laundry bin. "It'd look bad if I stopped helping you right before the final showdown, as it were."

She grinned, swatting my arm lightly. "As if you'd actually stop if you got the chance. You just have a hard time admitting you like it here."

I rolled my eyes, smiling. "I will openly admit I like it here. But my point still stands, Miss Avie."

She giggled, stopping at the back door. The nickname had come to me randomly, and I'd dropped it on her just as randomly, but I couldn't get enough of how much she loved it.

"Do you want to go see what's open for dinner tonight?" she said, gesturing to the door. I sighed, sinking back against a counter.

"Frankly, no. I don't want to go wandering around that much. Let me just use your kitchen, cook something for you here."

"What?" She put her hands on her hips. "Excuse me. You're cooking for me? I know how to cook for myself, woman."

I quirked an eyebrow at her. "I've noticed. We wouldn't be in your restaurant otherwise. But I just want to cook for you."

She waved me off. "Oh, fine. You know I'm a pushover. But I'll make dessert."

"Or you could be dessert," I said, which made her stumble on the flat floor, turning red.

"Oh, uh... why not both?"

I licked my lips. "I like the way you think."

But the whole time cooking alongside her in the kitchen, laughing together with her over inside jokes we'd made over the weeks of fake-dating that felt more and more like real dating, watching her prepare a tiramisu felt like I was watching her from miles away. My thoughts were everywhere but here.

She noticed while I was reducing a sauce, looking at me with concern in her eyes.

"Something's bothering you," she said.

I shook my head. "I'm all right."

She leaned against the counter. "You're doing that thing you do with your nose when you're not all right."

"Son of a..." I sighed, shutting off the stove and taking the pot off the heat, turning to her. "What even is that thing with my nose?"

She gave me a lopsided smile. "I'm not telling. You'd stop doing it."

I sighed. "I'd rather talk about it over food."

She nodded, but she put a hand on my arm and squeezed. "I'm here for you no matter what," she said, which should have made me feel better, and on one level it was everything I wanted to hear, but on another I knew it was just getting me worse and worse.

I *really* had it bad for her.

Once we were sitting together with a chardonnay and seared chicken breast with a raspberry lemon reduction and asparagus, Avery raised her glass in a toast to me, looking like the most perfect human being I'd ever seen, sitting there in that crisp black button-down with her hair a little messy from being worn up in a net, over here in the corner in front of the massive window out over the water, the low lights of the restaurant after closing and the moonlight through the window gleaming in her eyes.

"Here's to some less wilty asparagus," she said.

"You are incorrigible yourself, sometimes," I said, clinking my glass with hers. She grinned.

"And I choose to take that as high praise, thank you, Miss Mason."

I sighed, settling back into my seat, staring out at the waves rolling up along the water. "Avie... Avery. What are we doing? After all of this?"

Her eyes went wide, and she set down her wine glass. "I..." she started, studying me. "Well, assuming this segment is all the time we get together pursuing Mike Wallace, if what he said about his backdoor dealings with your showrunner was true."

I clenched my jaw. "I have zero doubt it's true. Gavin always went along with everything... grudgingly. And I already knew Mike was getting in with him. Seems likely he's telling the truth."

"Then, uh..." Avery looked down, kicking at the floor. "Whatever works best for you, I guess. I mean, I don't want to pressure you into anything."

"I'm not pressured. Not into anything at all."

"Okay." But she kept that uneasy demeanor about her, and I couldn't find words, either. How could I express to her that I was terrified I might end up hurting her? Letting her down? If I couldn't date her...

But I really, *really* had to wonder why I couldn't date her. I knew keeping to myself was the responsible choice, and I was good at being responsible—and Avery had her own reasons for not wanting to date me—but I wondered what I would have said if she just outright asked me to be her girlfriend.

I'd promised myself not to get into all of this again. But... Avie really wasn't like the others.

"Well," she said, after an uncomfortable minute of silence, "I would like to keep being, uh... around you."

I raised an eyebrow. "Being around me? Is that all you want or is that a euphemism for me fucking you senseless at least once a day?"

"*Wow,*" she said, blinking slowly and looking out the window, face going pink, and she cleared her throat. "Whatever I can get, frankly. Just being around you, that'd be fantastic. The... latter option? That'd be even better."

I sank back into my seat and stared out the window, watching dark clouds drift in over the horizon.

It felt like a metaphor.

"You don't have to," she said, quietly. "I mean, you don't have to do anything. I only want what makes you—"

"Avery." I put a hand up. "I would love that."

She stared for a second before letting out a long, slow breath. "Okay. I mean... great. Yeah. I'd love that too."

I sighed, running my hand through my hair. "Tell me I'm not the only one who sees the problem here."

She stiffened, drawing her arms in closer to her sides. "What is it? Is it something I did?"

"Well, yeah, I guess so." I rubbed my forehead. "You do that thing where you suck in one corner of your lip while you're thinking about something, and it's so damn cute I just want to kiss you."

She blinked, another pink flush creeping into her cheeks. "Uh... do you want me to stop?"

I laughed. "No. Maybe you should, though, if you want to stay around me." I sighed, shoulders sinking. "I'm not making any sense, am I?"

She smiled sweetly. "No, but I think it's cute when you ramble."

I gave her a dry laugh before I reached out and touched my fingertips to the cool glass, just staring out and watching the bay darken as clouds moved in. "Avie... I think if we keep doing this, if we stay close. If we keep sleeping together, certainly. I think I'll end up falling for you."

Out of the corner of my vision, I saw her eyes go wide, letting out a short, sharp breath. "Oh," she whispered, lips parted. "Holly. That's... not what I expected you to say."

"And why on earth not? You're sweet, you're funny, you're charming, you're hardworking and ambitious and you make me want to be better, too. You kiss me like I've never been kissed before, and you look at me in bed after we're done like I've never been looked at before. What else am I supposed to do, Avery?"

She swallowed hard, that flush spreading back over her cheeks again, and she looked down and breathed out, "I mean, you're not the only one."

My heart surged, but I just glanced at her, raising an eyebrow. "I thought we agreed we'd clear it with each other before we had anyone else."

"What?" she squeaked, face going crimson. "No, no, that's not—Holly, I'm not—I don't mean—"

"I'm teasing you, Avie."

She slumped over the table. "Incorrigible," she said, but she laughed, running her finger around the rim of her wine glass, avoiding my gaze. "I've been... you know. Thinking the same thing. When you take me out somewhere and we play it like it's a date, when you call me your girlfriend... uh. It does things to me."

There was the flash of hope in my chest, and the sinking feeling at the same time. Part of me said to throw it all away, ask her to just ignore all reason and make this into something more, into everything. But the rest of me knew it was irresponsible to overlook everything I'd promised myself and unfair to ask her to do the same, and if she'd been feeling the same thing, then that meant our... arrangement, it absolutely wouldn't work out in the long run.

I took a deep breath and said, "Whatever happened to how you didn't want to date another Andrean chef while on an indefinite stay here?"

She laughed nervously, sipping her wine before she said, "That's a silly little thing. That's not really why I felt like I couldn't date you. I just didn't know how to tell you the real reason."

Christ. Which meant the real reason was probably more compelling. I chewed my cheek. "You don't have to tell me anything you're not comfortable, but you can tell me whatever you want to."

"It's embarrassing," she mumbled, looking out the window.

"It's just me, Avie."

And she softened at that, giving me the sweetest look, her eyes sparkling, and she said, "Yeah. That's true. Um... the truth is, I'd never dated anyone before Cecilia."

I raised my eyebrows. "When you're that pretty?"

She laughed awkwardly. "Me being pretty is sort of up for debate. Point is, she was my first partner—mostly because it didn't feel right until I was really through my transition, you know? But obviously, she was miles out of my league. And I think she was just screwing around, having fun, while I fell in love with her alone. And I learned a lot from all of that, and I don't regret it, but... but I also learned not to, well, aim too high with dating, I guess. Not to date anyone where I'd always be worrying about not being enough when I was next to them, where I'd be embarrassed to meet all their friends and admit to how absolutely nothing I was in comparison, to always be waiting for the other shoe to drop. I learned that wasn't as fun as I thought it would be, dating someone really out of my league. And... well. You're even further above my level than Cecilia was."

I just... watched her for a while, trying to get my head around it all. I already knew I didn't like Cecilia. The more Avie said about her, the less I could stand her.

My voice felt small when I said, "From our meeting at Rosco's, I'm not surprised she made you feel small. She seems petty and self-centered."

She looked down. "She's a really lovely person, I don't want to talk her down. We just... weren't a good fit. And I learned my lessons from there."

My stomach churned. I knew I should have laid off, but I couldn't really help it. "She taught you—*you*, Avery Lindt, not to aim high? To dream smaller? Just from that, I already know she was horrible."

She blinked, looking up at me with wide eyes. "What? Well... I don't think that's really the same as aiming high somewhere else. A partner

isn't an accomplishment, or something. It's just...
you know... love should feel comfortable, I think."

"And what? You think just because
someone else makes more than you, or is more
famous than you, or is better connected than you,
that you can't be comfortable together?"

"Well—" She flushed. "I mean, no, I don't
think that, but..."

"But you'll specifically avoid even someone
you might feel comfortable with, just because you
think they're too good for you. Doesn't that seem
self-defeating?"

She chewed her lip. "I... guess so. I mean,
I've always felt nervous, intimidated around
people who are out of my league. Maybe I just
psyched myself out with Cecilia, got worried over
things that weren't even there. I'm just always
comparing myself. But..." She fussed with her
silverware, aligning them neatly on her plate.
"Well... I haven't felt that around you. I mean,
sure, I did at first. I was so tense that first time I
was in your apartment, I felt like I might have
snapped. I told Liv and she told me to just be
comfortable and be myself, and she also said to

bang you, which turned out to be a great idea. Even though you're the one who bangs me." She scratched her head. "Wow, I'm rambling."

"Say what you need to," I said.

"But—but you *weren't* intimidating. And you didn't try to make me feel smaller, or lesser than. And all you ever wanted was just for me to treat you like a normal person, and eventually, I just... realized I could do that. And I've never been so comfortable as I am around you." She sighed, sinking back into her seat. "Holly, I really want to be your girlfriend. I really do. I just feel like it can't possibly work."

Dammit. She was speaking directly to me, saying the exact words *I* was feeling. I looked away. "I care for you, Avie. Honestly, I do. You've been a lot of things that really mean a lot to me. But that just means I would never want to hurt you, and I'm afraid if we kept going... you'd end up getting hurt."

She looked down. "I won't pressure you into anything. I know you're taking the responsible decision."

I chewed my lip. "After all this, maybe we should just... put the whole friends-with-benefits thing on pause. Just be friends for a while. I want to make sure that, whatever we decide, we're not rushing into it."

She nodded, still keeping her gaze on the floor. "Right. And it's only a theoretical discussion, anyway, unless we show up Mike in the live interview I kind of screwed us over by suggesting tomorrow, and even then, only if Paramour does well after you're done helping."

I took a long, shaky breath. "Yes. You're right. Thank you, Avie."

She smiled sweetly at me, but the wistful look in her eyes was obvious. "Well... it's been really wonderful. Thank you for all of this time. And I'm still happy to be just regular friends. You're amazing."

"We're not through with it yet," I said, raising an eyebrow. "I was planning on taking you home with me tonight."

Her smile dropped, eyes going wide. "Oh. Yeah. Okay. I'm not complaining. We're not supposed to be—like—strategizing for the interview?"

"We'll do that in the morning, with Tay. For now, I just want to enjoy this with you. And there's nothing we can do, no more information we can gather. We never found who was ghostwriting those articles, so we don't have our silver bullet, but we'll have to make do."

She looked out the window. "I'm sorry. Maybe she'll come forward with the live interview being close."

I stopped, staring at her, just going over again and again what she'd just said. My heart sank, slowly, a sick feeling settling into my stomach. "She?" I said, after a minute, and Avery froze.

"What? I mean—they. I mean—"

"Who is she?" I said, my voice quiet, distant. Avery's eyes went wide, searching around frantically.

"I... I don't know," she stammered, but the flush that crept into her face this time wasn't the soft pink one I loved seeing, but the dark, hot one when she was uncomfortable. "I'm sorry. I misspoke. I meant—"

"How long have you known who she is?" I said, feeling my throat tighten. "How long have you *had* all the information and just had us running around uselessly? When were you planning on telling me?"

"I—Holly, please," she said, quivering now, lips drawn in a tight line. "I didn't mean that."

"Avery. Please. I want the truth. It's been long enough, now, hasn't it?"

She hung her head, shoulders slumped. "I... I've only known for the past week. I promise I wasn't trying to keep it from you."

That took some of the weight out of my chest. Thankfully, Avery was a terrible liar, and it was easy to see from the defeated look she had that she was telling the truth now, but that didn't mean it didn't sting like hell to know she'd been hiding it. "Who is it?" I said again, punching into each word.

"I—I can't tell you," she said. "I'm sorry. I promised her I wouldn't tell anyone."

"Avery, we *need* that information. If she just comes forward with her contracts—"

"I can't ask her to just sink her own career, putting it out there publicly that she did it!"

"What about *our* careers? They're banking on this moment, and you're just holding back to give the person who tried to ruin your dream restaurant a break on their conscience?"

She screwed up her face, giving me a smoldering expression, and then, slowly, she sank back in her seat, looking down. "I'm sorry, Holly. But I can't. I promised her, and I'm not about to go back on that."

Dammit. *Why* she'd promised that, I had no idea. "Then talk to her about it. Lean on her. Convince her that coming forward with it is the right thing to do. It's the least she can do to make up for it."

"I told her I'm going to support whatever decision she makes," she said, still not meeting my gaze. "I'm sorry."

"So what's your plan, then? You propose a live interview with Mike Wallace in the Julius, and you don't even have anything to show at the interview?"

She chewed her lip. "I think my plan is to roll with the punches, and to find a way to work with everything the universe gives me."

"For crying out loud," I sighed, rubbing my temple. "That's all well and good when it's just your own career, your own dream, but you're holding mine at stake, too, here, Avery. Between me and the person who wrote smears about your restaurant, you're choosing her?"

She frowned. "It's not like that, Holly. You'd do the same thing if you promised someone. That's why you were so mad about this whole pretend-dating arrangement, wasn't it? Because it looked like you were throwing away your contract for some girl you're too good for?"

Dammit. I didn't know if I was angry with her or myself. Why not both? Angry with her, angry with myself, angry with Tay for setting us up on this—I could have just been showing Cameron how to fix up Blue Sail, something I knew how to do, not thrown in the middle of all this. Just because they wanted me to do something fresh, something exciting?

"Fine," I said, standing up, leaving my food unfinished. "I respect that. You're right. I would do the same thing. And so I'm going to go spend the rest of the night looking for leads on who it is, now that I know it's a woman and someone who talked to you around a week ago."

"Holly," she said, standing up with me, guilt and worry written all over her face. "Please, wait. We don't need some silver bullet. It's really okay."

"Maybe we don't," I said, turning and walking away, hating the fact that the ugly feelings in my stomach only churned harder the further I walked. "But I'd be a damn fool to let you drop a lead like that into my lap and miss the opportunity. Good night, Avery. I'll see you tomorrow."

She walked after me, stopping by the door. "Holly... please don't be mad at me for this. I'm sorry."

I glanced over at her, over at those eyes that looked like she was about to cry, and I hated that I was the reason for it.

Christ. Maybe Mike was right. Maybe all I ever did was get close to people, get their hopes up, use them, and discard them when they were inconvenient.

I was a horrible person. But I could work on being a better person once I was sure my show wasn't about to go belly-up.

"Sorry," I said, and that was all, pulling open the door and stepping out into the rumbling stormy weather of Port Andrea near to midnight.

CHAPTER 20

Avery

Liv gave me a nervous sort of smile as she stepped inside, looking around the apartment. "Hey, Aves," she said. "Nice place. It's cute."

"I think what you mean is *small*," I laughed, closing the door behind her. "Hard to get an apartment around here much bigger than a postage stamp when you're worried about going flat broke. But I like it like this."

"Well, if it's your cramped prison cell, you've at least made it a homely prison cell," she said, taking her shoes off at the door and hanging up her raincoat, streaked with the light drizzle of rain I still heard pattering against one of the two windows total I had in my apartment.

"Definitely more of a cook than an interior designer, but I know what I like, at least. Sit down anywhere there's space. Do you want a drink?"

Liv perked up. "What've you got?"

I gave her a tired smile, trying my best to be perky. It was hard when everything felt heavier, the constant questions running through my head of if I'd completely ruined things with Holly. "I'm a chef, Olivia Harper. I've got whatever you're looking for."

"Rum and coke?"

"Have you eaten? I'm not giving you alcohol on an empty stomach."

She put her hands up dramatically. "Okay, Mom. Rum and coke and a sandwich."

"I didn't offer you food," I laughed, hitting her lightly on the arm. "But sure. What kind of sandwich shall I whip up for you, Your Majesty?"

"Something that looks at least a little responsible so I feel better about my drink."

"Raw kale on wheat bread, coming right up," I said, heading into the kitchen while Liv dropped into the loveseat in the living room, a cramped space in dark browns with a thick, plush rug and the walls crammed full of wall art, coffee table and end table and side tables all stuffed with cookbooks and magazines. A minute later, I came out with a couple of veggie sandwiches on sprouted grain sub rolls with carrot sticks and a seltzer for me, Liv's rum and coke in front of her, and she nodded slowly at the sandwich.

"For something responsible, it sure looks good," she said.

"It's still a lot of carbs, but I've found over the past couple years that once you start obsessing over healthy eating, you can never do it right enough. Life is about learning to embrace the imperfections in everything we do. And no better way to celebrate that than with a sandwich that has plenty of garden spread."

She raised her eyebrows. "Is that like saying grace in the Lindt household, you sit down for food and say a mission statement?"

I laughed. "Just eat, you weirdo."

So we ate, but we were quiet, for the most part, whatever Liv had wanted to say when she'd asked to meet me again sometime waiting on the back burner. I certainly wasn't going to start talking about *my* life, feeling like I'd been dumped by someone I was never together with and certainly wouldn't have had a chance with.

Liv caught on eventually, though, because she gave me an odd look and said, "So what's eating you, Aves?"

"Oh, you know. The weight of the world, and all that."

She grinned. "Emo Avery is a new take. You nervous about your big interview with the big bad guy?"

I shrugged and gave her a not-very-convincing, "Yeah, guess so."

She set down her half-eaten sandwich and wiped the crumbs from her mouth, and she said, "You know, you can talk if you've got something on your mind. I know our friendship's a little unconventional, but I'm here for you."

I smiled sadly at her. "Thank you. I'm just trying to focus on this interview, and then unpack everything."

"I'm surprised you're not with your fuck-buddy every second prepping for it," she said, which just made me sink more into myself, feeling like an air mattress with a slow leak.

"Er... she's been pretty busy."

The look on Liv's face said she understood, but she wasn't going to press it. She sipped at her drink, setting it down and looking around the apartment. I took it as my cue to change the subject.

"Your turn," I said. "What'd you want to talk about?"

"What do you think I should do?" she said, still looking away from me. There was an uncomfortable sort of vulnerability on her face as she said it, and I softened.

"That depends," I said. "About what?"

She snorted. "Well, okay. Say, hypothetically, I'm a loser with no direction in life."

"And this hypothetical person wants to find some direction."

She sighed, shoulders dropping. "Ugh. Is that the next step? I feel like I don't care about anything. I don't even know what the first step should be."

"Well, you could see a therapist. I've done therapy a few times, and it's always gone well. You need a good therapist, though." I paused. "But as for what you can do yourself... I guess find what excites you, you know? Just look around. Watch the world happen around you, see what makes you feel things. Look for something that makes you feel alive, and go after that. No holding back, even on the silly things you'd be ashamed to tell as dreams to someone else."

She gave me a wry smile. "Just get excited over everything like I'm a kid?"

"Hey," I laughed. "We have a lot to learn from kids. Just go out there for a day and look at the world with a sense of wonder, like you're seeing it all for the first time. Notice everything. Notice what kinds of things you notice. And when you start looking, you'll probably find something that makes you start caring, and then you never let go of that feeling."

She set her drink back down, looking away. "This all still feels silly. I feel ridiculous even talking about this. I have to learn how to feel things again?"

"Look at it this way. Two people have the same problem. They both feel silly about it. One of them never does anything, and sits in the problem forever. The other talks about it and finds a way out of it. Which one is sillier?"

"Ugh, I can't stand thought experiments. Fine. Yeah. I get it." She shifted uncomfortably in her seat. "Just don't ever tell a soul about this."

I laughed. "My lips are sealed."

"I've already been going around places, doing things. That's what I've been doing all this time I've been out of college. Just kind of... doing crap. Nothing feels any different."

"Were you expecting to feel any different?"

She scowled at me. "I mean, honestly, no. Life's just felt like an obligation."

"If you don't expect it to change, it will never change." I shrugged. "I think you just have to... open up to the thought. Before you can do anything, you have to believe it's possible."

"Ugh. Mission statements again."

I laughed. "You're so cynical. Is it just that anything that sounds good is a mission statement?"

"I don't know. I'm just not here for self-help gurus to give vague advice."

"It's not vague. It's extremely specific and actionable." I shifted forward in my seat. "Was there ever a time in your life when you felt like something really excited you?"

To my surprise, she took the question seriously, chewing her lip before letting it go with a *pop*. "Yeah, guess so. When I moved to Port Andrea and started going to UPA, it felt amazing. I'd never lived away from my parents before, and I felt so alive. I was so thrilled I was like a real adult and I could do what I wanted, and it felt like the world was mine. Like I'd never run out of things to do." She fussed with her shirt sleeve. "Well... guess I ran out of things to do."

"Tell you what," I said, turning in my chair and fumbling around in the drawer of one of my end tables, the stacks of books teetering on top. I pulled out a notebook, all cute pink and yellow, and I dropped it in front of her, and I said, "Take that and use it."

She made a face. "It's so... pink. I'll feel like a ten-year-old girl."

"Yeah, welcome to being a trans girl in your early twenties and wanting to have everything pink and sparkly and frilly and rainbows because you're looking to live the little girlhood you missed out on. That one's mine. From when I moved to Port Andrea the first time to be with Cecilia."

She wrinkled her nose. "What, you're giving me your lovesick diary you wrote while hanging with your ex-girlfriend?"

"If you want to be really reductive, I guess so," I laughed. "It's more than that. I was in the same position you are. I went out to pursue my life, as my own independent person, and the world was full of excitement and possibility, but I felt like I was missing something. Some kind of spark. So I took that notebook with me everywhere and wrote down whenever I felt really strongly about something, whenever I found something I really cared about. Sometimes I just sat down and wrote in it for an hour at a time. It's full of me finding my dreams, when I was in the same place you are. I only wrote on one side of the pages. Why don't you take it and do the same thing with the other sides? Keep it with you and write it down whenever something makes you feel strongly. See if it helps you the same way it helped me."

Her expression was suddenly alarmed, eyes wide. "Wait. You want me to take it and just... write in it myself? Isn't this thing, like, a precious keepsake for you?"

I shrugged. "Objects are just that, objects. They don't do any good unless they're helping a person. It wasn't to record the actual thoughts and feelings for me, it was to teach myself to pay attention to what I cared about. I'm done with it. I think it would do more good in your hands."

She stared at me for the longest time, until I started to wonder if maybe I shouldn't have given it to her—if that was a weird gift and maybe a little overly familiar—but after a minute she just looked back down at it and opened to the first page, running her finger down along the text.

"How old were you?" she said.

"I turned twenty-three halfway through the book, so, same age as you."

"Your handwriting was so good."

I laughed. "Thank you. I like handwriting."

And she was quiet again for a while, tracing through it, flipping reverently through the pages, just reading. I expected snarky comments and dry jokes about the silly little musings and overly-excited dreams I'd written down, along with the alternating gushing and insecurities about Cecilia, but she didn't say anything, just reading like it was the most important thing in the world. After a minute, I stopped staring at her, giving her the space to just read while I finished my sandwich, until she shut the book.

"Thanks," she said. "I'll, uh... I'll do that. You think it'll help?"

I beamed. "No idea. But I know it won't hurt, to give yourself some more time and space to think consciously about what's going on inside your heart."

She chewed her cheek and nodded, slowly, and she took a long sip of her drink before she spoke again. "Hey, I, uh... Avery. You know I'm really grateful, right? I mean—for everything."

I smiled wider, the feeling in my heart happy and sad all at once, a bittersweet wistfulness. "Of course," I said. "I'm happy if I can help."

"You've paid well enough I've been comfortable, you've trusted me with lots of stuff... it feels like you just—respect me and all. And you didn't get mad about the, uh, articles and stuff."

I shrugged, finishing off my drink. "Life's too short to get mad over things."

"You're just... I know I'm pretty cynical and crap, but—it means a lot. Thanks. Uh... I give you a lot of snark, but genuinely, you're a really good person. The world could use more of you."

I sank back into my chair, a little more warmth reaching my heart. "I think you'll be that for someone else before long, too. Someone unexpected who comes in and means a lot."

"Weird to think about." She riffed through the book again before she snapped it shut. "Yeah. Okay. Wow. I'll get to work on this book, and I'll let you know how it goes. In the meantime, though, I really need to pee."

I laughed. "Bathroom is right there," I said. "The only door aside from the exit and the bedroom. Like I said, it's small."

"I kind of like it, too. Like there's nothing here but the essentials." She stood up. "Okay. Give me a minute," she said, and I did, sinking back in my seat and just looking at my notebook on the loveseat, thinking of the million memories I'd made with it in hand.

Port Andrea had always been a city full of dreams for me. And somehow, I felt like I was blowing all those dreams by losing Holly, like all the memories led back to her.

And apparently, thinking about her had summoned her, because I hadn't even gotten through the thought before I heard a knock at the door, and I scrambled to my feet, remembering keenly Holly was the only one who knew where my apartment was.

My heart raced wildly in my chest as I paused at the door, my hand hovering over the handle, mind going to a million different places. Maybe she was here to say she was sorry for last night and she wasn't mad. Maybe she was here to say she never wanted to see me again. Maybe she was here to fuck me and I'd have to find a polite way to ask Liv to leave because I'd say yes. I didn't *know.*

Probably it was faster to open the door and find out. I took a long breath, steeling myself, and I opened it to where Holly stood in the narrow corridor outside with her hair up in a ponytail, wearing a runner's tank and leggings with a loose raincoat over top, and an expression on her face I didn't like to see. More likely this was something on the *never wanted to see me again* side of things.

"Hey," she said. "Can I come in?"

"Uh—yeah. Of course." Neither of us had asked permission to come in in a while. I pursed my lips as I stepped back and watched her come inside, my hands folded at my waist like I was waiting for an order. "Do you want a drink or something?"

She glanced across the living room to the two plates of food, and she raised an eyebrow at me. "Am I interrupting something?"

"Liv is visiting. She's, uh, in the bathroom."

"Just water. I'll only be a second."

I squeezed a lime wedge into a glass of water with a few ice cubes, and Holly laughed uncomfortably as she took it.

"I knew you'd do something fancy with it," she said, downing half of it in one go. "Thanks. Avery, I can't find anything."

My heart sank. I knew right away what she was referring to, and we did *not* need to have this conversation with Liv hearing from the next room. "I'm sorry," I said.

"I've been up half the night looking for them. I told Tay what you said, too, and they can't find anything either. I'm serious, Avery. If you just *tell me* who wrote the damn articles—I'm not even going to try parading them on live television, I just want to see the contracts."

I looked down, a sick feeling in my stomach. "I'll... tell them about the situation, but I'm not going to pressure them."

"You don't need to hide her pronouns, Avery. You already blurted them at dinner last night."

I do, because she's listening to this conversation right now. I wondered if I was too soft, too weak. Maybe I was hurting more people than I was helping by giving Liv the cover of anonymity. But there was no way I could expose her while she was listening from the next room. "I didn't mean to say anything about it. I promised to keep it secret."

"Yeah, well, I promised to do everything I can to get this damn filming segment to work, and I intend to hold to it. Do you realize all of this has been for *your* restaurant, Avery?"

"I—I know."

"And you've refused to hand over the information that could make it all work."

I shook my head. "We don't need the person who wrote the articles. We can talk to Mike without the contracts. We have the interviews, we have the shipment information, we have the contracts Dylan signed…"

"We know exactly how Mike will explain all of those away. And they're not illegal. We're looking for proof he's breaking the law, and you're hiding it."

"You know how he'd explain away the contracts, too. He'll say they're fake. It's not a court case, it's a live interview, and there's no rigorous evaluation of the case, we're making an appeal to the viewers."

"And that could all be *so much easier* if you just handed over the damn contracts," she snapped, and I flinched, eyes going wide. She sighed, rubbing her forehead, and she downed the last of the water before she set it down on the table by the door. "Look... Avery. I'm sorry. I know why you're doing what you're doing. I'm angry with a whole hell of a lot right now, and I'm taking all of that out on you. I'm sorry. But that doesn't mean I can accept this arrangement."

I chewed my lip, finding it impossible to meet her eyes. Every part of me felt so heavy, it was like I was wearing a lead jacket. "I'm really sorry. I understand why you're angry at me."

"So that's it? There's nothing I can do?"

I shook my head, feeling like it was the only decision I could have made and simultaneously the worst decision I could have made. "I'm sorry."

She sighed heavier, a deeper sigh than usual, and the look in her eyes was just crushed. Like some fundamental part of her had gone missing. "All right," she said, her voice distant, looking away, out the window at the drizzling rain. "Well, if you change your mind before the interview, let Tay know. They'll arrange everything."

My stomach churned. "If anything changes, I'll text you first," I said, and she shook her head.

"Don't worry about it, Avery," she murmured. "We knew this from the beginning, didn't we? It's unprofessional, dangerous, and inconvenient to get in too close with one another. I think we reached that point, and it's affecting our judgment." Her voice fell off when she said, "Or at least, it's affected mine."

My heart missed a beat, a sick anxiety settling in my chest. "Holly... are you saying you don't want to see me anymore?"

God, I did *not* want Liv to be hearing this. Especially not framed this way, so it sounded like it was her fault.

Holly just ran her fingers along her scalp and down through her ponytail, looking away from me. "I do want to. And that's the problem. From the beginning, we knew this would be casual, and that it would end. I've enjoyed filming with you, Avery. I hope your preparation for the interview goes well. I'll see you at the studio tomorrow for it."

"*Holly,*" I said, something curling up in my stomach, feeling like curdled milk. "I know you're angry at me because of the interview and the circumstances—"

"I'm not angry at you," she said, her voice too sharp to not be angry at me, but then she softened and said it more quietly. "I'm not angry at you. I'm angry at myself. I told myself I'd quit doing this. Quit... quit getting attached to people who have something to gain from me. Quit putting too much of myself on the line, letting myself get hurt when our needs diverge. I promised you I'd behave myself. But..." She rubbed her temples. "Christ, you just *looked* at me in that way you did, and I was too weak. I'm sorry, Avery. I know you must be upset with me for this, for leading you on. Guess that's all I ever do with people, in the end. But I can't keep seeing you like this."

"But..." I said, uselessly, watching her turn back to the door with a gnawing loneliness in my chest. "You know I haven't regretted one second of it, right?"

She paused, her back to me, her hand on the door handle, and she was quiet a minute before she said, her voice low, "I know. Me neither." She paused again. "And it's best to end it there. Before that changes."

She turned back towards me, her eyes filled with something I couldn't read, and she took me by the chin with two fingers, and she pulled me into the softest, sweetest kiss—into the saddest kiss I'd ever felt, feeling the way she was steeled against me, holding everything back.

I dropped my hands to her hips, holding her against me, desperate, lost, not sure how to handle this being our last kiss, and the way she held me by the back of the head was everything in the world and just not enough at the same time.

Her lips felt so much colder than usual. It must have been the rain.

When she pulled away, she had a distant look in her eyes, a sad little smile on her lips, and without another word, she turned, opened the door, and stepped out into the apartment hallway, closing the door behind her and leaving me to listen to her footsteps receding, smaller and smaller until I couldn't hear them anymore, and there was nothing there in the room with me but silence.

CHAPTER 21

Holly

The next morning found me with a headache that hurt like my brain was trying to escape, which would have worked out fine for me, because I clearly hadn't been using the damn thing.

I woke up around six, which was hours earlier than I'd wanted to sleep until, but the throbbing pain in my head told me I wasn't getting back to sleep, so I took painkillers and downed a glass of water before pulling on my running clothes and heading out to see if fresh air and what little bits of sunlight I could get from the overcast day outside would help.

I didn't push it, more of a light jog, so when I got in the area of Production Corridor, I was just feeling brisk and energized and *still* with a headache, and as far as I could tell, caffeine was the only answer I had left. I made my way towards the Den, luckily getting in on the tail end of a rush so that it was just clearing out when I got inside, only one person in line ahead of me. When I got up to the counter, the barista, Amber, grinned at me.

"Con panna, Holly?"

I rubbed my forehead. "I've got a killer headache and I don't think cream would sit right at the moment. Let's just do three on ice."

"Can do," she said, punching into the register while Cait started shots behind her, giving me a quick smile. It was only once I stepped to the handoff plane to watch her add the ice and espresso to a shaker that I noticed, sitting out in the lobby, was Avery's friend Liv, blonde hair pulled up into a high ponytail that spilled wide over both shoulders, wearing a loose tank, chewing one corner of her lip while she wrote into a notebook.

"Here you go, Holly," Cait said, setting down the iced espresso in front of me.

"Thanks, Cait," I said, taking it absently, my mind still on Liv. "That book you're writing going well?"

She smiled, brushing her hair back. "It hasn't been writing itself, for some reason. I've been worrying about it almost nonstop, but it still won't respond by magically writing itself."

I laughed, the sound feeling awkward in my throat. Everything I did felt awkward and wrong since Avery's and my last kiss yesterday, and the aching look she gave me, the last thing I saw of her, while I left—watching me go.

I shook my head, getting my thoughts back to reality. "Keep at it," I said. "I know it'll be worth it once you get it done."

She smiled sweetly at me. "Thanks, Holly. See you around."

"See you," I mumbled, turning back and pausing there to sneak a glance at Liv again. The sight of her just made me think of Avery, and that was exactly the kind of thought I was avoiding right now.

God, I'd been ridiculous and awful every step of the way. It was hard to believe I'd managed to make every decision wrong.

And I knew I'd make the wrong decision here, too, because I should have just left her to her work and gone about my business, meet with Tay again, try to figure *something* out, anything, but instead, I found myself walking over to her and saying, "Hey, Liv. Good morning."

She nearly dropped the notebook, startling up to her full height, eyes wide. "Oh," she said, looking up at me, closing the notebook. The sparkly pink and yellow was a bit... cuter than I expected from her. "Hey, Holly. You a regular here? I've seen you in here twice now."

"Yeah. Usually in the mornings. Do you mind if I sit here?" I gestured to the thick faux-leather chair next to her, and she nodded, a little stiffly.

"Explains why I don't usually run into you. I'm not much of a morning person. Yeah, go for it, I'm here alone."

I sat down, not sure why I was doing any of this but apparently going through with it. "And yet, here you are, in the morning."

She looked down. "Well, sometimes your body just decides to wake up early and then spend the whole day complaining it didn't sleep enough. Because for being the most complex systems in the known universe, human bodies aren't very smart."

I gave her a thin smile. "I'm in the same boat myself. I don't have anything today except Avery's and my interview with Mike Wallace tonight, but I woke up with a throbbing headache, and I figured caffeine might help."

Liv sighed, sinking back in her seat. I wondered how much of... yesterday she'd heard. I'd been trying to keep my voice low, but I'd sort of lost myself, and I'd forgotten Liv had been in the next room. When she didn't say anything, I looked away and I spoke.

"Sorry for everything at Avery's apartment yesterday. I'm assuming you didn't want to be audience to that."

"It's totally fine," she said. "I, uh... I know you've been acting out for the press that you're dating, and I won't tell anyone the details."

"Thanks," I said, and we sank into silence for a while before I looked back down at her notebook and said, "What are you working on?"

"Oh, uh," she said, fumbling with the notebook like she'd only just noticed she had it. "This—it's not mine. I'm not this pink and sparkly. Don't judge me."

I laughed, and the feeling kind of made me want to cry. Dammit. I was close to my period, too, and that was the wrong time to have emotional experiences like a breakup with someone I hadn't even been together with. I kept wanting to cry at the smallest things, and that didn't suit my image. "I wasn't about to judge," I said. "You can like all the pink sparkles you want to, Liv."

"It is not mine," she repeated, scrunching up her face. "It's, uh... Avery's. She let me have it. Kind of a... diary of feelings, I guess. She thought it'd help me with some problems I've been dealing with lately."

Christ. Everything came back to Avery. Like seeing her name spelled out in the clouds, she was so *there* in my mind. I took a long sip of my coffee first to give myself a second before I said, "Makes sense. Seems more her style."

"Yeah, she said that's what happens when you're a trans girl in your early twenties, you just want all the pink sparkles you can get." She paused, rubbing her neck. "I mean, she told me you knew she was trans, anyway."

I paused. Avery and Liv were closer than I thought, if Liv knew too. "I did, yes," I said. "That makes sense. A diary of feelings seems like her style, too."

She grinned. "Right? She wrote the thing back when she was in Port Andrea before, when she was my age. Full of wonder and excitement in the world and kind of... finding her place." Her smile faded, and she dropped her gaze to the floor. "I've been working on that, too. Finding my place. Aves gave me the book and told me to write my feelings in it, too, to help me find my place like she did hers. I feel... I don't know, I guess, small, not good enough for it, but Aves insisted. Of course she did. She's really good."

My heart ached. I didn't know why. Thinking about Avery, about the girl who'd been my Avie, despite all my best efforts to keep a cool distance from her. Thinking about just how damn good she was. "Yeah," I said, quietly, looking down at the book. "Her diary from finding her feelings, huh?"

"It's pretty powerful reading it, honestly. She's so bright and open with how she's feeling, it's weird to see her grappling here with all these insecurities, learning how to be a better person. It's... I mean, that's what it is. It's powerful, isn't it? A person's growth." She sighed, sinking back in her seat, kicking one foot in Converse up onto the ottoman. "Aves got me talking in lofty statements. Guess I'll have to hand it to her, she's good at them."

"I think you're right," I said, distantly. "When she was with Cecilia, right?"

"Yeah. Lots of talk about worrying she's not good enough for her..."

It felt almost voyeuristic talking about her in this way, seeing her through this portal into her thoughts when she was younger. I felt guilty and I wasn't even sure why. It wasn't like I was reading it. "Sounds like Avery," I said, my voice sounding dry.

She set the book aside, sighing, and she seemed to face some kind of internal resolution before she turned to me and said, "Hey—that girl, Avery. She *really* likes you, you know."

And therein lay the problem, because I also *really* liked her. I looked away, watching as the line built up at the counter again. I didn't say anything, and Liv didn't take the hint.

"I know you two have had, uh, kind of like, a thing, right? And I don't want to stick my nose all in your business, but Aves is my friend, and I don't want to see her hurt like this. The least I can do for her is try to convince you that you're making a huge mistake giving her up."

I rubbed my forehead. "Is *relationship repair* in your job description?" I said, and it wasn't lost on me that I'd implied what Avery and I had was a relationship. Because it *had* been, hadn't it? We'd *been* girlfriends. We just hadn't called it that.

"Uh, no. It's a part-time restaurant job, the only job descriptions you get there are *uh, I don't know, whatever the fuck we can get you to do to make sure the store doesn't burn down.*"

I laughed despite myself. "Touché. And I guess in a roundabout way, trying to get Avery and me together is keeping the store alive."

"Yeah, see? You get it. I'm doing my job. Hell, I should clock in."

I sighed. If Avery was going to trust this girl with things like her transness, I might as well have trusted her too. "Thing is, I really like Avery, too," I said, my voice sounding distant. "And I know that if I went along with that, it would get in the way of my career, put my show at risk, and it wouldn't be fair to ask her to be in that position."

She furrowed her brow at me. "How in the world does that make any sense? Does logic work differently in celebrity land?"

"I couldn't possibly keep work and my relationship separate if we were together. We tried that. It didn't work. I got too personally involved, and... when she made her own independent decision, it affected my show. My career. All of it. And inside, I want to blame Avery, even though it's her own prerogative what kind of bleeding-heart decision she wants to make, and it's all my own damn fault for letting her into that position. For letting my guard down."

Liv sighed, running her fingers through her ponytail, tugging out the knots. "Look, this is because of all that stuff you were arguing about yesterday, right? Her finding out who'd written the smear articles, and she won't tell you who it is?"

I frowned. "You know about all that? Is there anything she doesn't tell you?"

She tried to look casual, tossing her head back, but there was a deep anxiety under the surface as she said, "She's pretty open about stuff. But to be fair, I told her about that one."

I studied her for a second. "You... told her about who wrote the articles?"

"Yeah. Uh, truth be told, it was me," she said, fussing with the collar of her shirt, and I just... stared at her, the words not really settling in right. "I mean, I'm the one who wrote them. So in that case, I guess I'm the one who was opening up."

Jesus Christ. All this time, she'd been right there, and I'd been looking at just about everyone *but* her.

And didn't it make sense? I'd seen Avery's friendship with Liv deepen over the time I'd known her. She took Liv under her wing, wanted to help her, support her. Of course she wouldn't want to throw her to the wolves by putting her on air to talk about what she'd done.

That was just like Mike to target the staff working there. There was just something *extra* vile about it that fit him like a glove, and I felt sick at the thought.

Avery was willing to go flying blind for the sake of keeping *Liv* safe. And when I thought about it, all I could think was *of* course *she was.*

Liv shifted awkwardly. "You're staring at me, and I don't know if I just broke your brain, or if you're thinking of a way to murder me."

I didn't know, either. I should have been furious. I should have been relieved. I wanted to cry instead. I didn't think I could blame my hormones this time. All I said, though, was, "Why are you telling me?"

Liv shrugged. "It's the right thing to do, I guess. I mean, I stood there in front of the bathroom mirror staring at my own reflection while I listened to you break up with Avery because of what I did, and I thought back to what I even did with the money Mike's guy gave me for it. It would have been one thing if I'd used the money wisely, but hell. I blew it on nothing just to get rid of it. How am I supposed to stand there in that kind of situation and not go find a way to tell you the truth?" She rubbed her arm. "Whatever you may do about it. I'll understand if you're going to make me go on air. It's fine if this sinks my career. But for fuck's sake, if I'm trying to be a better person, this is the damn place to start."

I felt like I was floating untethered in the sea, just drifting. I heard myself distantly as I said, "You did it for some money?"

She shrugged. "I don't know. I guess. I think I did it more to feel important and powerful. That's an even worse excuse, but hell, it's the truth."

I dropped back into the seat, setting down my coffee and just looking around the café like I was expecting this to be a prank, cameras to come out. I didn't understand. I should have been so damn relieved right now. I'd spent so long looking for whoever had done it, and I'd just given up, just accepted that I wouldn't, and then here she was, walking right on up to me and saying, *hey, I did it. I'm the culprit.*

Instead, I just churned with this uneasy feeling like everything was so damn wrong, and somehow it was my fault.

Liv sighed hard, dragging a hand down over her face. "Could you just, like, start yelling at me or something now? This silence is a lot worse than anything I'd expected this would be."

I just shook my head. We were quiet again for a minute before I said, not really even conscious of it, "No. It's fine. I'm not going to ask you to come on air, either."

"What the fuck?" Liv put her hands up. "Are you *serious?* You and Aves both? The—I don't— are they putting something in the water at your studio? Why the fuck are you just going to let go of it?"

I shrugged. "To tell you the truth, I'm not sure. But I think it's because Avery did it."

She blinked, slowly. "I... uh... really don't get it."

Neither did I. And yet somehow, at the same time, I did.

Ugh. It was that damn notebook. If I hadn't seen that notebook, hadn't thought about Avery writing down her feelings like that, I would have felt comfortable telling Liv she had to come on the interview or I'd threaten legal action. And then I'd probably still threaten legal action.

But Avery had always just listened to her heart. She had a whole book right there detailing what her heart was saying, so she could learn to listen to it better. And if I listened to my heart, it told me that I didn't want to force Liv on the interview, either.

In ten years, the show would be gone. That much I knew for certain. Maybe I'd have gotten one last season and run it to the end. Maybe Mike would have taken over, and he'd have run it for three, four years before it ended. Maybe I'd have stayed on and gotten more seasons, and run it another few years. But whatever happened, in ten years, *Kitchen Rescue* would be gone, and I wouldn't.

I'd still be around. And I'd remember what I'd done to keep it on air even one season longer. And suddenly I realized that was exactly what

Avery had thought, too, and suddenly I felt impossibly small in comparison to her.

I realized I'd rather end up regretting putting it all on the line to keep one girl safe, even a girl who had screwed us over, than to end up regretting putting her on the spot and ruining her reputation for—life, maybe—just to keep *Kitchen Rescue* on air for another season.

And I guessed it was Avery who taught me that, with her pink-and-yellow sparkly notebook full of feelings.

I sighed, standing up. "I'm not going to try to make you come on air. You can send me the contracts, if you want to. I'll try to keep your name out of it as much as possible, and we can pursue a libel suit against Mike outside of the public eye, but only if you want to."

She jumped to her feet with me, eyes wild. "But—the whole damn interview, all of it—you were just freaking out to Aves yesterday, acting like your life was over because of this, and—now that you've got what you wanted, you're just going to brush it off? What was the point of being such an asshole to Aves, then?"

I raised an eyebrow at her, and she went wide-eyed. "Not a lot of people willing to just up and call me an asshole. I kind of appreciate it."

Liv blinked, and slowly, she shrugged. "It's an honor, I guess?"

"I don't know what the point of being such an asshole to her was," I said, picking up my drink and turning back to the door. "I've made a lot of bad decisions. I think we can all empathize. I'm sure I'll see you around, Liv."

"Yeah, no kidding. I mean, I know I can. But... uh... yeah. See you around, Holly. You are beyond bizarre."

I really was.

But, I noticed when I got outside the door and breathed in the warm air pregnant with the chance of rain—I didn't have a headache anymore.

I turned and headed up the way towards the studio.

CHAPTER 22

Avery

I felt like I'd drunk an entire bottle of vodka, and I hadn't even had any alcohol. I probably just got drunk on Holly and was hungover now that she was gone.

Ugh. That didn't make any sense. I was trying to be poetic, and I wasn't a poet.

But as I trudged to the studio, feeling lightheaded and heavy-hearted, I couldn't help reflecting on the similarities. The fact that I knew it would happen when I started, and yet I did it anyway. The fact that I managed to forget in the middle of it all that it would happen. And then waking up in the morning feeling listless, aimless, and so damn tired that all I did was make toast, butter it, and eat one slice before putting the other in the fridge for later.

I wasn't sure why I'd decided to preserve toast in the fridge. My mind hadn't been working at full capacity, and it just seemed like a good idea at the time. But floppy and cold toast with coagulated butter on it seemed like a good metaphor for my life right now, too.

Maybe I was a poet.

"How's it going, Avery?" Tay said when I got into the studio and nearly bumped into them in the lobby, talking to a receptionist. They jerked their thumb towards the elevator and said, "I'm about to head upstairs. You're just in time. Also, parenthetically, you look like shit."

I gave them my best smile, and I was sure it also looked like shit. "That's what we have makeup artists for," I said, and Tay clapped their hands together.

"Hear, hear. Give me one sec," they said, turning back to their conversation with the receptionist, and then a minute later, we were in the elevator together, heading up. "Kyle and Mason are already in the meeting room. We're going to go over everything we can and strategize for this live interview, which—for the record, I *love* that you got a live interview. My senses for drama are throbbing."

I cringed. They didn't need to use the word *throbbing.* "I feel like I ruined everything," I said.

"No such thing as ruining everything. Just making things more exciting. Here's our floor," they said, pushing the Open Door button as if the doors didn't know how to do that themselves. I figured they just liked pushing buttons.

The meeting room was set up by some tasteless designer, everything in tacky red and black, with intense but rounded angles on everything. Some kind of modern style I'd never gotten the appeal of, but I understood in every possible way the appeal of Holly Mason sitting there with her hair expertly styled down over one shoulder, dark makeup with a deep red lipstick and a black one-shoulder dress with the faintest shimmering accents.

And *completely* avoiding my gaze, giving Tay a swift smile and returning to her conversation with Kyle. It crushed my heart like a butterfly under a steamroller.

I dropped into a seat somewhere around the awkwardly-shaped table where I wouldn't have to look directly at Holly, and Tay sat across from me, but even with the odd angle, I found myself sneaking just a glance out of the corner of my eye at Holly. And then the glance stayed there until it was absolutely not *just a glance* anymore.

Was I a confident and skillful restauranteur and consummate professional, or was I a lovesick teenager blushing at her crush? Little bit of column A, little bit of column B, I figured.

"Great, we're here, we're starting," Tay said. "Let's dive right in and talk about the plan. And by plan, I mean whatever the hell we can throw together to make Mike Wallace look bad, which, as far as I know, could really just be a recording of him hitting on a girl. Badly."

I distantly recognized that I would have laughed at the remark if I weren't gazing at Holly, looking down at the table every time she cast her eyes even vaguely in my direction. It felt like someone had pulled out all my insides and put them back in the wrong order, and my heart was trying to find its way up from my knees, my stomach was drifting aimlessly through my shoulders, and my brain was absolutely nowhere to be found.

Holly, Tay, and Kyle all launched right into discussion, leaving me far behind. I watched with glassy eyes as talk pinballed between them, and whenever the pinball of conversation struck me— whenever someone asked me a question, threw a glance at me, or just said my name, everything would pause, all of them looking expectantly at me, and I'd swallow hard and say, "Sorry. What was that?"

The fourth time it happened, when Kyle said, "Avery can speak to that, if you remember exactly?" it took me a second to even remember that was my name. I shook my head, blinking.

"Er—I apologize. What are you referring to?"

And *that* was when he snapped, rolling his eyes and putting his hands down on the table, half-standing. "Avery, this is our all-or-nothing moment. Where the hell are you?"

Shame burned through my face, and I looked down. "I am so sorry. I've been—distracted. It's a lot for me. But that's no excuse not to pull my weight."

"You're damn right it's not," he said. "This is a hard enough task with the damn live interview *you* got us saddled with!"

"Kyle," Tay said, putting a hand up. "Relax. You're going to make the poor girl cry."

I wanted to cry for a million different reasons. I swallowed hard, adjusted my blazer, and I straightened my back before I said, "No, it's really okay. He's right. I'm the one who got us into this position. I need to—need to do... do my..." My brain got hazy, and I burned with embarrassment as I searched for words. "Do my part. I'm present."

Holly kept her gaze on the table as she spoke. "I'm sorry. Give me just a minute to talk with Avery privately?" she said, and immediately everything I was feeling changed. For better or worse, I wasn't sure—hopeful and terrified at the same time—but I sat rigid and watched as Kyle scowled at her, and then at me.

"I'll give you five minutes," he said. Holly bit her lip.

"Ten," she said, which just made my heart jump again.

"For fuck's sake," Kyle groaned. "Ten. Not a second longer. The timer starts now."

Holly glanced over at me, and for the first time since that last glance in my apartment, she met my eyes, and I felt a deep sigh of contentment in my heart at how damn pretty they were. "Sorry, Avery. Just one second."

"Of—of course," I fumbled, getting up and following her as she led me to the side, through a door and into a smaller meeting room that was empty right now, only the two of us and the view from the window over Production Corridor out towards the bay. My heartrate shot up to levels that couldn't have been healthy when Holly shut the door behind us and turned to look me in the eye again.

"Liv told me," she said, which—of all the things I'd possibly expected, that was last on the list. I blinked.

"Told you... what?"

"About the articles."

My heart sank. But then—it didn't make sense. I shook my head. "So then—she's coming to the interview, right? Why didn't you tell—"

She put up a finger. "She's not," she said. "I told her to only come forward with whatever she felt comfortable with, and I wasn't going to pressure her."

I stared, my mouth falling open. "I... what? But... Holly. You were so..."

She looked down, frustration flashing over her face. "Avery, I'm... sorry. I've been stressed lately, and I've acted in ways that aren't fair to you. I've said things I don't mean." She took a long breath and looked up, meeting my eyes again, and the intensity of the look she gave me made my heart flutter. "I told you the other night in my apartment, when Mike had gotten to me, that I'd tell you more about it all later."

I didn't need to think about that right now. *That* being the night she'd tied me down and edged me until I'd nearly passed out and made me come so hard my vagina might have broken. Well... maybe it wouldn't hurt to think about it. "Uh... yeah," was all I came up with eventually.

"I told you I'm afraid of myself," she said, steeling her expression, and I noticed she was... nervous. The look of vulnerability in her eyes made my heart soften. "And the more I've thought about it, the more I've realized how true that is. I always hurt people. I always let people down. Every single person I've thought maybe I could fall in love with, I called it off. And they cried. Some called me awful names. Some told me they loved me. I told all of them I couldn't see them anymore. I've spent all this time trying to find ways to justify being afraid around other people, but all this time, I think I've just been afraid of myself. Of doing that again and then having to live with the way I'd hurt them. Having to live with hurting you."

My head spun. I needed to sit down. "I... that wasn't exactly where I was expecting this to go."

She smirked. "Did you think I was taking you to a private room for a ten-minute quickie or something?"

"No!" I blurted, face going molten, hands shooting up.

"Wouldn't be the first time," she said with a one-shoulder shrug, which made me melt even more.

"I mean... admittedly, no," I mumbled. "But I always preferred the longer sessions. You know. Always gave us more space for creativity."

I had no idea why I was talking. But Holly laughed, tossing a strand of hair out of her face.

"You can be *very* creative. I'm fond of your creativity."

I cleared my throat. "It's okay if you hurt me," I said, which made her frown, shaking her head.

"I don't want to—"

"No, I mean it," I said. "You hurt me, I hurt you, we all hurt each other. We're clumsy. We make mistakes. We're all human. When you really care for someone, it doesn't mean you'll never hurt each other. It means through all the mistakes, you care enough that you want them there anyway. That all those tiny hurts and mistakes are insignificant in the big picture."

She stared at me for a second before she softened, shoulders sinking, a strange sort of smile settling in on her features. "You always did have a way with words, Avie."

My heart thrummed so hard at the nickname, it nearly burst right through my chest. I gave her a shy smile and said, "I just say what's on my mind. I try to be real about everything."

"Liv was filling in a notebook she says was yours," she said, one eyebrow raised. My spirits soared through the stratosphere.

"Oh! She was filling it?"

"She told me about what it was," she said, softly, eyes studying me. "Has anyone ever told you that you might just be too good for this world?"

"Um..." I laughed nervously, scratching the back of my neck. "See, that hasn't actually come up. People must be just assuming someone else has taken care of telling me that."

She came one step closer and laid a hand on my arm, and my pulse shot off the charts, the touch electric and tingly through every part of me. "I think you're right," she murmured, the eye contact between us so understated but so fiery, it could have burned me up. "When she told me all about it, I realized you were right not to make her expose herself as the smear writer."

My heart thumped so erratically, I was worried it might have just overclocked and shut down entirely. "I, uh... but... you worked so hard on all of this. This segment. This whole show. Everything. And we have the answer right there, and we don't know what we'll do without that answer..."

"Hey," she said, a teasing tone in her voice, and she reached up and ghosted her knuckles along my jawline, which was more sensual somehow than the things we'd done naked together. I felt a warm flush through my whole body, chills down my spine, and Holly gave me a little smirk. "What happened to that *roll with the punches, work with everything the universe gives me* attitude? I'd really grown to like that thing."

"If it's convincing you to back me up against a wall and touch my face like this, you can absolutely count on me keeping it up."

Here we were—me and Holly, back the way we were supposed to be. Trading barbs just to watch how the other reacted. It was natural, it was right. And when Holly licked her lips like she did then and raised an eyebrow, it was mind-numbingly hot, too.

"And that's supposed to convince me to stop pinning you up against the wall?" she said, moving closer.

"On the contrary," I said. "You've known from the day of the balsamic incident I liked being pinned against things. And I've known from then that you like it when I get a little difficult with you, don't you, Holly?"

She laughed, trailing her thumb up to brush over my bottom lip, and it gave me enough chills my succulent back home had to warm up. "I must say, you have an excellent read on me," she said, and she leaned in and brushed her lips against mine, just the faintest, tenderest touch.

And my heart could not take it. We'd kissed before. We'd had some incredible kisses before. I mean, hey, she'd tied me to a kitchen chair and strapped a vibrator between my legs and watched me come before. It wasn't like we were a stranger to intimacy. But—this was—different. This was charged. This was meaningful, and I didn't know what to do about it.

We'd had an agreement. No kissing outside of sex. Holly Mason was kissing me outside of sex, and I never wanted her to stop.

I angled my head towards her, pressing my lips up against hers, kissing her back, and she sighed softly into me, reaching a hand up into my hair and holding me by the back of the head. I dropped my hands to her hips, held her into me, and I melted into her when she deepened the kiss, nipping at my bottom lip, letting out soft moans against me.

And then all too soon, it was over, Holly pulling back and leaving me feeling the loss keenly, but the way her eyes sparkled and she brushed her thumb over her own lip as she met my eyes told me she didn't want that to be the last time any more than I did.

"Come on," she said. "Kyle will be waiting for us. We've got an interview to give our best shot at, and see how well we can do while keeping Liv safe."

I sighed, chewing my lip, just staring at her for a second. *How am I supposed to stop myself from falling in love with you?* I almost said it out loud, but I kept it in. Partly because it would have been ridiculous.

And partly because I knew I'd given up on stopping myself. I was falling fast and hard for Holly, and I never wanted to stop.

"Let's," I said. "We'll compare glazes. His will probably be runny."

Her eyes sparkled. "Terribly runny. Enough to ruin an entire evening."

CHAPTER 23

Holly

Dammit. This was useless.

I sat in the wings with Avery next to me, her hand in my lap, camera crews swirling around us, preparing the set for the live broadcast. Avery kept glancing at her phone, anxiously checking the time, and I squeezed her hand.

"We'll get this," I said. She gave me a nervous smile.

"Holly. Are you manifesting?"

I laughed despite everything. "I figured I'd give it a try."

She leaned against my side, looking up into my eyes. "You look so nervous, Holly. Are you sure you're going to be okay?"

I let out a heavy sigh. "It's not good. We don't have anything. But what we can do is try to control the narrative. Find a way to get people talking about the shady dealings, the facelessness of the restaurants, anything."

She squeezed my hand, and I realized, setting out to reassure her, I'd ended up with her reassuring me. "We'll make it work. I know we will."

"How do you know that?"

She beamed. "I asked the universe really nicely."

I raised an eyebrow. "And... what makes you think that'll work?"

She lifted her hand to my cheek, brushing her knuckles along the skin, and it sent tingles through my whole body. "Because it worked for getting me you," she said, which—well, it did its job in getting me to forget about Mike Wallace completely.

This woman was really everything good in the world. All she did was love, love, love. It was amazing, and my heart raced unevenly wondering what happened after all of this. After that kiss earlier, which had been the most powerful thing I'd ever felt, even with a small, sweet kiss stolen in a small moment.

"Give me the universe's number and I'll ask, too," I said, and she laughed.

"Just ask. It's already listening."

I looked up to the sky. "Any spare miracles up there?"

She laughed again, leaning in to plant a kiss on my cheek. "I'm sure they'll be looking for your sake now," she said, checking her phone again. A text popped up, and immediately she was nervous-texting.

I couldn't blame her. My mind was everywhere. And as the minutes counted down, Tay burst in, like a whirlwind in a white suit as always, and they came over to the two of us and gestured to the heavy doors that led onto the set. "Showtime," they said. "Get a move on, you two lovebirds."

Avery put the phone back and gave me another kiss on the cheek before she stood up and headed for the door. I felt a nervous flutter in my heart, amazed at just how... casual, how comfortable it felt.

I realized I was staring after her when Tay said, "Damn, you've got it bad for that girl."

I sighed. "Look, can you blame me? I was always a sucker for green eyes and brown hair."

"Somehow I don't think it's just that," they said, nudging me in the side playfully with their knuckles. "Look at you. I've known you a million years and I've never seen you look at someone like this. You're falling in love, aren't you?"

I frowned at them. "Is this the time for this conversation, Tay?"

They laughed. "Love is always the priority."

"Love is—love can wait a minute," I said, feeling strange even using the word. It was too early. I wasn't using the word yet. But... it was a strange sort of realization that I knew I *would* be using it, if Avery would stay with me. I changed the subject. "How are you so relaxed about this?"

They shrugged. "Either you ace it and get one last season, and then I can retire this whole *Kitchen Rescue* thing, or Mike gets it, in which case I'm out faster than you can say literally any single syllable. Either way, I get to retire to a life of luxury in the Bahamas."

"You have other clients you'll still be—"

"Shh. They're practically a life of luxury in the Bahamas compared to dealing with you."

I rolled my eyes, smiling despite myself, and I shoved their shoulder. "You're awful. What kind of agent are you?"

"The kind who got you your best shot at keeping Mike Wallace off the show, *and* a girlfriend. Feel free to pay me more. Now get on that stage and show me what they pay you for, girl."

Girlfriend, huh?

I was thinking about entirely the wrong thing as I followed Avery out onto the set, where Mike was already waiting behind a desk like this was a damn talk show, and that entirely wrong thing that I was thinking about was the pretty brunette with the stunning green eyes in a blazer and pencil skirt, sitting down in the sofa by the desk and looking up to beam at me.

"I was wondering if you'd ditched, Hol," Mike said, leaning back in his chair I unfortunately recognized from his YouTube series, all of his private filming locations decorated with his preferred black-and-chrome look. "Looking good today, babe."

I soured, but it was Avery who cleared her throat loudly and said, "That's my girlfriend you're talking to, Mike."

I gave him a thin smile. "And you're looking patently awful," I said, before I sank down next to Avery and took her hand, a motion that felt as natural as breathing. She squeezed it like it was as natural as breathing for her, too.

Christ, I did have it bad for her.

The staging coordinator came out to talk us through shooting and direction, and before I knew it, we were getting the countdown. With the lights blinking on across the cameras, we were live, and Mike started off before I could get a word in.

"Hello and welcome to a special episode of *The Perfect Sear*, recording live from Port Andrea. I'm your host, Mike Wallace, and I'm joined tonight by a good friend of mine, Holly Mason, and her girlfriend. Let's hear a round of applause—"

"Her *name* is Avery," I snapped before I could help myself.

"Now Holly, I'm sure you've got plenty you'd like to say," Mike said, completely ignoring my interjection. Avery took it in stride, just smiling with that perfect TV face she'd developed in no time. "But let's first introduce our audience to what this episode is about. I'm sure most of you have heard the buildup to this—we're here tonight to talk Holly Mason's *Kitchen Rescue,* and about her controversial latest segment that's stalled out in recording now, on struggling luxury restaurant Paramour."

"Thank you, Mike," I said, squeezing as much sarcasm into it as I could. "The truth of the matter, as you know—"

"Now, lots of you are wondering, I'm sure," Mike went on, not even looking at me, and on my earpiece, I caught Avery's and my microphone being faded out, just dropping us off entirely. Christ. I *knew* we shouldn't have engaged on his home turf. "What ever happened to the stories of Mike Wallace taking over *Kitchen Rescue?* Plenty of fans of my show and *Kitchen Rescue* both have been asking for it, citing concerns that Holly doesn't seem to be enjoying her role on the show anymore."

"Mike, this was *not* on the interview agenda," I said, raising my voice to try to get his mic to pick us up, but I knew it was no use. "We're here to discuss your restaurant partnership, and concerns about unethical behavior—"

"Well, I'm excited to announce," Mike said, puffing out his chest, "starting from season seven, I will be costarring on *Kitchen Rescue* after all. I know! I know. The ink is still drying on the contracts, and I'm as amazed myself."

My stomach sank deeper with each word. Was he even here to talk about the partnerships? Was this all just a way to legitimize his claim on my show?

"But as exciting as that all is, that raises some questions. Unfortunately, trying to help out a restaurant dug as deep as Paramour led Holly Mason and her girlfriend into a vendetta against my own restaurant, the Julius, a thriving modern restaurant in luxurious Southport. The million-dollar question here tonight is how does Holly's little quest play out, and how does it lead to me ending up on the show side-by-side with her?"

"You are *not* on the show," I said, not even caring if the mics picked it up. "Your contracts are still subject to a dozen different reviews and approvals, and you know Tay Atkinson isn't going to—"

"Hold on just a minute there, Hol," he said, gesturing for me to stop. "We'll get to you in one second. As many of you know, the Julius has started a philanthropic association of restaurants, a cooperative effort to make sure independent restaurant owners get to run their businesses safely. Holly here has taken some issue with the way we run things, and so tonight, we're facilitating a debate on the merits of our partnership. But first, I'd like to introduce a good friend of mine who's been an owner I'm proud to work with: Cecilia Davis, from Rosco's Point!"

My shoulders fell. Avery's fell harder, eyes going wide, as the curtains to the right of the set moved, and sure enough, there was the snarky-looking blonde woman from Rosco's Point, who had tried to suck up to me while talking down to

Avery in the same breath. She strode on, looking sharp in a pantsuit and her hair pulled up in a neat bun, glasses gleaming in the light, and she waved to the imaginary audience before she shook Mike's hand, taking a seat to his left.

"Cecilia, I really can't emphasize how wonderful it's been to work with Rosco's," he said. "You've been amazing, and your restaurant is really the pride and joy of our partnership."

"It's really my pleasure," Cecilia said, giving Avery a smug look, and I seriously wanted to kick her chair out from under her.

Mike Wallace, with the bold-faced audacity to cut our microphones, upstage our interview with a declaration that wasn't even true, and then bring on Avery's ex-girlfriend to throw her off. I found new ways to hate this man every day.

"Remind me, Cecilia, you've been in our partnership for how long?" Mike said, with that tone like he already knew.

"Six months!" Cecilia said, feigning surprise at the idea. "Six months. It's amazing, isn't it? It's been a rollercoaster, but it's always so wonderful knowing the association is there for us when we need someone."

"Oh, of course," Mike laughed. "You remember that time when a rumor went out about frozen steaks—"

"Oh, absolutely!" Cecilia said, her tone and gestures too practiced. Clearly, *she* had the actual script for this interview, unlike some of us. "Didn't the person who spread the rumor eventually come forward they were just holding a jealous grudge against the system?"

"Ah, something like that," Mike said, rubbing the back of his head. "It's a lot easier to clear up a rumor like that when you have a whole team behind you. And you've given plenty back to the team, too. When Shoreline Blues had a manager poached, and you sent Marjorie right on over? Drake there still tells me all about how he needs to find a way to get Marjorie down there more often."

Cecilia beamed. "Marjorie's a treasure. And she loved the opportunity, too. It helps us all improve our restaurants having a little exposure to others. I think we all have a lot to learn from each other."

Christ, it was like watching a 90s commercial, the kind with the fake candid conversations with two people talking about how great such-and-such company was. Recognizing our mics were still cut, I raised my hand, and I loved the way Cecilia's expression soured.

"Right," Mike said, turning back to me. "Holly, you've come here to air some grievances with our system. Tell us what you have to say?"

I heard my microphone level back on enough to be heard, and my heart surged. I was getting one shot to put everything out there.

"Thank you," I said. "First of all, your contracts with *Kitchen Rescue* have already been denied, because you made them without getting proper approval. I'm sorry to break it to you on live television, but my producer has settled you won't be on season seven. Secondly—I'd like to talk about how your partnership is a multi-level marketing scheme, and how you threaten your owners to get them to convince other people to sign up. Let's go over the payment structure we got in an interview with Kisha Greene, assistant manager at Parkwood Grill, to show that not only are your *owners* not actually owners of anything but just corporate middle managers, but that they're paid to convince—"

"I'm going to stop you right there, Holly," he said, putting a hand out—and he *did* stop me right there, because my microphone cut again. "Our partnership is not a corporation. We have the documentation to show it. This is an association, a loose partnership, and I think Cecilia will be happy to speak to how readily she signed up and what kinds of benefits she gets from it."

"Absolutely, Mike," Cecilia said, and so it went on—Cecilia droning on with a list of benefits, recited from a list she'd rote-memorized. Mike reacted to all of them like he was hearing about them for the first time, as if he hadn't written the list in his own damn blood.

"This is ridiculous," I muttered, just to Avery, who was still looking down at the floor. "They're not even going to let us say a word."

"It's all right," she said. "We've got this."

But no matter how hard she manifested, the next time Mike turned the microphone over to me, I got even less time to talk before he cut me off, taking it back to Cecilia to drone on about how wonderful things were. And the next time it was on me, I just snorted.

"Tell you what I think? What's even the point if you're going to cut me off?"

Mike frowned. "Hey now, Hol. Let's keep this sportsmanlike, okay?"

"Sportsmanlike?" Avery said, quiet enough it didn't pick up, but the way she looked up at him was unmistakable. "You're bringing—you cut our microphones. Put my microphone back on."

Mike turned back to Cecilia. "You were just saying," Mike started, but Avery turned and waved clear to the camera crew.

"Hey!" she called, waving and pointing to her lapel mic. "Can someone turn my microphone back on?"

Christ. I had to admit, she was taking an honest approach. I *had* told her honesty was the best policy.

It caught Mike off-guard, too, because he turned back to her, frowning, and he didn't seem to clear the request, because he looked surprised when Avery's mic started picking her up again.

"Thank you," she said. "Can we just keep the mics on? It seems to me *sportsmanlike* doesn't include interrupting Holly every time she speaks and cutting off her microphone so you can give all the airtime to Cecilia."

He gave her a thin smile. "Well, you can talk to the sound engineer if you're worried about balancing, but let's keep the discussion on this partnership—"

"No, we're talking about this," Avery said, shifting forward in her seat, leaning towards him. "Because this is just the thing about you, Mike. I watched your YouTube show. I mean, I tried to. I didn't get far, because all you do is stand there and talk about how great you are. You dated Holly for two months all of four years ago, and you still call her *babe,* right in front of me, like you did just before we started recording here tonight. And you won't even use my name. Why do you think that is, Mike?"

He glowered. It was Cecilia who spoke, though.

"Aves, please. Let's relax a little—"

"And how about *that,* huh?" Avery said, gesturing at Cecilia. "You have twelve different owners under you, and you *happen* to bring on my ex-girlfriend? Did you think that would throw me off?"

Mike reddened. I just watched with my heart in my mouth.

"Look," Mike said, "I don't want to resort to insults and name-calling here. Why don't we discuss—"

"The partnership. We are discussing it." Avery's tone got sharper and sharper with each word, and the way she straightened her back and threw her shoulders back more and more was unmistakably dangerous—and more than a little sexy. "Because why *are* you so worried about me, Mike? Why do you dislike me so strongly, you won't even use my name? You've referred to me as Holly's girlfriend, her sidepiece, her arm-warmer, everything but my name. Given that you treat Holly like she's your property, years after she left you, is there any chance maybe you have a grudge against me because I not only told you to get out of my damn restaurant when you sauntered in and tried to buy the place, but because Holly is with me instead of you?"

He shook his head. "*Avery,* if you want me to say your name that—"

"I'm talking, Mike," she said. "I've seen your type. A million times. You're the kind of pushy man who thinks he's entitled to a yes whenever he wants one. That's why you made up rumors to try to steal Holly's show, why you made backdoor deals with unenforceable contracts and then told the public you have contracts when that didn't work. That's why you harass people into joining your partnership, and then make them change their menus, change their ingredients. That's why you hate me enough to hire a ghostwriter to write up a fake smear campaign against Paramour. And you only hate me more because Holly is *mine* now, and you can't stand the thought of someone else having two things you want: Paramour, and Holly Mason. Can you, Mike?"

I had not expected this direction at all—least of all from Avery—but it worked. Mike screwed up his face, and the tightness in his arms told me he was gripping something under the desk. "There was no *smear campaign* against Paramour. And frankly, *Avery*, I couldn't care less if you want to stay out of the partnership with your—"

"Mike, it's okay," Cecilia said, which pulled him back to reality. "She's trying to get under your skin. She knows how to do it to a person."

They were really just rolling with Avery pointing out he'd brought on her ex-girlfriend, weren't they? "Please, everyone," I said, trying to cut in before my stomach was sick, "let's focus on the partnership numbers. You haven't given me a chance to tell you Kisha Greene's report, and if you don't—"

"No, let's go with what Avery brought up," Mike said, a sneer coming onto his features. "Since she's so eager to *not* talk about the partnership, let's. Let's talk instead about your relationship. It's been exciting, hasn't it, Holly? You, who've never publicly dated before, suddenly going so public with a relationship that you're willing to break a contract and throw your show into disarray for it. Funny timing, how it should happen right when you needed a refresh for your image, isn't it?"

My blood ran cold. The look on Avery's face told her she was feeling the same thing. "It's true," I said, my throat feeling tight. "Given the circumstances, everything happening at once—a strange smear campaign organized against Paramour, and threats of you trying to make backdoor deals with my show—we made a somewhat hasty decision to go public with it. But I don't regret it."

"I have to say, Avery, I'm impressed," Mike said, raising his eyebrows at her. "Holly never opens up publicly like that. And the Swanson charity dinner... funny the way she only started going again when she had a girlfriend to show off. Amazing how you managed to get her to do it in... how long were you together before you revealed your relationship?"

Avery chewed her lip. My heart pounded. I was the one to speak up. "This is irrelevant. This isn't a gossip rag. Why are you avoiding Kisha Greene's—"

"Impressive, especially, since you only moved to Port Andrea in May, when you opened Paramour," Mike said. "So you were only together for a month before then?"

"And especially for Aves," Cecilia said, giving her a look that just *dared* her to say something. "When we broke up, she told me she wasn't going to date someone *out of her league* anymore. Seems like that didn't hold up. Impressive for a girl who doesn't do things quickly."

"Impressive, definitely," Mike said. "Or maybe the truth is that you two were never actually dating after all. Maybe all of this was just a distraction from reality: that Holly Mason's show is tired and boring, and in order to keep it interesting, the studio had you jump the shark. Had you start a fake celebrity romance and take on my restaurant partnership—"

"We're dating, Mike," I said, my stomach churning hard. "And we shouldn't have to prove it to you. You've proven an expert in unfounded rumors, after—"

"None of it adds up, Hol," he said. "And it's too convenient, isn't it? The timing. The fact that Avery just moved into town. The fact that Cecilia assures me it's very *not like* her. So tell me, Holly. Don't you think you're being a bit dishonest?"

Christ. It didn't matter what I responded with. No matter what I did, people didn't care about Kisha Greene's report. Hell, I doubted they cared about the partnership at all.

He wasn't trying to get us to admit to it. He was trying to change the conversation, and he'd done it, airtight. Everyone was going to be asking *are Holly and Avery actually together,* no matter how compelling a case we put forward.

Checkmate. We'd been playing with half the pieces on our side, and we'd been delaying the inevitable as long as we could, but there was no moving from here that got us out.

Or—I thought that. But Avery found a different move to play, because she said, "Well, to tell you the truth, yes. It was a fake relationship," and it seemed to suck all the oxygen out of the room.

Mike paused. It seemed to catch him off-guard, and he didn't have an answer. Avery took advantage of it, standing up and leaning over Mike's desk.

"Yes. It was a stunt to change Holly's image, and to bring more publicity to the investigation. Neither Holly nor I really liked it, but those pictures of us at Holly's place were leaked before we were ever consulted, so we figured we didn't have much choice but to go through with it. But you know something else, Mike? Holly and I spent a lot of time together. We filmed together. We went to different restaurants together. We made sure to appear around town together to look like we were on dates, and soon enough, that line blurred," she said, looking back at me. The look in her eyes, intense and fiery, made my heart catch, and I thought I could have looked into them forever. "And soon enough, I wasn't sure if the dates we were on were pretend or not. She kept brushing the hair back from my face and smiling at me in that way that made my heart beat faster even when we were off camera. And when you tried to harass Holly at the charity dinner, talking about your past together, the jealousy I felt was real."

"Avery," I said, standing up with her, my heart pounding so hard I felt dizzy. I put a hand on her arm. "Are you—"

"And—when I kissed you there, Holly," she said, turning to level with me, "that wasn't pretend anymore. I couldn't keep my eyes off you from the start. I care for you, Holly. I don't *know* what we are now, but I know every second we've spent together, even if we told ourselves we couldn't act on these feelings for each other—I know every second has been real."

And then—just like that, as if she hadn't pulled my entire soul out of my body, shaken it awake after a lifetime asleep, and put it back in upside-down and backwards for me to realize that I'd had it in wrong all along—she spun on her heel and turned back to Mike.

"You want to talk about dishonest, Mike, let's talk about dishonest. Let's talk about the frozen food shipments you send out labeled with strict orders not to reveal are shipped into the restaurants. Let's talk about the staff who have seen changed menus showing up without anyone being consulted on them. Let's talk about the smears you had written about my restaurant. And let's talk about the way you gave us a fake script on what would happen in this interview, and then turned around and violated your own agreement by bringing Cecilia on to give her all the airtime instead. You want to talk about dishonest, Mike? Do you *really* want to talk about dishonest? Then let's *talk* about those smears."

Mike snapped, putting his hands down on the desk and rising with her. "You keep saying that word like it's a get-out-of-jail-free card. *Smears?* They're bad reviews, Avery. They happen to bad restaurants all the time. And frankly—"

"Oh, did I ask you?" Avery said. "That's funny. I really didn't mean to, but I guess when you're Mike Wallace, you think every woman is talking to you. No, Mike. I'm not talking to *you* about the smears. You violated the agreement and brought Cecilia on air, so it's only fair I also have a dear friend coming on to talk the smear campaign. Someone I think you may have heard of." She glanced off to the curtain on the side of the set, and changing the world, she called, "Let's hear it for Olivia Harper!"

My stomach fell, and I found my head spinning.

She hadn't been nervous-texting. She hadn't been checking the time. She'd been coordinating Liv to come on the show.

Mike went the color of marble, and Cecilia just looked around lost and confused as the curtains pulled back to let Liv through, wearing a black dress and looking different from any time I'd seen her at Paramour, with the stage hair and makeup. Her expression was somewhere between confident and terrified, but she strode on, keeping an even pace in her heels, and Mike turned to her before swallowing hard.

"Who—when did anyone let you in?" he said, and Avery laughed.

"I told her to tell the staff she was an owner here at Mike's orders. Looks like no one's very well-informed around here." Avery stepped out and offered a hug to Liv, who took it, squeezing her a little too hard.

"Hey," Liv said, as Avery moved her lapel mic to pick her up. "I'm a little nervous to be here, but... hi. I'm Olivia Harper, waitress at Paramour, and Mike Wallace paid me to write eight different anonymous smears against Paramour. I'm aware no one is going to want to hire me at their restaurant now, but..." She gave Avery a small smile, almost shy, and she said, "But Avery's said my position at Paramour is safe, and I like working there anyway. So I've decided to put my career on the line and share the contracts, the emails, and everything."

And as if that wasn't enough, Cecilia paled, and she turned on Mike, and she said, so quietly I could barely hear her even with her microphone on, "Mike. If you *did* smear Paramour, then our refrigerant failures when we delayed on signing... was that *you?*"

And I watched—breathless—because what else was I supposed to do?

Avery hadn't been lying that time in Paramour, when we'd first met, when she'd told me her plan was to roll with the punches, and to find a way to work with everything the universe gave her.

I really did have it bad for her.

CHAPTER 24

Avery

I couldn't lie. The rush after that interview felt great.

I was paraded around the studio like a hero. Kyle gave me a high-five that turned into a handshake, and then he got emotional and turned it into a hug that went on too long, squeezing me, and he said, "Avery, if you want a career in television, give me a call. I swear, you saved this whole season. Damn, you are good."

I squeezed him back and laughed. "Right now, I'm just planning on celebrating with Holly, but I'll definitely keep that in mind."

Tay, too, crossed their arms and shook their head at me, giving me that funny Tay smile, and eventually they said, "I am so damn smart getting you two together like this. You see? Never question the inspir-Tay-tion."

I laughed. "I won't tell Holly you said that."

"No, please tell her. And take a picture of her flipping me off and send it to me."

But in all of it, I didn't get to see Holly much, not until after everything and she was waiting for me outside the studio, eyes sparkling, looking so beautiful in that dress I just wanted to cry.

"I already thanked it," she said, and I cocked my head.

"Thanked... what?"

She jabbed her thumb upwards. "The universe. It gave me that miracle I was asking for."

Laughter burst up from me, more than I could help. Laughing right now was the only thing I could do, everything feeling so right. "Liv coming through was a miracle for me too. She texted me half an hour before filming, and she said, and I quote, *fuck it, I'm coming clean with everything on the show, and you and Holly can't stop me.*"

She smirked, raising one eyebrow. "That was great, but it wasn't the miracle, Avie. The miracle was you."

My laughter took a sharp turn onto a road marked with *awkward blushing* and *what even is the English language.* "Uh," I stammered, eyes going wide. "I mean—uh—oh."

She took my hand. "Come back to my apartment. I have an Emiliano Russo vintage 76 I'd like to open with you."

Wow. I thanked the universe for my miracle, too.

And that miracle was still going when we got back to her apartment and she opened the bottle of vintage 76, which must have cost something I didn't even want to know, and poured a glass for me. I almost sank down in a seat at the kitchen table, but she snaked an arm around my back and led me to the sofa with her, sitting down with my side pressed up against hers, watching the city lights outside the full-wall window, and my heart hammered so hard I might have spilled the wine.

"Here's to you," Holly said, raising her glass.

"Here's to the look on Mike Wallace's face when Cecilia started yelling at him."

She laughed. "Here's to exactly that," she said, clinking her glass with mine, and we took a sip together.

The flavor was incredible—complex and marbled, deep and mature and elegant, while still crisp and sweet. I could have spent hours with this wine, dissecting it, understanding it, but it was a shame, because my mind was kind of elsewhere. Like the incredibly beautiful woman next to me who I wanted *so* badly.

"Avie," she said, a minute later, setting down the wine glass on the end table. She didn't look at me, just resting her hand on my thigh as she stared out the window. "I don't know how to say this enough, but... thank you. Not just for bringing Liv out. If it had just been Liv, he would have still found a way to deflect. What you did on that set—calling out the engineers on your mic, deliberately aggravating him, admitting to our relationship, and *then* bringing out Liv—you saved the show, and I don't know how to thank you."

I set down my own glass, looking down at where our legs pressed together. "I didn't know what I was doing. I was making it up as I went. But I... was thinking about things you'd said."

She glanced over at me. "Like what?"

"Things about... honesty, I guess. About false pretenses. About trying to be something we're not. What I did on that set—all I did was tell people exactly the truth, unvarnished, undecorated. And somehow, it worked. I think maybe you're right, Holly. I think... maybe I've been trying too hard. Losing myself being something I'm not. I think maybe I'm enough, just like this, as the woman I am."

My heart hammered, and it only got worse when Holly put her hand on the small of my back, turning to face me. "Avie... Avery." She reached up with her other hand and brushed the hair back from my face, that little gesture that was everything to me. "I think you've underestimated just how good you've been at that this whole time. You're honest. Real. You're the most real person I've ever known, Avery. And that's the reason I..."

I needed to know what came after that *I*. Like, *needed* needed. I squeezed my hand on her thigh. "The reason you what?"

She looked down at the space between us, and her voice was almost... shy, once she spoke. "The reason I know you're different, Avie."

"Different... from what?"

"Everyone else." She looked up and met my eyes, vulnerability flashing in hers. "All the people who just wanted to get close to me. You're different. You're not here to be close to a celebrity. You're here to be close to me. You're here because you care. And I've never... felt that before you, Avie."

I stared—just stared into the warm, dark brown eyes staring back at me, and I wondered how on earth I was supposed to not kiss her. I glanced down at her lips, dark red gloss looking too kissable, and back up at her eyes. "I was always interested in you as a celebrity. You have no idea what the show meant to me. When... after I came back from Port Andrea the first time," I mumbled, my voice falling off.

Holly raised her eyebrows high at me. "When you broke up with Cecilia?"

"Yeah. I'd come here to try pursuing my dreams. That breakup, and going home, it felt like a failing grade on an assignment. It felt like an indictment on my dreams. I gave up on it. All of that. I just went to work and didn't even care if it took me nowhere." I took a long breath, staring down at where our legs pressed together, and when she put a hand on top of mine and squeezed, it gave me just a little more strength. "But then a couple years later, I saw your show. And I saw you helping restaurants just like one I wanted to start. I saw you taking bad beginnings and making them beautiful. You gave me permission to give myself a second chance. I watched the whole thing again, and again, and slowly, I started to realize you were right. Change is always possible. Growth—reinventing ourselves—it's always possible, no matter how rough the beginning was."

"Avie..." Holly's voice was just a breath, a whisper. I glanced up into her eyes, my heart pounding.

"You gave me my dreams back. Three years of watching *Kitchen Rescue* later, I started off to make the dreamer's story my own. You're the reason I'm here, Holly. But... you on the show, that was just a snapshot of who you are as a person. You told me you were less interesting in person, but the more I got to know you, the more I saw the human being you wanted everyone to see. Fun, flirty, confident, and full of dreams—a girl who just wants the world to see her." I turned more towards her, sliding a hand to her back. "I see you, Holly. And I've seen you since the moment you told me about your thing for runny sauces."

She laughed, leaning in and touching her forehead to mine, and my heart burned so warm it was like I had a star bursting inside of me. "And that's supposed to convince me to stop telling you that?"

I stuck my tongue out. "For one, I don't even *get* runny in that way."

She raised an eyebrow, which was a new feeling when it was with her forehead pressed against mine. "Are we talking about something other than salad dressings, Avery Lindt?"

"Perish the thought, Holly Mason." I glanced down at her lips again, and back up to her eyes. "I don't think Andrean chefs are all bad after all."

She smirked. "What changed your mind?"

"Well..." I flushed, but I smiled, holding her tighter. "Maybe a certain Andrean chef who convinced me to give it all one more try. You're my best friend in the world, Holly. And I think that's why it's safe to say I'm really... really... falling for you, and I don't even mind."

My heart thumped erratically in my chest, watching the emotions play over her face—her smile fading, something I couldn't read in her eyes, and I wondered if I'd said too much—if I'd shattered the moment.

But instead, she slipped a hand around my waist, holding me closer to her, and she said, "You know what's funny?"

"Mm. Tell me."

"You're my best friend, too," she said, sliding in and placing a single soft, tender kiss against my lips, but it was somehow more powerful than all the sensual kisses with me on my back. She pulled away just far enough I could feel her breath on my lips, and she said, "And you have no idea how much it means to me that I was able to reinspire your dreams. Maybe... maybe it's too early to call it quits on *Kitchen Rescue*."

I lit up, my heart bouncing in my chest. "For real? Because of me?"

She planted another soft kiss against me, leaving me tingling through every part of my body. "You're responsible for quite a few miracles. And that's why I think it's safe to say I'm falling for you quite a bit faster than I'd planned."

My heart jumped through the roof, and there were still at least six more stories above us for it to go through. I felt a smile coming on so wide it hurt, my hands falling to her waist too, holding her into me. "You mean... you... plan your schedules for falling in love?"

"Ha, ha. You're hilarious, Avie."

I grinned. "Aren't I, though?"

"Avery," she sighed, letting her eyes flutter shut as she slipped her hands up to my hair, holding me by the back of the head, and she kissed me again, softly, sweetly, still tasting of the wine. "I admire your honesty, so let me admit honestly that I am... terrified to ask this question. But I have to." She paused, still barely an inch away from my lips. "Will you... be my girlfriend, Avery?"

"I was expecting something a lot scarier than that," I said, and she cracked one eyelid.

"Is anything scarier than this?"

I grinned. "Terrifying, exciting... sometimes I can't tell the difference." I kissed her, my heart swirling, dancing, swooping, the chorus in my head chanting *my girlfriend, Holly, my girlfriend, Holly.* "Only on the condition that you'll be my girlfriend, too," I said, and she grunted, kissing me back.

"That's just—that's how being a girlfriend works, Avery. It can't be one-sided."

"So, you agree to the terms and conditions?"

She laughed. "And you called me incorrigible?"

"I did, and I stand by it. I mean, takes one to know one."

She kissed me harder, taking my bottom lip in her mouth, a sensual feeling that sent shivers through my whole body, down and up my spine until I let out a soft moan into her. "So that's a yes?" she murmured, after she let go with a *pop.*

"It's a yes. Now and forever." I spoke in between kisses, my arms slung around her neck as she eased me onto my back on the sofa, resting on top of me. "Your girlfriend. I'm happy to take any risk with you, Holly."

"God, you are perfect," she whispered, pinning me down to my back. "I don't know what I did without you."

"Well, you didn't have any fun grabbing balsamic vinegar, that's for sure…"

"Mm. When you give me sass, I've found it usually means you want me to take your clothes off."

I raised an eyebrow as best I could. I knew I couldn't do it right. I knew Holly loved seeing me try. "Projecting, much, Miss Mason?"

"Deflecting, much, Miss Lindt?"

I licked my lips. "Why don't you try taking my clothes off and seeing how it's received?"

"Oh, I wonder," she said, slipping my jacket off and flinging it over the back of the sofa.

"Aren't these the studio's clothes?" I said, more absently than anything else.

"Tay will know exactly what the wrinkles are from, and they'll be delighted," she said. "But I am resolutely not thinking of Tay right now."

"Oh. Good call."

"Take this shirt off," she said, tugging at the offending garment.

"Two for two on the good calls."

"I'm going to make a lot of calls, and you're going to be a good girl and follow them."

I wasn't sure what possessed me to reach up and catch her hand as she slipped down my sides, but I did. "Wait," I said. "Let's just..."

She was immediately alert. "Do you not want this?"

I squeezed her hand. "I do. Just... can we be gentle? Slow? Take our time?"

She stopped, studying me, eyes smoldering as she met mine. "Are you... asking me to make love to you?"

I felt myself flush ridiculously, and I didn't even mind. "I mean... would you say yes?"

She stared a second longer before she sighed, sinking into me. "Oh, Avie," she said. "Of course I would."

"Holly..." I paused. "Um... just to be clear, the answer is yes, then, that is what I'm asking."

She kissed me before I could ramble any more, pressing her lips against mine, and I melted into the soft, but fiery sensation that was her lips moving slowly with mine, her tongue darting into my mouth, as her fingertips trailed along my skin. I surrendered everything to her in a way that felt more vulnerable than times I'd been tied to her bed naked, and it was unbelievable to find the more I let myself feel vulnerable with her, the better it felt.

And I was pretty sure it was only going to get better.

We only broke the kiss in short intervals to strip the rest of our clothes off, her dress landing in a pile with my skirt, tights stripped off, bras and panties dropped to the floor, and then naked and open and honest and raw, we kissed, hands tangling in hair, legs lacing around one another as we kept feeling one another there, holding on like Holly was my tether to this world and I was hers.

Her taking my nipple in her mouth felt intensely erotic in a way it had never been before, and I wondered if that was what love did— because that was what this was, a tiny little burgeoning love that was just waiting to sprout, to break the surface, and it made everything feel beautiful. I felt myself breaking a sweat already, arching my back against her, gasping out her name as I held her tightly against me.

She kissed her way back up to my mouth as she slipped a hand down between our legs, and I found myself mimicking the gesture along her body, reaching down to the wetness of her folds, circling around her entrance as she teased over my clit. It was all too easy to slip a finger inside of her, feel her walls clenching around me, and feeling the way she tightened and shifted around my finger while her hand worked over my clit was like an otherworldly experience.

"God, Avery," she groaned.

"You are so perfect," I sighed, moving in to kiss her again, moving my finger slowly in and out of her. "And so beautiful..."

"You're everything, Avery," she moaned, and I couldn't get enough of hearing my name in her voice like this. "So perfect... so damn good with your fingers."

I bit my lip before I moved back in to bite down lightly on hers. "I want to make you come first this time," I murmured against her lips.

She let out a hungry groan, moving her hips with my finger, grinding against me. "Is this the slightest bit of top energy from you, Avie?"

"Just a little bit..."

"Then you're going to need a second finger. Please."

I pressed my lips back to hers, slipping my tongue into her mouth while I slid a second finger inside of her, feeling the way she clenched around me and groaned against my mouth with the added finger. She kept circling around my clit, but slower and slower as I directed focus to where I picked up the tempo, finding a rhythm that her hips matched naturally, thrusting into her and dragging back out. The gasps, the noises she made, and the feeling of her tight and wet around me, it was all so obscene, so *good,* I felt like I could have come from her barely touching me.

"Fuck, Avery," she groaned against my mouth. "You feel so fucking good."

"I want you to come for me."

"I'm eating you out after this," she breathed, shaky and heavy.

"God. You're going to make me come just thinking about it." I renewed my energy, kissing her, thrusting in and out of her, gripping her tightly by the back and burying my fingertips into her. The desperate thrust of her hips, the way she moved faster, harder, the way her gasps picked up in intensity until she was just about crying out with each thrust, I felt the biggest wave of my own pleasure building up as I watched Holly break away from the kiss to bury her face against my collar.

"Fuck, Avery, I'm going to come," she moaned, and then—she didn't really wait for a response, gritting her teeth and gripping me tightly, pressing her face harder into me, and I felt her clench tighter with her orgasm, grinding against me all through it, and I couldn't get over how it was every kind of sexy watching her press her body into mine like that as she came.

Every kind of sexy, and almost unnervingly beautiful, I thought, once she came down slowly, gasping hard against me, her chest rising and falling as she kept her grip tight on me and slowly rolled her head up to look at me, hair fanned out messily over my chest, that blissful look of satisfaction in her eyes.

I wanted to bottle up the moment and keep it forever, like a fine bottle of Emiliano Russo.

"You are so beautiful like this," I whispered, brushing a hair back from her face. "My sweet Holly."

"I've—never felt anything like this before," she admitted, another flash of vulnerability over her face. I bent my head down to kiss her forehead.

"Me neither. And there's no one I'd rather feel it with than you."

She looked up into my eyes for a second, filled with every kind of emotion there was, before she buried her face into my chest and just nodded against me. "No one I'd rather feel it with than you," she murmured, and I just held her against me, feeling the sensation of her wetness on my fingers still as a physical mark of how good she felt right now. I rolled my head to the side with her, and we just stared out the window, looking at the city lights all alive below us, the whole world just waiting for us to live it all and see it all, together.

Holly could absolutely eat me out, but—in a minute.

I was really enjoying the moment.

EPILOGUE

Holly

Thanks, Kyle," I said, taking the envelope from his outstretched hand. He leaned against the corner of the wall, fussing his scarf back into the proper position.

"Nice seeing you, Mason. Looking forward to the season seven filming."

I paused in the doorway out to the studio reception, shooting him a playful smirk. "Be careful what you wish for, there. You blink and the time will be gone."

"Oh, I wish it were like that. I'm working on a home and garden show that honestly I can't figure out why I signed up for it. I'm about to die of boredom just thinking about it. Maybe I need to get Atkinson on that team and see if we can spice things up with a celebrity romance?"

"Hm. Somehow I think you can only pull that one so many times."

He waved me to the door. "Yeah, details. All right, Holly, shoo. I know you've got a pretty girl waiting for you to take her that delivery. I'm sure the time until season seven will pass quickly for you two. Bring her round to the planning meetings once it's time, will you? The fans will be dying to see her pop up here and there."

"Will do, Kyle. Thanks again," I said, waving the envelope at him, before I slipped out of the building and hit the road, winding my way down to Komodo's to pick up my con panna and the ghastly cinnamon mocha Avie had gotten so fond of lately. I kept an eye on the sky the whole rest of the way to Paramour, aware of how the early September air and the gray clouds drifting in promised a drizzle soon, but they held off for now.

I got to Paramour right on the dot, pushing open the glass doors at the front with my hip like I'd done so many times already, nodding at Diane on hosting.

"Avery was wondering if you'd get soaked out there," she said, watching me head towards the back.

"Still plenty of time for me and Avery to get soaked later," I said, which I only realized once I'd gotten to the back sounded like an innuendo. I winced inwardly.

"Avery's in her office," Dominic said, looking up from where he was stirring soup, somehow looking tranquil even in the middle of the kitchen whirling with activity around him. "She was pining over you the whole open. I don't really see the appeal, frankly."

I gave him a tired smile. "Dominic, I will never get tired of your honesty. Thanks a ton. The caramelized wafers turned out well?"

He shrugged. "Big hit. Seasonal ice cream with the wafers, people pay a lot. I think they just like the sound of *caramelized wafer*. Makes them feel pretentious."

"Glad to hear it," I said, heading for the back office, waving to him. "Tell Liv I said hi!"

"What's even the point? She'll just say hi back," he called, but I brushed him off, knocking twice on Avery's office and pushing it open, coming into where the unfairly beautiful brunette who I somehow got to call mine sat there at her desk, scrolling through her laptop with her face scrunched up, but she lit up at the sight of me.

"Hey, Lemon Bread," she said, standing up and coming around the desk, giving me a quick kiss on the cheek.

"You really do have the strangest pet names," I said, handing her coffee over.

"Don't pretend you don't like it." She took a long sip of the coffee, tilting her head back and brushing her hair away from her shoulders. "Ugh. God, that's good."

"Your bizarre mocha just tastes confusing. I don't get it."

She nudged my shoulder. "It's an acquired taste, Holly. You'll learn to love it because your girlfriend does."

"We can love different things, and it can be complementary," I said, dropping the envelope down on the desk. I waited until she was sipping her coffee again before I said, "For example, I don't love being tied to the bed and fucked face-down, but..."

I watched like it was a comfort movie I'd seen a hundred times—first the widening of the eyes, then the tightening of the throat, the quick spread of pink over her cheeks, and then, the crowning moment, her sputtering her coffee back into her cup and coughing, wiping her mouth and looking away. "Okay," she said. "Yeah. Point taken."

I gestured to the envelope. "It's for you, Avie. Early copies made their way to the studio."

She set down her cup on top of the filing cabinet, eyes going wide as she came over next to me. "Is it...?"

"Well, you could try opening it. That would be a good way of finding out."

"Oh my god. If it is, this is no time to be giving me sass." She nestled up against my side, working intently as she pulled open the strip sealing the envelope, and when she reached inside, I felt her breath catch against me. "Oh, Holly. It is. And you didn't tell me before you got here?"

I tilted my head to look at her, at the look of wonder in her eyes, sparkling and shimmering like gemstones too pure for belief. "I wanted to see your reaction," I said, and she laughed, her voice thick.

"Well, here it is. Oh, wow. Is it—does it look good?"

"Pull it out and see."

"Holly," she groaned, burying her face in my shoulder. "Just tell me something."

I kissed the top of her head swiftly, moving my hand down to squeeze hers. "It looks amazing, Avie. And I'm proud of you."

"See?" she mumbled into my shoulder. "Was that so hard? Did the world end?"

I kissed her forehead this time, secretly just falling a little more in love with her every time she made a little comment like that. "Go ahead, Avery."

She took a long breath, and she slid it out of the envelope, and—of course, it came out backwards at first, but she flipped it around to the front, and the small, soft breath she let out, the way her eyes flared at the sight, it was worth every second of the wait.

In her hands, the glossy cover of Foodie Magazine looked up at us, the picture of me and Avery on the front together casting side-eye glances at one another looking even better on this one than in the proofs.

Avie didn't say anything for a second, just holding it, brushing her fingers lightly over it. I started to worry for a second she hated it, but she pursed her lips, shook her head, and she wasn't able to help the smile spreading over her face anymore.

"Look at us," she said, her voice crackling just a little at the end. "We're so cute together."

I laughed, feeling the nervousness in my heart too at this point, and I snaked an arm around her waist and pulled her into my side. "What, only on the magazine cover?"

"Ha, ha. Oh my god. Holly. Look at it."

I had looked at it, plenty—the simple cover of me and her on the studio background, the big text *PARAMOURS: How Holly Mason and Avery Lindt exposed a Port Andrea restaurant racketeer, and fell in love in the process* just reminding me of every second of those two months together with Avie. Tumultuous, certainly. And I wouldn't have changed a minute of it. "It looks amazing," I breathed, holding my hand against the small of her back. "How does it feel? Dream come true?"

"Well, I mean, yeah," she sniffled, wiping at one eye. "I look so good."

My heart swelled up for her, but I gave her a teasing smirk. "Oh, and I'm a washed-up mess there, am I?"

"Don't be silly," she laughed, just tracing her finger over her own face in the picture. "For the longest time... in the middle of my transition, you know. When I tried to visualize myself on the cover of Foodie, I wasn't sure what I'd look like." She sighed, softly, holding the magazine in both hands. "And I was worried I wouldn't look right, but this... me here, you here... it's right."

My chest welled up with a million different thoughts, different feelings, a million different things I needed to say to her. Instead, I just held her tighter into my side, and I said, "I'm really proud of you, Avie. You do look perfect. I think you always have."

She set it back down on the desk, leaning her head on my shoulder and just breathing, slowly, with me. "Hey... Holly."

"Yes?"

She trailed her fingers down my arm, down to slip them between mine and squeeze my hand. "I know this has all been a little weird, because everyone thinks we said this ages ago already, but... I kind of have to get this out there," she said, speaking a little faster. She took a breath, held it a second, and let it out slowly. "I love you, Holly."

The moment—that moment where Avery glanced up at me with those half-lidded eyes, the moment she held her dream in her hands and shared it with me, the moment she said those words, I felt every little bit of it—every sight in the office, every sound back from the kitchen, the faint smell of the soup cooking mingling with the bread baking, and every inch of Avery's face, the expression she had like there was nothing else in the world to do *but* to tell me she loved me. The moment was just that—one moment, infinitely small in time—but like a beautiful painting in the smallest space, it was a masterpiece in creation, and I wanted to frame it and keep it hung in the gallery of my heart as long as I lived.

And god knew I would—that this moment would be preserved forever.

I turned to face her, slipping my hands down to her hips, holding her against me, and I leaned in, resting my forehead against hers, and I breathed the words I'd been aching to say. "I love you, too, Avery," I whispered, feeling like it was releasing a buoy underwater, feelings shooting up to the surface so suddenly and so fiercely it couldn't be contained. "I love you so much, I don't ever want to let you go."

She smiled—slightly at first, and then wider, and then wider, until her eyes crinkled at the corners, sparkling with that light that I couldn't get enough of—seeing it next to me in the mornings we woke up together, at her place or mine. Seeing it when we worked together, in her kitchen glancing up over a counter and meeting my eyes and sparkling in that way she did, or when we interviewed somewhere together, a common activity for us these days, and she'd sneak a glance over at me and just gaze at me with that look like I was everything. Seeing it when we'd have dinner together, over her kitchen table or mine, or over a restaurant table.

I wanted to keep seeing it forever.

"Then... how about we say that you don't?" she said, and I laughed, brushing my forehead against hers.

"What a brilliant plan. You never told me you were such a genius."

"Well, I prefer to let the results speak for themselves, don't you know?" she murmured, leaning in to kiss me, and I met her in the middle—kissing her, and kissing her, and feeling the way she held me, like the whole world was here in this space between us, and neither of us ever wanted to let go of it, not until the door flung open without even a knock.

We threw ourselves away from each other, Avery flushing and looking down, and I shot a death glare at Tay, who'd come into the room in, to no one's great surprise, a white suit.

"Ooh, sorry to interrupt," they said, waggling their eyebrows. I glared.

"If you're actually sorry, then you're going to step back outside that door, close it, wait ten seconds, and then *knock* before you come inside."

"Guess I'm not that sorry," they said, shutting the door behind them as they strolled over to us, picking up the magazine. "Damn, Avery. Did they photoshop your boobs bigger in this?"

"What?" Avery paled, picking it up, looking it over. "No, uh... I think they just look big in the camera angle..."

"Well, we can ask Mason, she's an expert on them," they said, with another eyebrow waggle at me. I wanted to rip their damn eyebrows off and see how they liked that.

"Or we can ask you what in the world you're doing barging into the office when I was *positive* you had a meeting in New York City?"

"Canceled. The girl's got pink eye. I can't stand NYC, so I refunded the ticket the second I heard. Lucky you, getting to have your best friend Tay stick around."

"You are my agent whom I sometimes tolerate. Don't get ahead of yourself."

Avery giggled, looking between the two of us. "I can never get tired of you two. What's on your mind, Tay?"

"See, Mason? Avery likes me. You have no choice but to keep me around. It's for your gal pal's sake."

"Oh, yeah," Avery said, furrowing her brows and nodding at me. "Gal pals over here."

"Gal pals kissing in her office before my agent comes in and, quite frankly, ruins the moment. What do you want, Tay?"

"Ah, you'll change your tone when I tell you this," they said, putting a finger up. "Mason."

"Atkinson."

"Offer. For a studio takeover of *Kitchen Rescue.*"

I stopped. My head spun until I felt dizzy. "I... a takeover? What are you talking about?"

"I'm talking about shedding Gavin and the other crusty old white men who latched themselves onto *Kitchen Rescue* like leeches and tried to sell you out to Mike Wallace. Abby Parker's team wants to meet with you and talk about a completely new direction moving forward, inspired by everything you did with Paramour. Going beyond kitchen rescues, and uncovering other shady business dealings, finding other people taken advantage of in the industry, and sticking up for fairness and independence in Port Andrea. In between the classic kitchen rescues we all know and love."

I sank back against the desk, my chest feeling lighter and lighter. "Abby... Abby Parker, like *Quick Fix* Abby Parker? *Simple Food* Abby Parker?"

"The one and only. She wants to meet with you next week." They raised an eyebrow. "And the you is plural."

"Plural—what?" I scowled. "Don't you dare tell me this is another scheme to get Mike Wallace on air with me."

They laughed. "Mike Wallace's brand is dead in the water. His partnership dissolved after everyone in it realized all the shit that happened to their restaurants before they signed were Mike's doing, and his show's tanked ever since his disastrous live. All he's got left is the Julius, and rumor has it that's struggling too. It's beautiful. I love schadenfreude." They shook their head. "No. You and Avery. She wants to see Avery get a major role in the production, too."

"Me?" Avery said, shoulders dropping. "You—want me to stay on *Kitchen Rescue* to help other restaurants?"

"Look, people love you two. They've been eating up the whole honesty and openness thing with your relationship coming along ever since that live, and interest in *Kitchen Rescue* is the highest it's ever been. You should see the pre-launch interest ratings in this season. People are about ready to murder to get to watch it. It's incredible. And Avery's a part of that."

"I..." I looked between them and Avery, still feeling like I was spinning. "I mean... I can't believe I might get the chance to work with Abby Parker. Of course I'll meet her. But—Avery, I want to be clear you don't have to do this," I said, turning to her, my brows furrowed. "I know Paramour comes first and foremost. And I don't—"

She cut me off with her finger to my lips, stepping in closer. "Holly," she said. "Do you really think I watched all the episodes *just* twice? You know how important *Kitchen Rescue* is to me. I'll meet with Abby Parker. I can't wait to do this together."

"Avie," I breathed, my heart racing. She grinned.

"Holly?"

I shook my head, short for words, and I settled for what I think was going to become a new staple.

"I love you," I said, and I leaned in and kissed her again, not even caring Tay was watching.

"Aww," Tay said. "You said the three little words?"

"Truth be told," Avery said, not parting far from my lips, glancing at Tay out of the corner of her eye, "We were kind of in the middle of doing that for the first time when you barged in."

"Without knocking," I added. Tay laughed.

"Come on. A little appreciation for the genius who got you two together?" They winked. "A *thank you* would be nice."

"I will *thank you* to leave us alone now," I said, still holding Avery closer to me. "Tell Abby we'll be happy to meet with her. And that I'm looking forward to it."

Tay rolled their eyes, but they were grinning, spinning on their heel back to the door. "All right, all right. Can't interrupt the teenage girls making out. I'll just keep doing my job incredibly well with no appreciation, as always," they said, striding out of the room and pulling the door shut behind them.

"They're funny," Avery laughed.

"Give it three years, you'll want to strangle them too," I said, brushing my forehead back against hers again. "Now... where were we?"

"Kissing," she murmured, ghosting her lips along mine, smiling against me. "And saying I love you."

"Aah, yes." I pressed my lips back against hers, a soft and sweet kiss, feeling Avery giggle against my lips like she had the same—just boundless *happiness* I did right now. "And how long, pray tell, do you think we'll be doing that?"

"Mm. Quite some time, I think. Until you've kissed me enough. I don't see that happening any time soon."

It sounded like it could be a lifelong endeavor, trying to kiss Avery enough.

But what a way to spend a lifetime.

The End

About the Author

Lily Seabrooke is a lesbian, trans woman, and writer of tender, heartfelt lesbian romance. She lives in central Michigan with her family (an espresso machine and a houseplant), and she writes soft stories that make you feel good—they're cozy little books to read in cozy little nooks, and she hopes they make you feel a little warmer.

You can find her on Twitter under @lilyseabrooke to be in the know on everything she's doing, and you can check out her website at lilyseabrooke.com. You can sign up for her mailing list there and be the first to get book announcements or get free copies of her books before they release in exchange for honest reviews.

She thinks you're amazing, and she hopes *Fake It* was as fun and warm for you as it was for her.